Caroline Hemingway

RECKONING

THE DESTINY CHRONICLES BOOK 2

This is a work of fiction. All names, characters, locations and incidents are products of the author's imagination and any resemblance to actual people, places or events is purely coincidental or fictionalized.

ISBN 978-0-9942028-1-9

Published in Australia in 2015 by Carroway

This book is first and foremost dedicated to:

My amazing husband and children, who are my number one fans. None of this would have been possible without your incredible love and support and I am truly grateful to have you in my life.

Thanks especially to my daughter Michaela, who has proof-read and tirelessly worked to help me get this book published – you have been a gem.

This book is also dedicated to:

My awesome parents and siblings who have shown me what it is to truly love and the value of family – despite the distance between us, you are all constantly in my thoughts.

And finally a big thank you to:

Erin, a godsend in my life when I needed it most –your challenge to me to write saved me in a dark time and set me on this crazy, adventurous journey. For that I am so grateful.

Name Pronunciation Guide

In order of appearance:

Aislinn	ASH- lin
Struan	STREW- en
Imogene	IM - uh - j EEN
Legion	LEE – jin
Falstaff	FALL- stof
Eion	Owen
Rozanne	Rose- ANN
Ziah	Z (long i)-uh
Aedan	AY- dan
Daemon	DAY – min
Nuada	NU-ah
Sephtis	Sef – TIS
Cillian	KILL-yan
Beathan	Bay - an
Phoenix	FEE - nix
Ailith	Ay-lith

PROLOGUE

HER SCREAM reverberated through the little cottage, bouncing off the wattle and daub walls like an echo, terrifying the young man who looked on helplessly. There was nothing he could do to help her - he felt useless. They were well past the encouragement and placating stage – he could see agonizing pain in her eyes but there was something else there too – he was too afraid to acknowledge it as he was certain it was mirrored in his own eyes – fear! Tears rolled from her eyes as she labored to bring their baby into this world. *Something was wrong*, she could feel it – pain ripped through her abdomen again as another contraction came in unrelenting force. The old midwife clucked as she made her as comfortable as possible and tried to feel the position of the baby once again. She muttered under her breath and it did not bring any reassurance to the young man who stood wringing his hands helplessly.

'The wee one is breech,' she said to him.

'What does that mean?'

He had never been at a birth before and he wished he could be anywhere else at that moment. Listening to her in pain was more than he could bear.

'It means the baby has not turned the right way for birth,' she explained patiently. She did not want to frighten them but this was a serious complication and many a woman had haemorrhaged as a result of this very thing, usually resulting in the death of mother, baby or both.

'Lie as still as you can,' she instructed the pale woman who was heaving as though it would be her last breath. 'I am going to try and turn the baby.'

Minutes ticked by as Martha did her best to turn the little life within the womb. She rubbed the belly trying her best to encourage the babe to turn.

'Come on little one, you can do it,' she coaxed the bulging belly.

At last she looked up and shook her head. Now he really felt panic. There had to be something they could do. His eyes implored the old woman. She had seen this look in many a husband's eye in all her years as a midwife. Some could be saved and some could not.

'This is not how it is meant to end,' he blurted out frustrated. 'This baby is a gift to us from the Great One. He would never be cruel enough to give us this treasure only for it to be snatched away right at the time of delivery.'

'Well I don't know about this Great One or how he operates,' Martha said, 'but I do know that there is nothing more I can do to turn the baby. I certainly hope your faith is enough to see her through. We need to deliver this baby, feet first. I cannot guarantee that either of them will come through this unscathed.'

'Why can't you turn the baby?' he asked angrily. 'Aren't you supposed to be trained to do this?'

'Trained, yes but able to perform miracles – unfortunately no. The babe is rather chubby, and there is simply not enough room around it for me to turn it externally.

I have done everything I have been taught. Sometimes it works and other times not – your baby decides whether it will turn or not and it seems to me this little fellow or lass is quite content to stay the way they are.'

She groaned again, low, like a wounded animal.

'I'll be back in a minute,' he said striding out the cottage. He needed some air and to regain his composure. He needed to be strong for her – he could not let her see his fear.

'Great One, we need your help – she can't do this alone and I need her. You gave us this promise child and I believe that we are meant to parent that beautiful baby together. Please don't take them from me yet – not now when we are just discovering true happiness.'

His prayer was interrupted by her scream followed by another low moan. He rushed back into the cottage and held her hand as she struggled against wave after wave of pain that washed over her exhausted body.

'All right we are almost ready to deliver – baby's feet are coming. I need you to encourage your wife and help her as best you can. Can you do that for me?'

He nodded numbly.

As the next contraction came she was instructed to push as hard as she could. Her effort was immense, but so too was her pain.

'Well done lass, baby's feet are out. Take a deep breath and relax – the next contraction won't be long now and you'll need all your strength.'

With each contraction a little more progress was made.

'Push! Yes you're doing well lass. Now we mustn't rush the next push as we don't want to tear anything – I won't have you bleeding out on me now. The next part is getting baby's torso out and will be a lot trickier.'

He relaxed just a little – it would all be okay. It had to be.

That was the last logical thought he had. Things went from progressing nicely to pandemonium in a matter of seconds. The baby's shoulders became stuck and there was no way for Martha to get her hands in to manoeuvre the one shoulder for delivery. This was a well-nourished baby which made it more difficult. She feared the lack of oxygen would kill the child or rupture the mother causing a bleed out. The young woman no longer screamed or moaned – she fell unconscious from the excruciating pain. Without her able to push, the last bit of hope died. Fear edged its way back into the room like a silent partner – waiting to consume the inhabitants the moment they acknowledged its ugly presence. They needed a miracle.

CHAPTER 1

GENESIS

"There are far better things ahead than any we leave behind"
– C.S. Lewis

SHERBROOKE - MID-WINTER 1624

SHE WOKE as the winter sun crept through the little window glistening against the frosty morning air. She smiled to herself as she lay in the warm folds of her quilt, thinking of the adventure that awaited her. Today was the beginning of another chapter and she relished the thought of all the knowledge and the experiences she would gain. She stretched her limbs like a content cat and thought of the day ahead. Aislinn Hamilton could hear her mother moving around in the little kitchen below as she readied the household breakfast. Her father Mac would have been up and about early preparing the thatch bundles for another days work. Keeping them dry in the icy winter was vital and no easy feat. Aislinn felt extremely happy. Her parents had rediscovered themselves and were following their dreams. Now it was her turn. This was the day her dream began.

Most young eighteen year old girls in her village were already married off by their fathers, but she had been fortunate, although some of her peers pitied her lack of marital status. She did not care what they thought. Her parents recognized her desire and passion to make a difference in this world and had allowed her to reach for her dream. Thank goodness they also believed she should choose her own suitor and marry for love. They had been living proof that love makes a great deal of difference in marriage and she wanted what they had in her own marriage one day. She would not settle for less. There had not been a lack of suitors, each had tried to woo her and had asked for her hand in marriage, but she was not ready to settle down yet, and besides she had not yet met a man who made her heart leap in her chest and her knees weak. She thought back to the day that awaited her – a day she had worked hard for and had eagerly dreamed of. She would officially become a recognized midwife today. The village doctor had overseen her training with an older woman called Martha who had coached her the last four years and taught her all she knew about childbirth. Aislinn had been a quick learner and an eager student. She had a natural empathy and compassion for the birthing mothers but at the same time she was able to remain calm and focused in times of trouble and she had certainly seen a few of those. It was the only time she did not enjoy her work. Seeing a birthing mother fade away and die of infection or blood loss was never easy but in the times they lived in it was also not uncommon. This was her dream – to change the way childbirth took place and to make it safer for all mothers.

She thought back to the birth of the first baby she had ever attended. It had been frightening and yet exhilarating at the same time. It's what made her decide to follow this path and she did not regret her decision one bit.

Aislinn was mature for her age. Although she was just eighteen she had seen and experienced things most girls her age had never had to face up to. She had weathered the responsibility of her siblings when they had been captured by the Dark Lord and she had experienced the pain of thinking her parents were dead. Her life experiences had taught her much and made her wiser than her eighteen years. While the other young girls in Sherbrooke aspired to becoming the wives of reputable young men, she set her heart and dreams on something greater, something that would impact the world and make a difference. The realization that life was short and could be taken at any time had given her a sense of responsibility and a desire to live it to the full.

'Aislinn.'

She was pulled from her reverie by her mother's voice calling her to breakfast. She swung her legs over the side of her bed and pulled herself up out of the warm cocoon of blankets. Shivering, she quickly pulled on her clothes and washed her face. Her chocolate brown hair was a riot of curls that cascaded over her shoulders with a life of their own. She pulled her hair back into a neat ponytail taming it. Her blue eyes sparkled in her pretty face and she pulled a tongue at herself in the mirror and then giggled. She was a young woman now – she couldn't behave like a child anymore even if she felt not a day older than fifteen.

'Aislinn,' her mother called again a little louder this time.

'Coming,' she yelled back as she bounced down the stairs of the cottage.

Her siblings were all sitting at the rough wooden table. Struan looked half asleep and rubbed his eyes as he yawned loudly.

'Struan, that's enough,' his mother said sternly. 'You need to go to bed a little earlier at night.'

He grunted in response then tucked hungrily into his porridge.

'Ouch, it's hot,' he yelped burning his tongue on the steaming food.

Maddy giggled and was rewarded with a scathing look from her brother.

'Eat up everyone,' Imogene said.

One needed the patience of a saint. Having teens in the home was a new and challenging experience for Mac and Imogene Hamilton. They were like creatures from another planet and trying to understand their thinking or behavior was vexing and mostly just plain confusing. Struan was sixteen years old now and considered a young man. He towered over his mother and was starting to develop some muscle tone due to his work with Mac in the afternoons after school. He had dark brooding good looks that would have the girls hounding him in years to come. Maddy was twelve and starting to grow in leaps and bounds. Her body was gangly and long-limbed and she was a little awkward the way she carried herself. Her feet seemed too big for her body and yet in many ways she was still like a little girl. The transition from child to teen was creeping in slowly leaving her a muddle of both. Her long brown hair was straight like her mothers and a complete contrast to Aislinn's magnificent curls. Mitchell sat on his chair and scraped his porridge bowl. He was an energetic six year old and curious by nature. He asked numerous questions and had a very inquiring mind. He had started school at the local village and loved the time he spent with his friends and learning new things. His fair hair was starting to turn brown as his siblings had. He had a smattering of freckles across the bridge of his nose which made him all the more endearing.

'Come on you lot – eat up or you will be late for school.'

Maddy moaned. School was not her favourite place – she would much rather be at home with her mother.

'Are you ready for your big day Aislinn?'

'I can't wait. It's hard to believe the day has come - I'm a little nervous but very excited.'

'You'll do well – you have a gift and I know you will make a difference in many people's lives,' her mother encouraged.

The children all collected their lunches from their mother as they readied themselves to leave.

'Now walk together all of you. Struan make sure they get to school safely,' she yelled after her eldest son as he made his way out the door. Sometimes he needed reminding that Mitchell was only six. The younger children kissed her, pulled on their warm coats to keep the cold at bay and ran out the cottage to catch up to their long-legged brother who was already striding over the rise.

CHAPTER 2

FIRST IMPRESSIONS

"Don't judge a book by its cover."

'WELCOME Aislinn,' Dr. Williams smiled at the eager young girl who entered his rooms.

They were not grand rooms by any means but they were spotlessly clean and he had a thriving practice in their village of Sherbrooke. Aislinn loved this old man. He was in his early sixties now, but had a wealth of experience and a delightful bedside manner. She was very fortunate that he had taken her under his wing and mentored her over the last few years. Not many young women would have had this opportunity. The times they lived in did not encourage women to work and many midwives were viewed as devilish. This had not deterred Aislinn – she felt called to help others. Dr. Williams did not believe in all that hocus-pocus nonsense and despite his age, he was progressively broad-minded.

'You must be very excited that today you begin your work.'

Aislinn smiled, unconsciously biting her lower lip which betrayed her nervousness.

'Don't fret child,' he reassured her. 'We all have to start somewhere. You were born to do this.'

'It's just that I am so used to assisting Martha – I will need to get used to working alone.'

'Well you won't have to. I have decided that for the first three months you will work with another doctor going from village to village to help deliver babies. When he feels that you are confident enough on your own, we will set you free to fly solo young lady.'

Aislinn was not sure whether to laugh or groan. On one hand she was glad to have someone to share decisions with, but on the other hand she wanted to venture out on her own – to take the bull by the horns or fly solo as Dr. Williams referred to it.

'Speak of the devil,' he said as the door opened and a young man entered the rooms. He must have been about twenty-six years old Aislinn thought. He had a strong jaw and deep violet eyes. His almost black hair was thick and wavy and just reached his collar. He was a handsome man.

'About time you got here young man – I was beginning to think you weren't going to show up.'

The young man ignored the doctor's jibe and eyed Aislinn up and down as though he were inspecting a horse at market. She almost expected him to wander over and check her teeth. Her face reddened at his audacity.

How dare he make me feel insignificant! This is my big day – I won't let him spoil it, she thought angrily. In defiance she lifted her chin ever so slightly but it was not lost on the young man. She could see the amusement in his eyes and it further infuriated her. Her hand itched to slap his smug face.

Who was this rude man?

'Aislinn, this is Dr. Drew Williams – my son.'

She almost choked at this revelation.

Dr. Williams has a son.

No, this couldn't be happening. Surely he wasn't the doctor she would be working with? She guessed that he wanted to be stuck with her as much as she wanted to work with him. How would she survive three months of this insufferable man? It was bad enough that she would be supervised by him but to know that he would be reporting to his father made the situation worse. Her mind went into overdrive as she pictured them discussing her over dinner every evening rating her performance out of ten. She pulled herself together. She would not give him the satisfaction of seeing her discomfort. It was only three months she had to endure the arrogant sod. She smiled sweetly and introduced herself.

'Aislinn Hamilton – pleased to meet you Dr. Williams.'

His warm fingers enveloped her tiny hand, sending sensations up Aislinn's arm that confused her. She quickly pulled her hand away as though he had electrocuted her.

'I'll leave you two to get acquainted,' Dr. Williams senior announced as he left to attend to his first patient of the day – a tiny little red-haired boy who was yelling at the top of his lungs after a nasty fall. His poor frazzled mother tried her best to calm the boy with little success.

'Let's pop over to the Inn and get a coffee shall we?' he asked. It seemed more of a command than a suggestion and again Aislinn wished she had some smart quip to throw back at him. He was way too arrogant for her liking and needed taking down a peg or two. Today's excitement had turned a little sour. Nonetheless she meekly followed him out the door and down the street to the Sherbrooke Inn. At least she would get a warm drink. He just assumed that she drank coffee but if he had bothered to inquire he would have learned that she never touched the brew but preferred tea. He ordered for them and Aislinn sweetly changed her order to tea. He raised his brows and laughed.

'Coffee too strong for you?' he mocked.

'No I just prefer tea thank you.' She would not rise to the bait.

'My father has it in his head that you will be no trouble to me whatsoever. I however, am not too sure. I don't have time to babysit or to fix any mistakes you make. Frankly I think this is a waste of my time.'

He certainly didn't beat around the bush.

'Well now that you have that off your chest I can assure you that you won't have to babysit. I may be young but I am quite capable contrary to what you believe. I too don't have time to deal with self-absorbed, petulant individuals such as yourself, so we are both agreed on that score. I simply want to do my job and do it well. If that means I have to put up with your boorish behavior for three months then so be it.'

She smiled at him sweetly although her heart was pounding in her chest. Had she overstepped the mark?

She was surprised when he threw back his head and laughed – a deep laugh that reminded her of her father.

'Touché,' he responded. 'I guess I deserved that. It seems we got off on the wrong foot and for that I apologize. '

She silently heaved a sigh of relief. Their drinks arrived diffusing the awkwardness momentarily.

'Tell me about yourself?' he asked. 'I guess if we are going to be spending time together then we should make an effort to get acquainted.'

Aislinn described the moment she had come to know that birthing babies was the right thing for her. He watched her face intently as she described the first birth she ever attended and he could not miss the passion she emanated. It made her very attractive.

'Now you,' she finished. 'What is your story?'

'My mother died when I was born. I never knew her and yet somehow I have always felt partly responsible for her death. It was very difficult for my father in the early years so he hired a widow to look after me during the day until I was old enough to attend school. When I was eleven Rachel, the widow who cared for me, died and he decided that it was better for me to travel with him and learn all I could rather than to sit in school all day grieving for the two mothers I had lost. I think we kept each other from feeling lonely and sad in our own way. I would go with him to each appointment – a doctor's apprentice if you wish. I learned everything from him. By the time I was old enough to go to a medical school, I had practiced most of what the students were learning. As a result they allowed me to complete my studies far sooner than I would have. I have my father to thank for that.'

She could tell that he was very fond of his father and that the years of working together had given them a bond that was ironclad but she could also see the sadness that tinged his eyes when he spoke of the two women he had lost.

'How come I have never met you during my training?' she asked trying to cheer him up.

'I have spent the last four years travelling overseas to learn new techniques and practices. My father never had the opportunity to experience this so he felt it was important for me to learn as much as I could.'

'Where did you go?' she asked eagerly. She had never travelled much being a young woman but she had always wished she could see what the world was like out there. She envied him his freedom to travel.

'I went to Arles. Do you know where that is?'

'Yes, it is across the sea further east of our homeland. What was it like there?' she asked eagerly. 'Is it as sophisticated as people say?'

'It certainly is a different way of life – far more civilized some would say and yet I missed the simplicity of everyday living we experience here. Nonetheless I learned things I never would have here and for that I am grateful.'

They finished their drinks and each felt a little more comfortable with the other.

'Well I guess we should make a start for the day,' he announced. 'We have a house visit first to Mrs. MacGregor. She had her baby a week ago and we need to do a follow-up visit to check that all is well with them both.'

The rest of the day sped past in a blur of activity. Mrs. MacGregor welcomed them with open arms. She looked exhausted and had been having trouble feeding her new baby. Aislinn was able to sit with her and help her to master the technique. By the time they left the babe was greedily sucking at her breast as though making up for lost time over the last week. Drew looked on, watching the young girl helping the much older woman. She was confident and had a natural way with her patient. Yes, she would make an excellent midwife but he would keep that to himself. He had decided this beautiful young girl was a contradiction. In one sense she was very shy and sweet, but if you crossed her he was certain she would become stubborn and defiant. Today he had seen both aspects of her character and it intrigued him more than he cared to admit. For now, there was a truce between Aislinn Hamilton and Drew Williams. He was clearly very dedicated to his work and she could tell that he was a perfectionist in his practice. She held similar views and she hoped that they would not clash in any way. Maybe the three months would not be so unbearable after all.

CHAPTER 3

ILLUSIONS

"All problems are illusions of the mind." - Eckhart Tolle

GRISWOLD

LEGION, better known as the Dark Lord in Griswold, looked across the table at the woman sitting near him. She certainly was not a traditional beauty and yet she was striking in her own way. She had fair skin and light brown hair that was pulled away from her face in an ornate style and held in place with pearled hair clips. Her almond brown eyes were large and almost sad looking. He thought back to the day they had married nearly four years ago. It had not been a marriage of love – at least not from his side. He had married her to save face after Aislinn Hamilton had humiliated him in front of all his wizards and followers. She had made a mockery of them all – with her team of rescuers sent from the Great One. Yes, he had been defeated that day and made to look like a complete fool, but he had learned a lesson. Never give your heart to anyone or you would become weak. He vowed never to make that mistake again. When Gwendolyn was introduced to him by Wizard Falstaff, he felt this was a way to redeem his bruised ego. Up till that point his chief wizard had kept his children a secret as he knew of his Master's temper and selfish character. The day they were defeated by the young Hamilton girl changed his mind. As chief wizard of Griswold he had not been able to conjure up enough magic or sorcery to outwit Ziah and Aedan and he had been terrified that he would be banished and replaced by another wizard. He had seen the Dark Lord's fury when he realized that they were beaten and his fear had multiplied. If Wizard Morelock had still been around he would surely have been sent packing. The fact that the young wizard had mysteriously vanished just before the challenge was a blessing for the older wizard and his saving grace. He would have been doubly humiliated if the young wizard had outwitted the Great One's team. Losing Morelock to the Great One's side had made the Master even angrier and those few weeks in the castle after the defeat were like treading on eggshells.

It was then that Falstaff hatched a plan to bring Gwendolyn, his daughter, to the castle to meet his Master. If she could woo him into a marriage then his fate as chief wizard would be sealed for his lifetime. Of course neither Legion nor Gwendolyn had any idea they were being set up. Gwendolyn was feeling the pressure of becoming an old maid if she didn't marry soon. At twenty-two people were starting to view her as unmarriageable. As for Legion, his humiliation had been so great that he felt the need to prove to his subjects that he was able to tame a woman and find a wife. He was not getting any younger at forty and time was running out for him to provide an heir. Meeting Gwendolyn had been a stroke of luck and had solved all his problems. He believed love was for weaklings and played no part in his decision to marry her. It was purely strategic. The only emotion he felt was hatred for Aislinn and even after four years it had not waned.

He courted Gwendolyn, pursuing her with all the charm he could muster. It did not take long to win her over. The day after their wedding he changed. He reverted to his usual egotistical personality. Gwendolyn had spent the whole day in her rooms weeping at the change she saw in him.

Where was the caring man she had fallen in love with?

She fervently wished that man would come back to her.

So here they sat in the hall, two strangers eating breakfast – he feeling nothing for the woman who sat opposite him and she afraid of the man she had once loved. Leaving him was never an option – if he did not kill her, her father certainly would. She was trapped and now with the secret she had kept for the last month she would never escape or be free.

⌘

Mac and Imogene sat at the table with Eion and Rozanne. Their bouncy four year old son played hide and seek under the table around their legs with Mitchell Hamilton. He had the face of a cherub – sweet and rosy and his blond curls fell over his forehead. Gone were the days when Eion practiced wizardry for the Dark Lord. He was known as Wizard Morelock in those days, but thanks to his wife's persistence they had made their great escape from the Dark Lord's clutches. This sweet child was the gift they had been granted from the Great One after years of being childless despite Eion's sorcery abilities. The one thing he could never do was to create life through magic. Now he only ever used his gift to help others. They had been terrified for a long time that they would be discovered living in Sherbrooke by the Dark Lord's spies. They had made sure not to venture too far from their little cottage. Only Mac and Imogene and their family knew of their true identity and they preferred to keep it that way. Not a day went by where they didn't worry, even if for a second, that they would be caught and dragged back to Griswold to face the Dark Lord. Fortunately travel was difficult in the day they lived and so not too many people from Griswold ever ventured this way. Certainly no-one from their village ever wanted to go to Griswold – its evil reputation preceded itself.

'Look at those two boys,' Mac laughed as Mitch and Asher played around the table. 'They were made to be friends.'

The parents watched the two young boys, grateful for the blessing that each child brought to their respective families. Mitchell had almost been lost to them but thanks to Rozanne and Eion they were a family again. The Dark Lord had tried to ruin many lives and they had all fallen victim to his evil in some way or another. Thanks to Ziah, Aedan and the Great One they had learned that good always overcomes evil and that nothing is impossible if you just believe.

'I am leaving with Aedan in the morning. He is making a journey to Glen Morgan as there have been rumours of raiders pillaging the village,' Mac informed Eion. 'You are welcome to come along with us Eion.'

'Thanks Mac, but I don't think it's a good idea yet – if the raiders happen to be from Griswold then my goose will be cooked.'

'You can't let the Dark Lord dictate your future forever Eion – you live like a captive in this village – it's been four years since you left Griswold and it's time you got out and had some adventure with Aedan, Regent and myself. You would feel completely liberated if you were part of the team instead of watching from the sidelines.'

Imogene saw the alarm on Rozanne's face.

They still feared the Dark Lord – even after all these years.

'Mac, don't pressure Eion – he will know when he is ready to go with you on a trip,' she gently chided.

Mac let it drop. He loved Eion and Rozanne but it frustrated him beyond words seeing a man that was so talented wasting his gifts because he was so fearful to face the Dark Lord again. Granted, he hoped he would never have to face the man as he had seen his evil firsthand when Ziah was executed, but he would not allow it to stop him from doing what he felt most passionate about. Still, it had to be Eion's decision – if he chose to live his life this way then that was his choice. If only he would realize there was so much more.

They may be free physically from the Dark Lord but did they not realize they were still his captives?

Mac looked at the two boys playing – there was a sense of freedom and childlike enthusiasm in each of their games. That was how life was meant to be – fun and carefree.

'Well you know that you never have to wait for me to ask you to come along Eion. When you are ready you are always welcome.'

He did not miss the relief that flooded the man's face.

'Thank you for understanding Mac, you and Imogene have been true friends to us.'

For now the matter was closed but Mac hoped fervently that Eion and Rozanne would be able to overcome the fear that held them captive. They had simply traded one prison for another and yet they could not see it. He prayed that their eyes would be opened to the truth. Until then, he would have to be patient.

CHAPTER 4

THE CHILD

"A child is an uncut diamond" - Austin O'Malley

GWENDOLYN had been feeling off-colour for a few moons. It started with nausea every time she smelled food and ended with her emptying the contents of her stomach daily. Legion had been too pre-occupied to even notice her ill health. The truth was that he did not spend too much time with her anymore and Gwendolyn realized that she had been played, not only by her father, but by the man she thought loved her. Too late she realized that she was simply a trophy wife on his arm. It took her a few moons to comprehend that she was going to have his child. She decided not to rush to him with this news – she wanted to relish her new state alone for a while and get her head around it. She was not sure whether to be delighted at this news or terrified. Perhaps this child would change things in their relationship. Surely it would give her some leverage in the household? Even the servants kept her at arm's length, as though they were afraid of her. She felt so alone and miserable.

To help her cope she dreamed of Legion pampering her, falling in love with her all over again when he realized she was carrying his child. If that did not happen then at least she would have someone to love and receive love from in return. Up to this point she had been wondering whether the rest of her life was doomed to loneliness and isolation. She could not live that way. Now, this child would be her reason for living.

Her dreams came to a rapid end as she retched again, her stomach turning in a wave of nausea.

When would this awful sickness pass?

She could already feel the changes beginning in her body. Her tall reed-like frame was softening and filling out as her breasts were swelling in preparation for the young one. Her usually flat belly felt more rounded and her emotions were all over the place. One moment she felt joyful and the next a hopeless despair. She desperately wished she had someone to share it with. Oh how she missed her mother.

⌘

The Great One gazed in his Mirror of Time at the vulnerable young woman. Even though she was the wife of Legion his heart ached with compassion for her. He had to remind himself to think of him as Legion – to the Great One he was Sephtis – the man he had such hope for but who betrayed him. Poor Gwendolyn - she had been trapped and manipulated into a marriage that could only end in heartbreak for her. Now she would produce an heir and that child would be subjected to a father who was cruel and unloving – no child should ever have to experience that. Still, hope was the one thing he always believed in – that and a man's ability to redeem himself – he never stopped believing that Legion could be the man he believed he could be.

In the meantime, he would have to keep watch over Gwen and the child.

⌘

Gwendolyn retched again for what felt like the millionth time as her lady in waiting entered her chambers. Maeve looked at her mistress' pinched face, her green pallor evident. Her gaze dropped to the woman's breasts and belly and she knew the plight that affected her. She had seen this in many a young girl. Gwendolyn silently turned and walked to her bed where she lay down, just until the nausea would pass.

Her desire to keep the news to herself was short lived. Before long the kitchens were abuzz with the news that the Dark Lord would soon have an heir. From there it was only a matter of time till the Dark Lord's valet heard the news. He found his Master in his chambers poring over some new spell that Falstaff had concocted.

'I have some news Master,' he cautiously ventured.

'What is it Holgrimm?'

'There is talk in the castle that the Lady Gwendolyn is with child Master. Her lady in waiting swears that she is suffering with morning sickness.'

He waited unsure how the Dark Lord would react. He did not expect the look of utter shock that flickered momentarily over his Master's face before he pulled his emotions in check.

'Leave me Holgrimm, and tell the help to stop gossiping about matters that do not concern them,' he snapped.

Alone, he felt anger stir within him.

Why hasn't Gwendolyn told me?

He would not tolerate another woman deceiving him. He felt foolish that he was the last to hear the news and a little embarrassed that he had not noticed Gwen's condition. Then the reality of the news hit him – he was going to be a father, he would have an heir and someone to leave his legacy to. This was a good thing.

She heard her door open and was surprised to see him standing there – she could not read the expression in his eyes. Was it anger she saw, tenderness or just a plain question?

He knew.

She felt it in the pit of her stomach.

Who had told him?

She had been so careful.

'Holgrimm tells me that you have not been feeling well, my dear.'

He would give her the opportunity to tell him. What he was really doing was testing her. Intuitively Gwendolyn felt caution and knew her secret was over. If he caught her lying to him she would pay dearly for it. She was right to be afraid of him – he was devious and cruel when crossed.

'Yes,' she replied trying to calm the furious beating of her heart. She was sure he would see it thumping in her chest.

'It started off with nausea and feeling very tired. I wasn't sure until just recently and I've been waiting for the right time to tell you. We are having a baby Legion.'

He let out a silent breath of relief. Thankfully this wasn't going to be a war – she had been honest with him. He smiled and walked over to her, placing his hand on her belly. She tried not to recoil in fear at his touch. When had she become afraid of her own husband?

He was surprised at how round her belly was already. How had he not noticed? Had it been that long since he had touched his wife?

Was she lying about not knowing sooner that she was pregnant?

No, he had to give her the benefit of the doubt.

'When is the babe due?'

'I am not exactly sure but I think in about five moons.'

'You need to look after yourself Gwen,' he chided. 'This baby is very important and will be my heir – we wouldn't want anything to happen to him would we?'

Gwendolyn suddenly felt sicker than she had all day. Of course he wasn't concerned about her health – she was just an incubator for his heir and what if the baby wasn't a boy? She prayed that it was or that would be her fault too.

'In the meantime I will find the best doctor in the country to birth this child. You don't have to worry about that, Gwen. You really should tell your father that you are expecting – I guess he will be delighted.'

With that he turned on his heel and marched out the door.

Gwendolyn let out a sigh. She was relieved he was not angry but it was a sigh of sadness too. Clearly he did not love her. Most couples when expecting would feel closer to one another – more in love at this new bond or creation, but it was not so with them. All he cared about was having an heir. Why did he have to be so cold?

He was right, she should tell her father. She knew he would be delighted but again for his own selfish reasons. This baby was another bargaining chip in the game they played with one another. It sickened her.

Legion was on cloud nine. This would give him credibility amongst his followers again. Griswold would have an heir. An heir would have his loyal followers scrambling for favour and recognition in fear that they would be ousted from their positions. Yes he would use this news for his own benefit and get as much mileage out of his subjects as possible.

Now to find a doctor who could attend to Gwen. This child must be protected at all costs. He would have to ask around. His local physician was quite effective when it came to basic diseases and ailments but he was no great healer. Besides he doubted that the man had much experience with childbirth as he had worked here in Griswold for Legion for many years. Usually the birthing was left to the women but he wanted someone with more experience and knowledge than just an old woman from the village beyond his castle. He was not willing to trust his heir to anyone.

Maybe Falstaff would know of someone.

Wizard Falstaff was indeed very excited to hear the baby news. It was just as Gwendolyn had anticipated. This gave him an even stronger position in The Dark Lord's castle. Not only was he the chief wizard but he would be the grandfather to Legion's child. The Master could never get rid of him now.

'We need a physician Falstaff to attend to Gwen,' Legion stated.

'I will see who I can find Master,' he promised. He was secretly delighted that he would have an opportunity to control this part of Gwendolyn's care.

He would have to make some enquiries in the villages surrounding Griswold – only the best physician would be good enough for the Dark Lord's heir. Falstaff began to hatch another plan to weave himself further into the Master's graces. He had yet another secret he had not shared with Legion. Gwendolyn had been a well-kept secret from the Dark Lord until it benefitted him to reveal his daughter's identity. Now he would play his second trump card. He had a son, Daemon, that Legion had never met. The young man had been away following in his father's footsteps learning from the druids all about wizardry and witchcraft. Falstaff had kept him well hidden because he was afraid that his own son would usurp his position in the castle. Now Daemon was back home and itching to get working and all Falstaff's insecurities came flooding back. He had to keep his son away from Griswold castle for a while. He did not want Legion to meet Daemon just yet. What better way than to send him off to find a physician. He would be gone for at least one moon, if not two. That way he would be helping his sister whom he adored without the Dark Lord discovering his wizardry abilities. Falstaff smiled to himself. He would get all the credit for Daemon's hard work.

Falstaff lived with many secrets and he had kept one vital secret from his own two children.

Daemon was not his biological son.

Just like Morelock and Rozanne, he and his wife were unable to conceive. It had been a painful thing for them to endure. Falstaff worked for an apothecary in those days, concocting all sorts of remedies and potions to help people; yet the irony of not being able to make his wife fertile ate at him. The answer to their prayers had come twenty-six years ago when they adopted a baby boy whose mother had died during childbirth. The boy had been the saviour of their family, so it had come as a complete shock and surprise when just four years later his wife had fallen pregnant with Gwendolyn. The two children were inseparable growing up until their mother had died from illness in their teens. Then they had both withdrawn, each one dealing with their loss by isolating themselves in their pain. They still loved one another deeply but the closeness they felt as children had been suffocated by their individual grief.

Maybe this would bring them together again. What better way than finding his sister a physician.

CHAPTER 5

FACING FEARS

"If you want to catch your dreams, you have to drop your fears."
— Anton Rubaclini

SHERBROOKE - SPRING 1624

AISLINN and Drew soon came to understand one another as they worked side by side. He knew when to give her freedom to attend to a patient, and frankly he was impressed by her caring nature together with her ability to focus and get the job done. She in turn had growing respect for the young doctor. His overseas training taught her many new things and she was grateful to old Dr. Williams for pairing them together. She would not have learned half as much had she not worked with him. She asked many questions and he patiently answered them, explaining medical procedures and protocol. He even loaned her some of his medical journals to read through and every evening before bed Aislinn would spend hours reading and absorbing all she could about human anatomy and medicines. She found the knowledge fascinating and her thirst for it increased as she pored over the material.

They were becoming firm friends and Aislinn enjoyed her time working with him. She remembered the day they met nearly three moons ago and smiled. Their initial meeting had been as cold and as frosty as the freezing winter they had experienced. How she dreaded the idea of working with him then. Now she dreaded the day they would no longer work together – it wouldn't be long now before they parted ways and he would be free from tutoring and mentoring her.

She had misjudged him. He was not the arrogant young man she thought he was. His real nature was incredibly caring and gentle, yet underneath there was incredible strength. He was an excellent doctor and she had to admit that he was extremely good looking – too much so, as her heart beat furiously whenever she looked at him. When he smiled his violet eyes flashed mischievously and he had a dimple on his left cheek. Other times he would concentrate so hard during a procedure that his brow would furrow and his eyes would be intense, deep and dark.

'Aislinn, I do believe you have a little crush, but he probably sees you like a little sister,' she thought.

Aislinn tried very hard over the next few weeks to focus on her work, even being a little more distant than usual in her behaviour toward Drew. It did not go unnoticed and the young man wondered what he had done to offend his pretty co-worker.

'Is everything all right,' he asked one day.

'Yes fine, why do you ask?'

'You just seem a little distant Aislinn – not your usual bubbly self,' he added.

'No everything is fine,' she insisted.

Drew was not going to push it.

⌘

Gwendolyn felt incredibly uncomfortable. She should be over the sickness as she was well and truly into the second half of her pregnancy now, yet it still persisted. She felt debilitated most of the time and she prayed that everything was all right with the baby. Daemon had sent word that he was still searching for a good physician. She worried about the labour and how she would cope. She touched her blossoming belly and spoke to the wee babe. Legion checked on her daily now like an over-protective father and she found that she enjoyed the few moments he spent with her. He had softened a bit in the last few months and she liked the new version of the Dark Lord.

Maybe they could restore their love when this baby came.

She hoped so.

She smiled as she felt the child move within her womb.

⌘

'Aislinn, I've had a call to go to Trenton. There has been an outbreak of measles and they want me to go and set up a quarantine area. There are some pregnant women that need to be checked and if they are free of it, kept away from those who are sick. As you well know measles can have devastating effects on a pregnant mother. Would you be willing to come with me?' Drew asked.

She felt her blood run cold. The last time she set foot in Trenton was when she and Regent went to find Mitchell. Aislinn remembered the inn and their reception there and how they tricked the Innkeeper into getting her work with Rozanne. All the memories and fears came flooding back. There was no way she could go back there. It was too close to Griswold castle – what if someone recognized her? Drew did not know everything about her past – her run in with the Dark Lord was not something she usually mentioned in casual conversation and as yet she had not told him what had happened four years ago. She planned to tell him but up until now the time had not been right.

'I'm sorry Drew, but I can't go with you. Please don't ask me why – it's complicated and one day I will explain it all to you, but I have a really good reason.'

'I have all the time in the world to listen Aislinn.'

'I can't tell you right now – besides it's a long story and you have to prepare yourself to leave soon. It's a long journey.'

Her tone suggested that she was done talking. The little muscle in his jaw twitched and his eyes grew cold. He felt hurt that she did not trust him enough to share her past.

'I always knew that you wouldn't cut it,' he said cruelly. 'What kind of midwife do you hope to be Aislinn? Part of the job entails you caring for women before the babe is born. It's not just about the delivery you know. You leave me no choice but to put this in your review.'

With that he turned on his heel and marched out. She felt his anger and disappointment and punched the air in frustration.

Damn the Dark Lord.

He still managed to ruin her life four years later. Now Drew had lost all respect for her. It hurt her that he saw her as weak and fussy, that he did not believe she had a good reason. It dawned on her that his opinion really mattered to her.

⌘

'What should I do Papa?' she asked her father as they sat near the hearth that night, the warm flames crackling and licking the glowing wood.

Her mother sat nearby mending Struan's shirt. Struan loved to practice his sword fighting each afternoon after school and his clothing took quite a beating.

'Aislinn, I understand your fear of the Dark Lord and going back to Trenton. Being within Griswold's borders is worrying, but Drew does have a point sweetheart. You are training to help those who need it. Doctors don't have the luxury of picking their patients. It is their responsibility to care for the sick no matter what the risk. I remember a fearless young girl four years ago who stood up to The Dark Lord. Where has that girl gone?'

'I'm not the same person Papa.'

'Oh yes you are, but you are even stronger and more resilient now. You care for people. You are in a better position now than you were when you faced the Dark Lord all those years ago. You just need to believe in yourself Aislinn.'

'But what if someone recognizes me Papa?'

'That is a possibility Aislinn, but four years have passed and you are no longer a little girl but a grown woman now. People don't always remember faces. The Dark Lord has ruined our lives enough - don't live like Eion, Aislinn. He and Rozanne are still so afraid of the Dark Lord that they will not venture more than a few miles away from home. They live like prisoners here.'

'Thank you Papa, you are right as always,' she said wrapping her arms around his neck and planting a kiss on his forehead. 'I have to care for all people if I am going to make a difference. I won't let that man ruin my future. Ziah always told me that my destiny rested in my hands and that I could be anything I wanted. It's time to believe that again and trust my heart. Do you think Regent would escort me to Trenton? Drew left this morning and I don't want to travel alone.'

'There is no way you can travel alone Aislinn. I will get a message to him – I'm sure he will come.'

'Thank you Papa – I love you.'

He smiled at his eldest daughter – she was so beautiful and she did not yet realize what an amazing young woman she was – some man would be lucky to have her as a wife someday.

⌘

A day later Aislinn found herself on the road to Trenton with Regent. They laughed and reminisced over the old times and it was good to be in her old friend's company again.

'How do you feel about going back to Trenton, Aislinn?'

'I would be lying if I said I wasn't nervous,' she laughed looking at the truth ring she wore constantly now. It gleamed purple and she smiled. This ring had saved her bacon many times and she treasured it. The Great One had given it to her as a gift after their victory against the Dark Lord. She had tried returning it to him in Lionsgate but he would not hear of it.

'You have earned that ring young lady,' he said. 'Keep it as a reminder that goodness can always overcome evil and that nothing is impossible for those who believe.'

She knew the value of this ring and how special a gift it was.

'So how long do you think you will stay in Trenton?' he broke into her thoughts.

'I guess it depends how bad the outbreak is and how Drew manages to contain it,' she replied. 'Hopefully it won't be too long.'

'I won't be able to stay while you are there, but you do know that if you need me I will come.'

'Thank you Regent – I am sure Drew will look after me and I will be fine.'

'Nonetheless I will come and check on you. I want to know you are safe.'

'Thank you, dear friend.'

The suffering in Trenton was clear to them as they rode through the usually bustling village streets which were eerily deserted. Some houses had crosses painted in red dye to mark the contagious homes. Aislinn was glad she had come. She could be of help here. Deep in her heart she was looking forward to seeing Drew again. The way they left things made her uncomfortable and she cared deeply what he thought about her. It had taken her a while to realize what was happening - the truth was that she was in love with him. The telltale signs were all there – the butterflies in her stomach when she saw him, the way her heart skipped a beat when he smiled at her, her irrational attraction to him that affected her entire body. She had never felt this way about any man before. She knew that he more than likely did not feel the same way about her and her heart ached a little. Still she would focus on the job and just being near him for now would be enough.

She found him at the inn eating lunch. He looked completely surprised when she walked in the door, more so when he saw Regent standing behind her dwarfing her petite frame with his statuesque form. Aislinn introduced the two men and she could see the questions in his eyes. She had to admit it was a strange sight – a young girl with a complexion so fair travelling with a bear of a man as black as ebony. She smiled at the thoughts that must be running through Drew's mind. She had not told him much about her past at all.

'So you came after all. What changed your mind?' he asked. His cool tone was not lost on her.

'You were right,' her words tumbled out nervously as she ate humble pie. 'It is my job to help wherever I am needed and this is where I am needed right now. I'm sorry Drew it won't happen again.'

She could see the hardness in his eyes soften and he smiled, that irresistible dimple deepening. Her heart lurched. *Damn the man* – he made her lose her senses.

'Well I'm glad you are here. Won't you both join me for lunch?' he gestured to the empty seats at his table.

Drew filled her in over lunch as to what had been done and what still needed doing. They would visit some of the pregnant women that afternoon, making sure they were isolated from the infection. After they had eaten and her bag stowed away in her room at the inn they headed out to see their patients. Regent bid them farewell and readied himself for his journey back to Lionsgate. Aislinn hugged him as she said goodbye, grateful for this beautiful man in her life. She loved him like a brother.

'Thank you my friend. I know I can always count on you.'

'Take care Aislinn and watch your back. Remember what I said about being there if you need me.'

She knew what he meant.

'I will,' she promised.

'He's a good man Aislinn,' Regent said acknowledging Drew who had retreated to give them time for to say their goodbyes. 'Follow your heart and be honest with him.'

'I'm not sure what you mean,' she blushed.

'You can't hide your feelings from me Aislinn – I know you too well. I saw how you looked at him.'

She smiled. 'You always were astute,' she said as she kissed him on the cheek. 'Farewell my friend and thank you.'

⌘

Daemon urged his horse forward. He was tired as he had been on the road for more than two moons. His father had tasked him with finding a good physician to take care of Gwendolyn and he had visited many villages within Griswold's borders. So far he had found no one suitable for the job. He had hoped that he would find someone in Trenton as it was one of the bigger villages in Griswold and the closest to the castle but when he first passed through the village at the beginning of his search he quickly realized that the doctor was too old and set in his ways. He had found no-one suitable in Griswold and he would have to extend his search outside its borders. This was a concern as Legion's reputation preceded him and he was not sure anyone would be willing to accompany him back to the castle.

Time was running out.

He rode into Trenton and tethered his horse at the post outside the inn. His horse needed a break and he was looking forward to a tankard of cold ale and something to eat. After a good night's rest he would leave for the neighbouring kingdom of Ebondeen to search for a physician. He stepped into the warm inn, the smell of bread assailing his senses.

'Back already Dr. Williams. That was quick.' the young lady behind the counter flirted. Daemon was confused and looked around.

Was she talking to him?

He wasn't a doctor but he was glad to hear that there was one besides old Dr. Payne in Trenton. Why had she mistaken him for the doctor? He shrugged off the error and asked for a tankard of ale. Perhaps he and the doc looked similar. She probably realized her mistake and felt too embarrassed to acknowledge it. He would have to find out about this Dr. Williams before he left. This may save him a trip to Ebondeen after all.

He carried his ale over to the corner of the tavern and sat down where he would not be disturbed. He sipped the frothy brew thirstily, savouring the bitter flavour. It had been too long since he had enjoyed a good meal. He'd ask about the doctor later when he felt rested and his belly was full. He ate the delicious bread and cheese. He was famished after being on the road so many days.

'All right Betsy,' a buxom woman who appeared to be the owner of the tavern said jovially to the young girl who mistook him for the doctor; 'time to get home, lass, to your family. I'll take over from here. The evening crowd will be in soon though there's been a lot less business since the measles hit us.'

Betsy gathered her things and made her way out the tavern but before she left she smiled seductively at Daemon.

Was that an invitation?

He could have sworn she was flirting with him again. He would have seriously considered her offer had he not been too exhausted. For now he just needed a warm bed and a place to wash up.

He sat and watched as the tavern slowly filled up. The owner was right - it wasn't as busy as it usually would have been but he was glad for that due to his fatigue.

He was about to get up and ask for a room for the night when he noticed a man and woman enter the tavern. The woman was young and beautiful, her dark hair a little unruly as she tried to tame it in her hands. It was not her that caught his attention though. He sucked his breath in, shocked by what he saw. The man was his double – the strong jaw and black wavy hair. He did not need to see his eyes to know that this man was his spitting image.

'Good evening Dr. Williams, Miss Aislinn,' the buxom woman welcomed them. 'I trust you had a successful day helping those poor folks who are sickly.'

It was obvious that they were highly regarded here in Trenton.

So this was the doctor. No wonder the young girl had mistaken me for the man. But why does he look so like me?

Daemon's thoughts were muddled as he was still in shock. He could not approach the doctor now - not until he had some answers. It was just his luck to find a doctor who seemed to know what he was doing and not be able to approach him. His father would not be pleased with this delay. Legion was beginning to get angry at Falstaff's lack of ability to procure a physician and the old man was taking it out on him.

His father must know why this man looked so like him. What hadn't he told him?

Daemon waited in the corner of the tavern, his head down, hoping no one would notice him. After Aislinn and Drew had retired for the night, he slipped out of the inn. It was best that he and the good doctor were not seen together for now.

CHAPTER 6

MIXED EMOTIONS

*"Emotions don't tell the truth. Just because you have a feeling about
something doesn't make it a reality"*   - Joyce Meyer

GWENDOLYN clutched her belly and screamed in pain.
It felt as though this child was devouring her from the inside
out. Something was wrong. She was bleeding just a little but
she feared what that meant. If she lost this baby Legion would
resent her – no he would hate her for all time. The one thing
she yearned for most in her confinement was her mother.
Being pregnant made her loss feel even greater – she thought
she had dealt with losing the one person she loved so much
but now the pain was coming back to her. Her mother would
have known what to say and do to make her feel safe. She
missed her so terribly. She curled up in the foetal position and
let out another cry. Her lady-in-waiting rushed to get Legion.
Her mistress needed a physician now.

⌘

Daemon had rushed back to the castle, riding hard from
Trenton. All his weariness had disappeared the moment he
had laid eyes on Dr. Williams. Now he glared at his father
incredulously. Why hadn't his parents told him the truth
years ago? He felt anger stir in his heart.

'You have to understand the circumstances we found ourselves in Daemon. Your mother so desperately wanted a child. We tried for years to conceive so when the opportunity came to make you our son we could not say no. When Dr. William's wife died there was no way the old man could look after two babies. He wanted to; and he felt so guilty giving you up but he was grieving for his wife and could only keep one child. We loved you so much and we only ever wanted the best for you.'

'It's more than the fact that I am adopted father,' Daemon yelled angrily. 'I have a brother – a twin. It was like looking in the mirror. Do you know what that felt like - how shocking it is to come face to face with yourself?'

'I'm sorry Daemon – we should have told you. I had no idea that you and your brother looked so alike. I never wanted you to find out this way.'

'Were you ever planning on telling me the truth?'

'We always agreed we should tell you when you were older but the longer you were my son the harder it was to tell you. We also promised old Dr. Williams that we would not reveal his secret as this would come as a huge shock to your twin brother. When your mother died I guess I became afraid I would lose you if I told you – I lost her and I couldn't bear the thought of losing you too.'

'Well what do we do now father? How can we ask him to come and help Gwendolyn? He is the only doctor that has any clue what he is doing in the whole of Griswold and he has a woman who works with him which would be good for Gwen. She needs another woman's company at this time.'

'A woman you say? Is she one of the midwives from Griswold?'

Falstaff felt a little concerned. He had heard horror stories of some of the midwives within their borders. That is why his Master wanted the best for Gwen.

'I really don't know father. I have been away if you remember, but I do recall the innkeeper calling her Miss Aislinn. Do you know her?'

Falstaff felt like the air had been punched out of his lungs. Was it even possible that Aislinn Hamilton could be back in Griswold? The young woman certainly had some gumption if she was willing to come back. He was not sure whether it was courage or stupidity on the young woman's part.

'I'm not sure. In the meantime I'll think about it Daemon – somehow we will get Dr. Williams to come and care for Gwen.'

'How is that even possible without him finding out the truth, not to mention what a shock this will be to Gwen? I assume she doesn't know about my adoption?'

'I will make a plan, Daemon. In the meantime say nothing to your sister about this – the shock could affect her condition.'

The door flew open and Gwen's lady in waiting stood there panting, fear on her face.

'Come quickly Wizard Falstaff,' she urged. 'Miss Gwendolyn is bleeding and in pain.'

⌘

Legion was furious, mostly because this was out of his control. He was not used to feeling helpless and yet this time he honestly did not know what to do. He took his anger out on Falstaff.

'Where is this physician you have promised to find me?' he ranted.

'I have found him Master but he needs a little persuasion to come to the castle as he is from beyond Griswold's borders and fears coming here.'

'I don't care – just get him here no matter what. Do you understand me?' he threatened.

Wizard Falstaff understood all too well. They had to get that doctor here as fast as possible. Legion would have his head on a pike if anything happened to his child. Then a thought occurred to him. He knew how much the Dark Lord hated Aislinn Hamilton. He would use this to his advantage – it would be his double-edged sword. Daemon would be the key in getting her to the castle as she would never agree to come, even for Gwen's sake. Oh how the Dark Lord would reward him for delivering the girl to his doorstep. She would help Gwendolyn and then when her time of use was over he could do with her as he wished and Falstaff would have won his Master's favour back. It was time to set his plan in motion – he did not have much time as Gwen was starting to come down with a fever and was confined to bed rest. He had to act fast and he needed Daemon to cooperate for his plan to work. As Daemon and Legion had not yet met, his little plan might just work.

⌘

Aislinn and Drew had been in Trenton for half a moon. Their time was coming to an end as they had done all they could for the sick. No new cases of measles had been identified which was good news for the village. They would begin their long journey back to Sherbrooke in a couple of days. Aislinn was looking forward to getting home – she had missed her family and this was the first time she had been away for such an extended time. She unpacked her nightdress from her bag and put it next to her bed. She felt tired as she combed through her wild curls. It had been a long busy day and she looked forward to curling up under the warm down quilt. A soft knock at the door caught her by surprise.

'Yes,' she called.

'It's me Aislinn.'

She pulled the door open surprised to see Drew standing in the hallway. They had said goodnight only ten minutes previously.

'Is everything all right?'

'Yes,' he smiled reassuringly, 'but I was wondering if you would like to take a walk with me before bed,' he asked.

He appeared a little nervous, not his usual confident self.

'I would love a walk Drew. Just let me get my shawl,' Aislinn responded.

Her stomach did a little flip. This man had a very strong effect on her. She took a deep breath as she grabbed her shawl.

It would not do to behave like a lovesick girl in front of him she chided herself mentally.

They walked out into the moonlight and down the now quiet street of Trenton. Houses reflected flickering lamplight and murmurings of voices could be heard here and there. It was good to see the red dye crosses had been washed off the whitewashed walls of many homes and that things were getting back to normal in the village.

'Let's go down to the pond,' he ventured. The pond was in the middle of the village and surrounded by the natural plants that grew in the area. They could hear the frogs croaking and the crickets chirping as they approached it.

'The stars are so beautiful,' Aislinn said gazing up at the dark night sky that winked at her with a thousand shiny sparkles.

'Yes they are,' Drew said looking at her enraptured face.

They walked in silence for a while then spoke simultaneously. 'Do you...' she said, just as he said, 'Aislinn...'

They both laughed nervously.

'You go first,' he offered.

'I was just going to ask you if you wanted to know why I didn't want to come to Trenton.'

'I've been wondering about that since you said no. I knew it wasn't like you to back away from a challenge. You must have had a good reason for wanting to stay away from here. I'm sorry for the things I said Aislinn. I was angry and upset – I know that you are a brilliant midwife and that you truly do care about people. Can you forgive me?'

'I'll have to think about it,' she replied in her sternest voice, then giggled at his mock look of pain.

'Of course I forgive you Drew – I don't blame you for being upset. The truth is that Trenton has some bad memories for me and reminds me of another time in my life that was difficult.'

Aislinn told him all about her family's nightmare with the Dark Lord and Cillian and how she had ended up imprisoned by him.

'He truly hates me Drew. I humiliated him in front of all his subjects. I don't know what he would do if he ever caught me again. I guess I was fearful that if I came to Trenton someone might recognize me. I'm glad I came though; I feel that I have conquered a fear that was hidden deep within me. This trip has healed me more than I have helped heal the people here. I don't regret coming.'

'I'm sorry Aislinn. If I had known why you were loath to come here I would have insisted you stay in Sherbrooke. I want you to know that I would never do anything to endanger you. I always want to be honest with you and I hope you trust me enough to be honest with me.'

'I trust you completely Drew, that is why I came here – because I knew you would keep me safe.'

He took a deep breath as she spoke those words.

'The truth is I have developed feelings for you Aislinn that I no longer can ignore. I have tried so hard to pretend that we are just colleagues but I can't lie to myself anymore. When I'm not with you I feel as though part of me is missing, as though I am half a person. That is why I was so disappointed when you didn't want to come to Trenton – the thought of being away from you for weeks, was unbearable.'

'What are you saying Drew?' she asked breathless, not wanting to get her hopes up.

'I'm saying, you daft woman, that I am in love with you. I want to be with you the rest of my life Aislinn, unless you feel differently of course?'

She stared at him, unable to believe what he had just professed.

'Well, say something Aislinn please,' he said worried she did not feel the same way.

'Yes, oh yes. I love you too Drew,' she blurted out. 'I've been trying so hard to squash down my feelings. That is why I have not been my usual bubbly self lately as you put it. I was terrified you would think me a silly young girl with a crush on the doctor.'

She realized she was babbling.

He could not help himself. He pulled her gently into his arms and kissed her tenderly. Her legs felt weak at the intensity of the emotion she felt for him. These feelings were new to her, his kiss searing her lips and leaving her wanting him more than ever. She could feel the strength of his arms and body and excitement stirred in her lower belly. As impulsively as he had kissed her, he released her, his voice husky with passion.

'I'm sorry,' he apologized. 'It was not my intention to do that but you are just so irresistible. We need to do this right Aislinn. I will talk to your father when we return and get his permission to court you.'

She smiled up at him.

'That is fine with me. Can we leave for home right now?'

'Patience, darling girl, patience,' he laughed.

⌘

They walked back to the inn, their fingers entwined. She felt safe and loved and her heart felt ready to burst. He wanted to court her. This would be the beginning of a lifetime together – the great love she had waited for – it had come sooner than she imagined. She felt incredibly blessed. Entering the inn they found themselves face to face with a young woman. She must have been about twenty-two years old and she was very beautiful. Her emerald green dress was gorgeous and complemented her chestnut hair. Aislinn thought she must come from a very wealthy family to afford such finery.

'Drew, there you are darling,' she murmured ignoring Aislinn's presence. "I've been waiting ages for you to return.'

She swept past Aislinn throwing her arms around his neck and pressing her body brazenly up against the doctor before brushing her full lips seductively across his.

The same lips that had just kissed her with passion at the pond.

Aislinn's euphoria was quickly snuffed out.

'Your father said I could find you here. It's been so long darling, I've missed you.'

'Gabrielle,' Drew stammered, his face flushing crimson and Aislinn could not tell if he were embarrassed or annoyed. Clearly he looked surprised to see her.

Aislinn could not bear to watch the spectacle unfold any longer.

'I'll leave you two to catch up then. Goodnight Dr. Williams,' she said coldly. She did not want him to see the hurt etched on her face.

'Wait Aislinn...'

She did not wait to hear what his excuses were. She was furious with him and she cursed herself for her foolishness.

⌘

She lay in her bed remembering Drew's lips on hers. It was her first kiss and she would remember every minute of it – his manly scent in her nostrils and the feel and taste of his skin. Then she remembered the humiliation she felt downstairs a few moments ago.

What game was he playing – why did he tell her he loved her and that he wanted to court her when he clearly was courting Gabrielle, or whatever her name was? Was that his way of trying to have his way with her – pretending to love her so she would give herself up to him? Well he wasn't going to have her now. She would not be one woman of many in his life. She had saved herself for her one true love and she would find him one day. Obviously Drew wasn't the man for her.

Tears rolled down her cheeks as she silently cried into her pillow, her heart feeling broken. She thought she heard his footsteps at her door, hesitating and waiting, before they moved off down the passage to his room.

Was he spending the night with her?

⌘

Breakfast the following morning was awkward. Aislinn greeted Drew politely, if not a little coldly, and then focused all her energy on the bowl of porridge and scones set before her. She could not look at him. She had deep rings under her eyes from crying and lack of sleep.

'Aislinn, look at me please,' Drew implored.

She lifted her eyes to his. They were icy blue.

'You don't have to explain Drew. What happened last night is already forgotten. You don't owe me anything. As far as I am concerned we are work colleagues and that is all.'

'Is that really what you want? You don't even want to hear my side of the story?'

'I don't think there is anything to hear Drew. What I saw with my own eyes was enough to tell me that you have been in a relationship with that woman and clearly she thinks you still are.'

'I should have told you about her Aislinn and I would have if we had more time to talk. It's hardly the thing you talk about when you are declaring your love for the person you've given your heart to. I told you last night that I wanted to be honest with you and I have every intention of telling you all about my past, but not before you knew how I felt about you.'

'Well now is not the time either,' Aislinn said indicating Gabrielle who was approaching their table with predator strides.

Drew cursed under his breath.

'Drew darling,' she said kissing his cheek as he turned his face away. 'May I join you both?'

'By all means,' Aislinn said meanly, seeing Drew's angry look thrown her way. 'I am Aislinn, Drew's colleague. How did you two meet, I'm so curious?'

Gabrielle took over the conversation, needing no further prompting.

'We met when Drew was studying in Arles. My father became ill and Drew came with the attending physician, and the rest is history. We just saw each other and that was that.'

'Fascinating,' Aislinn said. 'Love at first sight.' Her sarcasm was not lost on Drew who frowned angrily at the two women sitting at his table.

Are they both going to talk as though I'm not here?

They were playing a game and he felt like the piggy in the middle.

'Gabrielle, Aislinn and I have patients to see. We can't sit here reminiscing on old times. For your own health I suggest you get out of Trenton.'

'Nonsense Drew, don't be so dramatic - the outbreak is over and Gabrielle will be fine if she stays,' Aislinn said sweetly enjoying his discomfort.

Served him right!

'Nonetheless we need to get started for the day.' He stood and pushed his chair in.

Aislinn followed him out the door. Once out of Gabrielle's sight he spun around grabbing her and pushing her against the cold wall.

'Don't play games with me Aislinn,' he hissed furious with her. 'What I said to you last night was not a lie – I meant every word. Just promise me that we can talk on the way home tomorrow and that you will listen to my side of the story, please.'

Aislinn was surprised at his anger. She nodded her head, realizing she had pushed him too far.

'All right Drew, I am willing to listen but that is all. I'm not making any promises.'

The rest of the day progressed slowly. They were both silent, unsure how to respond to one another. Drew wished that Gabrielle had not come to Trenton. The timing could not have been worse.

What does she want from me? Hopefully he and Aislinn could work this out. If he lost her his heart would break. *Damn Gabrielle!*

⌘

Drew paced up and down his room. The evening had not been pleasant. Aislinn had asked for her dinner to be sent to her room. Gabrielle had used that opportunity to pounce on him as though she wanted to devour him.

'Why are you so standoffish,' she had whined.

'Gabrielle, I have no idea why you have come here. I told you when we were in Arles that we would never be a couple – that I did not love you, yet here you are.'

'You didn't mean that Drew. I gave myself to you and you did not push me away then – you seemed to love me then.'

'That is not how I remember it. I remember you taking advantage of me the night I celebrated the completion of my studies. You bribed my friends to let you into my quarters and then in my drunken state you took advantage of me. I never was anything but a gentleman to you Gabrielle. It was only your word when I woke next to you in the morning that we had been together. I don't remember anything about that night. I certainly have never professed my love to you, then or now.'

'It doesn't matter how we got together Drew. The truth is I love you and want to be with you. We would make a formidable team the two of us. I have the wealth and social standing to make you a prominent doctor in Arles. Come back with me and live the life you were meant to. How can you bear to live in this backwater place?'

'I am exactly where I want to be Gabrielle. I have no desire to be your pet project or to return to Arles. There is, and never has been a relationship between us and the sooner you realize that the better.'

'It's because of her, isn't it? I've seen the way you look at her, I'm not a fool.'

'Yes Gabrielle, I do love her, but that's not the only reason I don't want to return to Arles. I don't feel that way about you – I want my marriage to be about love, not convenience. You deserve that too and I can't give that to you but one day someone will love you wholeheartedly.'

'I don't want someone else Drew – I want you. It's always been you. You have captured my heart and no one else will ever replace what I feel for you.'

'That's a bit dramatic Gabrielle. You only want me because you can't have me. Go back to Arles and your life. I don't love you – now or ever.'

He knew he was being harsh but she was not listening to him. She had a romantic idea in her head and he knew she was strong-willed enough to pester him. He had to crush any dreams she had concocted.

'You're making a big mistake Drew and it will come back to bite you,' she threatened. He could tell she was hurt and angry as she spun on her heel and stormed out the tavern.

All he could feel was an enormous sense of relief. He and Aislinn would make this right in the morning. They would start afresh.

⌘

Later that night as Drew lay sleeping in his room dreaming of his future with Aislinn, shadows lurked outside his door. The handle clicked and the door swung open creaking ever so slightly. The two men stopped dead in their tracks waiting to see if he would stir. When he did not move, they moved into the room creeping over to his bed. The good doctor was sleeping like a baby – well they would ensure he slept a lot longer. Drew awoke to a tap on the shoulder. He sat upright, startled, fearing that Gabrielle was up to her old tricks again. Instead he found his face connecting with a fist. Then he remembered nothing.

CHAPTER 7

OLD SCARS, NEW WOUNDS

"From every wound there is a scar, and every scar tells a story. A story that says I survived" - Craig Scott

AISLINN woke up and stretched in her bed. She felt so confused. She remembered how angry Drew was the previous day and how adamant he was about loving her. What should she do? She flew out of bed and washed herself. She couldn't worry about it now – they would work it out one way or another. She had promised she would hear his side of the story and until then she would not let her mind or heart think about it.

She headed down to the tavern where she met him daily for breakfast which usually consisted of toasted bread, honey and porridge. She waited, surprised he was not there. He was always up before her, something he never tired teasing her about.

'Good morning Aislinn,' he said as he entered the room.

She gave him a smile and was surprised by his formality. It stung her, as she had decided to try and be civil – to curb her tongue which got her into trouble too many times and to hear him out, but obviously he was still annoyed at her goading him the night before.

'Good morning,' she responded equally stiffly. He did not seem to notice her sarcasm.

'We have a very busy day today and some patients further afield to see.'

'I thought we were heading home today,' she said surprised.

'We are, but first we must make this stop.'

Breakfast was strangely awkward between them. Did he regret declaring his love for her? He was behaving very coldly toward her and it hurt. She would not play this cat and mouse game with him. If he wanted to pretend nothing had happened then she would not give him the satisfaction of seeing her heartbreak. She felt foolish.

How he must be laughing inside.

Was this his way of punishing her for refusing to come to Trenton? Well he would not have the last laugh.

'We had better get going then,' she said all business.

They rode for eight miles out of Trenton before they came to a small homestead. Aislinn felt uneasy.

Why are we coming this far out of the village and who lives here?

Her senses prickled, the response to flee ever increasing. She had to force down her trepidation.

Stop it Aislinn, you are being ridiculous!

She dismounted and followed Drew into the little cottage. She did not see anything inside that indicated a sick person. She was tired of playing games.

What is Drew up to? All I want to do is go home.

'Hello Aislinn,' a voice said. 'It's been a long time.'

She froze, her heart hammering in her chest, nausea threatening to overwhelm her. She knew that voice. Drew would never have brought her here after she had shared her story with him the other night. She spun around and came face to face with Cillian.

'Surprised to see me?' he laughed. 'I must say I never thought our paths would ever cross again.'

'Drew, what is going on?' Aislinn asked incredulous.

It was one thing to pretend he loved her but to bring her here to Cillian was quite something else. He did not love her but he hated her. Slowly it dawned on Aislinn that this was a convenient way to get rid of her so that he could be with Gabrielle. She realized that the old scars she bore from the past may have healed but now it felt as though a new wound had been torn open causing the old scars to bleed and hurt once again. She had been tricked, betrayed by him. He was a coward and in that moment she hated him.

'How could you? I trusted you.' The hurt was etched in her blue eyes and he looked away momentarily, unable to meet the pain he saw.

'It's not what you think Aislinn. I knew you would not come if you knew where we were going. The Dark Lord's wife is pregnant and they need a good doctor and midwife to help her. We are the best and it is our duty to help her, to save that child.'

Aislinn had no words. Just a few nights ago he had vowed never to endanger her and not even a few days had passed before he had not only broken that promise but actually betrayed her to the Dark Lord.

This man was unbelievable.

How could she love him after this? He had lost her trust forever. Cillian helped her to her horse and took the reins so that she had to follow. This was déjà vu all over again. What would her parents think when she did not return? They had no way of knowing where she was or how to find her.

'Great One, Ziah' I'm afraid I'm in trouble again and this time it's not my doing. Please help me get a message to my parents,' she prayed silently.

⌘

Falstaff was delighted his plan had worked. The two men he dispatched to the inn had been very successful. They had found the doctor, who he learned was named Drew, and brought him back to his spell chambers where he was shackled and nursing a very painful jaw. Daemon had switched places with him and would bring Aislinn Hamilton back here to the castle. It was all going splendidly.

'What do you want from me?' Drew asked.

'You'll see in time.'

'Who are you and where am I?' he persisted.

Falstaff sighed.

'I am, the Dark Lord's chief wizard and you sir, are in his castle. Your pretty little assistant, Aislinn will be joining us soon I believe.'

'No, please you can't bring Aislinn here, I beg of you. He will kill her. You know he will.'

'Not just yet, he won't,' Falstaff said. 'We need both you and Aislinn to do some work before the Dark Lord decides what should become of you. His wife, and my daughter, Gwendolyn is with child and you will see to it that nothing goes wrong with her confinement and birth. At present she is in bed with a fever and some bleeding which you need to attend to.'

'When is the baby due to be born?'

'Not for another two moons I would guess,' Falstaff answered.

'You can't keep us here that long. My father will come looking for me when we don't return as will Aislinn's family.'

'I have thought of that already. Your father will be notified that you have taken a case for an affluent family that requires you to be away from home for a while. I believe that there was a young woman who tried to make you an offer to return to Arles. Perhaps we will use her as our scapegoat. Don't worry; your father will be reimbursed for the loss of your services while you are away.'

Drew felt fear creep up his spine. They had been watching him in Trenton, had overheard his conversations. He had promised never to endanger Aislinn and he had done exactly that. Would she hate him for this, especially since he could not warn or protect her? He felt helpless and frustrated. Today was meant to be the day he made things right with her, where he told her the whole story. He knew she would understand when he explained it all to her. He remembered her sweet kiss – lord, he loved her.

Please let her be safe.

Wizard Falstaff had no intention of reimbursing old Dr. Williams for Drew's services. He had something better to hold over the old man. They had agreed when the adoption took place that they would never tell the boys of their separation. It would be too painful. He had lied to Daemon about telling him the truth of his adoption as he knew his son would not understand. Now if the old doctor wanted to keep this secret from Drew then he would go along with the plan for Drew to look after Gwendolyn. Of course Falstaff would omit the part about Daemon being back from his studies or of the Dark Lord's plans once they were finished their work. A messenger would be sent to Sherbrooke. He would make sure that Mac and Imogene Hamilton also received a message to allay their fears for their daughter. He was confident the old doctor would not share their whereabouts – he had too much to lose.

⌘

Legion had been distracted with Gwen's condition the last few days. He was worried about the health of his child.

'Come in,' he bellowed when there was a knock at his chamber door.

'Master, I have some wonderful news for you. I have managed to convince the physician and his midwife assistant to come to the castle. They will attend to Gwendolyn and make sure everything is all right. They are the best in their field and I'm sure they will be able to help her.'

'Thank you Falstaff. I knew I could trust you to get the job done.' He felt relief overwhelm him. Everything would be all right now.

'There is just one detail you need to know Master. It may come as a shock to you. The midwife is Aislinn Hamilton.'

The tension in the room was electric. Legion froze. He thought he would never hear that name again. Memories flooded back to his last meeting with the young girl and his hatred festered afresh. Worse than the hatred though, was the fear at what this meant.

'How did you manage to get her to agree to attend to Gwendolyn, Falstaff? I can't imagine she would have come of her own free will.'

'I have my ways and means Master. Put it this way, she did need some convincing but I had some help from Cillian with that.'

'Do you know what you have done you fool?' he roared.

Wizard Falstaff had not expected this reaction. He thought the Master would be pleased – even delighted, not furious and red-faced.

'I th..th...thought you would be pleased Master. It is your time to get revenge for the way she made fools of all of us. This way you can kill two birds with one stone,' he defended.

'Have you forgotten Ziah's threat when he left with her? This could start a war and frankly with a baby coming in the next few moons it is not a very good time Falstaff. My head is not in the game – I would lose a battle against him right now.'

The wizard could not believe his ears. The Dark Lord was becoming soft now that he was a father. His whole life had been consumed with defeating the Great One and now he had the opportunity but he was too afraid and weak to take it. Well, Falstaff would not let this go to waste. He would use this opportunity for his own gain to show everyone in Griswold that he had the strength of character to overcome the Great One. When he had done that, the Dark Lord would have few followers left. Yes, Griswold could become his if he played his cards right.

'Master, don't worry about it - I have taken care of it. No one will come looking for Aislinn or the doctor for many moons. We have time on our hands. Besides you did tell me to find the best to care for Gwendolyn and they are the best. We need them right now despite our personal feelings.'

Legion was angry but he realized that what Falstaff said was true – they did need the doctor and Aislinn if Gwendolyn was to carry this baby to term.

'Make sure she stays out of my way Falstaff, and treat her right – we don't want her to feel like a prisoner even though she is. I can't have her taking her frustration out on Gwen and the baby or summoning the entire Great One's army.'

⌘

Drew wondered when he would get to see Aislinn. He assumed they would both be taking care of Gwendolyn together. He needed to know that she was safe and all right. He missed her.

'When can I see Aislinn?' he asked Falstaff.

'I'm afraid she doesn't want to see you Drew. She feels betrayed by you. In fact I think the words she used were that you are a liar and untrustworthy. She blames you for getting her into this mess and worse she hates you for lying about that beautiful woman you kept hidden all this time.'

Drew's heart ached.

So she does hate me.

He couldn't blame her really, after all he had he failed to protect her.

How did they manage to get her here? Did they steal her out of her bed in the middle of the night too?

He had to see her and make things right. Dammit he loved her – she had to know that after the kiss they shared.

'There is another reason for keeping you apart. The Dark Lord wants to make sure there is no collusion between the two of you to harm his child. Let's just say that previous experience dealing with Aislinn Hamilton has left him skeptical. You will simply be giving medical advice, Dr. Williams. Aislinn will attend to Gwendolyn. We trust that you will concur on what needs to be done for my daughter and grandchild.'

'How am I supposed to give advice when I can't examine the patient?' Drew complained. 'That is simply irresponsible.'

'For Aislinn's safety, I suggest you try your best Dr. Williams.'

Falstaff had it all planned out. Dr. Williams would make a diagnosis based on the information he gave him regarding his daughter's condition. Then every bit of information would be passed onto Daemon who would then repeat all this information to Aislinn before she had her consultation with Gwen. That way Aislinn would be convinced that she was working with Drew. As long as she thought Daemon was Drew everything would work out nicely. She still believed that Drew had betrayed her to Cillian and the Dark Lord and she was curt and cold toward him. He must not let her discover the truth. He suspected from what Daemon had told him that Aislinn Hamilton had a soft spot for the good doctor. That could work nicely in his favour, especially if she believed he had used her. The thought of her nursing a broken heart pleased him and would surely please the Dark Lord too. His Master would thank him yet.

CHAPTER 8

PERFECT DECEPTION

"Oh, what a tangled web we weave...when first we practice to deceive." —
Walter Scott, Marmion

DR. WILLIAMS Senior had been working long hours since Drew and Aislinn left for Trenton. He was looking forward to their return until the letter from Falstaff came. He was shocked to receive correspondence from the man who had taken his other son twenty-six years ago. The guilt came back instantly as he thought about the child he had given up – the boy he would never know. It had been an impossible decision for him to make, so he had drawn straws to see which child he would keep. He believed that he would never see the boy ever again, but now his past was catching up with him. He hoped desperately that Drew would not come face to face with his twin brother. He had no idea how similar they looked now, but as babies they had been hard to tell apart. It would be a shock to Drew if he found out this way. He just hoped that Falstaff would keep his word and not let the cat out of the bag. The truth should come from him, if anyone. He was caught between a rock and a hard place and Falstaff knew it. He hoped that both Aislinn and Drew would be all right.

⌘

Mac and Imogene were equally surprised to hear that Aislinn would be away for about two more moons. She had written them a letter explaining the work she would be doing over the next few months. They would have been worried had the letter been penned by someone else, but it was clearly written in her hand. They also trusted Drew. He seemed a responsible young man. Imogene read the note again.

Dear Mama and Papa,

Drew and I have been asked to help a wealthy family for the next two moons. The Mistress of the house has had a complication with her pregnancy and they are concerned for the baby's welfare. We are being well taken care of and feel that it would be remiss of us to come home when we can make a difference here. I love you both and miss everyone back home. Please send my love to Struan, Maddy and Mitchell.

Please also thank Regent for escorting me to Trenton and thank him especially for the generous gift of the red ribbon he gave me.

All my love Aislinn.

'She seems happy enough. Do you think everything is all right?' she asked Mac.

'She's fine Imogene. Drew will take care of her – he's not some young boy but a well-travelled man. She will be safe with him. I'm sure.'

⌘

Aislinn examined Gwendolyn. Her heartbeat was too erratic and she was still bleeding. She knew what had to be done. She had seen Drew just before coming into Gwen's chambers and they had agreed about the course of action to take. Aislinn felt conflicted about her feelings toward him. She was still very angry for his betrayal but she could not deny that she still loved him - what was wrong with her? How could she continue to love someone who had used her? Love certainly was a complicated thing. Well she would tackle him about it the first moment she got alone with him.

'I am giving you False Unicorn root and Lobelia to stop the bleeding,' Aislinn said. 'I shall mix three parts of the False Unicorn with one part Lobelia. Then we'll make you a cup of tea using one small spoon of these mixed ingredients in boiled water. You must promise to stay in bed and use half a cup of this tea each half hour until the bleeding stops, then each waking hour for one day, while resting as much as possible and then three times in a day for the next three weeks.'

She cupped Gwen's stomach gently feeling every part of the baby's anatomy with her small hands. Her head was cocked to the side as she concentrated on the baby inside the womb.

'Baby is still moving so that is good and seems to be in the right position. Gwendolyn you must keep up your fluid intake. Should you become too thirsty this baby's heart rate will go through the roof and that is not good for the wee one.'

Gwen nodded, relieved to finally have some real advice.

'You're her aren't you?'

The question caught Aislinn by surprise.

'What do you mean?' she feigned ignorance to the question.

'You're Aislinn Hamilton. I heard your name a lot in the first few months of my marriage to Legion and usually not in glowing terms. I hated you then and thought you were the reason he could not love me. The truth is that I have come to learn that he can't love anyone – not even himself. I don't think he even loves this baby. I think he sees this child as another pawn in his power games.'

'I'm sorry Gwendolyn, I really am. He never really loved me even though he may think he did. The only reason he wanted me was because he couldn't control me and that drove him crazy. It was never about love - if anything he hates me. I'm afraid of what he will do to me if he sees me here.'

'Don't worry Aislinn, I will keep you safe. When your duty here is finished I will make sure my brother gets you to safety.'

'You have a brother?'

'Yes, he is the most important thing to me besides this baby. I'm glad you're here, Aislinn,' the young woman smiled.

'I'll get onto mixing those herbs for you,' Aislinn said feeling a little more reassured.

⌘

Falstaff was beginning to find it difficult to juggle all the balls he had in the air. Deceiving so many people at once was not an easy task and if this were discovered he would have a lot of explaining to do. He must keep Daemon and Drew apart so that the young doctor did not find out about his twin. He also had to ensure Drew and Aislinn remained apart whilst allowing Aislinn to believe they were working together by having Daemon impersonate Drew. Gwendolyn must never meet Drew or she would discover the truth of her brother and his twin which would tarnish the memory of her mother. Aislinn had become suspicious as to why Drew could not be present when she examined Gwen. Falstaff had made up a story about Gwen having an irrational fear of strange men due to an incident growing up as a child and so Aislinn believed Drew's absence was imperative to the young woman's health and state of mind. She consulted daily with Daemon, whom she believed was Drew, about Gwen's condition and they devised a plan of action. Daemon gave daily reports to the Dark Lord regarding Gwen's condition, to keep Legion believing that he was Dr. Williams and personally overseeing his wife's care. Falstaff was just grateful that Legion and Gwen did not have a close marriage and that their level of communication was virtually non-existent. If they had just discussed the doctor with one another they would have made the connection, but it seemed Legion found sitting with his wife for too long a period tedious and awkward. Gwen was just too tired to care.

Yes, Falstaff certainly had a lot on his plate. If he could just get this right then everything would work out fine. His Master would be furious if he knew how he was playing them all.

CHAPTER 9

LOVE AND LOATHING

"You don't love someone because they're perfect, you love them in spite of the fact that they're not" - Jodi Piccoult

AISLINN sat on the bed in her room. She hated this room. It was the same room in the south tower that she and her siblings had been locked in when they were the Dark Lord's prisoners. It seemed so long ago and yet it also seemed like just yesterday. Granted the room had been refurbished to look like a suite but to her she could only remember the feeling of helplessness she had felt all those years ago. That same feeling threatened to suffocate her. The bed was large and comfortable with a fabric canopy and there was a lush velvet rug on the floor. A writing desk took up one corner and an armoire with her few clothes covered another wall. The room looked nothing like she remembered it and yet it was still her prison – just a little more luxurious this time. She recalled how she was made to sit at the writing desk and write a letter to her parents to alleviate any suspicion of her whereabouts when she was brought here. She just hoped her parents realized she was in danger. A knock at her door startled her.

She opened, surprised to see Drew standing on the threshold. He had done everything possible to avoid her since handing her over to Cillian. The only communication they had was related to Gwendolyn's care. Her heart skipped a beat when she saw his rugged good looks. It annoyed her how her body betrayed her true feelings and how easily she fell under his spell each time they were together.

'Aislinn we need to talk about Gwendolyn,' Daemon played the role beautifully. He had her fully convinced that he was Drew.

'Is that all you think about Drew? Gwendolyn this, Gwendolyn that, poor Gwendolyn....' She let out her annoyance and frustration of the past few days as she yelled at him, completely out of character.

Daemon was surprised at her anger and did not know what to say or how to react to her outburst.

'I'm sorry Aislinn – have I offended you?'

'You actually have to ask you oaf? This is unbelievable. Don't pretend you don't know what I mean Drew. How could you be so cruel to me...first you lead me on and then you betray me,' a sob caught in her throat and she could say no more. Daemon did not know what had transpired between her and Drew but her face looked stricken and he could bear it no longer.

'Please don't cry Aislinn. I'm sorry,' he said pulling her into his arms. She did not resist.

The warmth of his broad chest and his gentleness enveloped Aislinn and she could not deny how much she loved this man, even after all he had done to her.

'Drew...'she whispered broken.

Daemon sighed. Deceiving her was part of his father's plan but he hated seeing the wounded look in her beautiful blue eyes. Clearly she was in love with the doctor. He had to admit he found her very attractive and realized to his shock that he wanted her desperately. He kissed her, slow and tenderly and then more urgently as though their time together would be cut short any moment. Aislinn responded, her body melting into his, her heart revealing how easily he could sway her.

No, her mind screamed – *think with your head and not your heart. Remember what he's done to you. Don't be such a fool Aislinn, he's playing you again.*

She pulled away, slapping his face as hard as she could. Daemon held his cheek and laughed at her pushing her roughly against the doorjamb.

'I know you enjoyed that Aislinn, Your body tells a different story to your attitude.'

'You're insufferable,' she spluttered. 'Let me go.' She struggled against him but he was too strong for her and the more she resisted the more he enjoyed her discomfort.

'I will take what I want from you, when I want it Aislinn,' he said as his head descended for another kiss, more brutal this time. He bit her lip gently but enough to make it bleed and she cried out in pain.

'Don't resist me sweet thing – it won't be in your best interest,' he said as he pulled himself away and marched out the door, leaving a red-faced Aislinn. He had to get away from her. His father would be furious if he manhandled her in any way and her sweetness entwined with her indignation and feistiness had aroused him more than he cared to admit. Yes, whoever ended up marrying Aislinn Hamilton would have their hands full.

Aislinn tried to stop her hands shaking. She thought she knew Drew better than anyone and yet he had completely pulled the wool over her eyes. He was that arrogant, rude man she met months ago in Dr. William's rooms. Her heart broke and tears ran down her face. She had fallen in love with a brute – a man who was as evil as the Dark Lord himself.

Why did she attract men with cruel and evil personalities? What was wrong with her?

⌘

Drew paced up and down in his room. He tried the door once more hoping this time it would magically open. He was sick of being a prisoner here. He was terrified Aislinn was in mortal danger and he was desperate to see her. He missed her terribly. How had they gotten into this mess? He wished he could turn the clock back a few weeks.

CHAPTER 10

THE REUNION

"Individually we are one drop but together we are an ocean"
- Ryunosuke Satoro

'IT'S SO GOOD to be together again,' Mac beamed. 'It's been far too long since we caught up.'

The men ate the delicious stew that Imogene had prepared, dipping their crusty bread into the thick gravy.

'We're always keen for one of Imogene's stews. Would never say no to it,' Nuada smiled winking at Imogene.

"Flattery will get you everywhere boys,' she smiled in return filling up Nuada's bowl once more with the thick, steaming food.

It had been a while since they had eaten together – usually Aedan, and Ziah would stop by when there was some task to undertake and Mac would join them on their latest crusade. However this time it was purely social. Imogene had urged Mac to invite them for a meal and at last it was a reality. She looked at the men around the table –each different from the others but a formidable force when partnered together. She remembered how they had saved their family from the Dark Lord and her affection for each of them increased. Ziah held a special place in her heart – he had brought her back from the abyss of death. Had he not been there she would not be here today. His love was so great that he sacrificed himself for their whole family. He loved life and this came through in his constant joy and his amazing sense of humour. Then there was Aedan. He was something else. His fiery red hair and piercing green eyes displayed his nature perfectly. He was wild and passionate, yet gentle and sensitive at the same time. He was a direct contrast to the dark Regent, who towered over everyone, his body a wall of muscle. Imogene was so grateful to him for all he had done to protect her children. Finally there was Nuada who was the first person to help them discover who they truly were after the Dark Lord's attack on their family. Every single one of these men made a difference to their lives and she was profoundly grateful to have met them, the Great One's family and they were part of that now.

'Have you heard anything from Aislinn?' Regent asked. He had not been happy leaving her in Trenton as he realized the danger she could be in being back in Griswold's borders.

'As a matter of fact we have,' Mac said.

'Yes Regent, she and Drew will be staying on longer than planned due to a difficult confinement,' Imogene explained. 'She did ask me to thank you for taking her through to Trenton and we are equally grateful. She could not have made the journey alone.'

'It was a pleasure – brought back some memories of adventures we had in the past, although I wouldn't want to relive any of it,' he smiled.

'Oh yes Regent, Aislinn also asked me to thank you for the red ribbon you gave her,' Imogene added.

Regent stopped, his spoon hanging in mid-air, the gravy dripping back into his bowl.

'What do you mean Imogene?' he asked.

'Well I assumed you would know. That's what she wrote in her letter.'

'Can I see the letter please?' he asked.

'Is everything all right Regent?' Ziah asked.

Regent did not reply as he quickly scanned the letter Aislinn had written and then looked up at the others, worry creasing his brow.

'No, everything's not all right. Aislinn's sending us a message in this letter. I didn't give her the red ribbon when I escorted her to Trenton. I gave her that ribbon four years ago when we went to rescue Mitchell. It was our way of communicating - if she tied the ribbon to her window latch then I would know she was in trouble. She's reminding me of that. We have to go and find her – she needs help.'

'What do you think could have happened?' Mac asked. 'Surely Drew would keep her safe?'

'Unless Drew is in danger too,' Aedan suggested.

Imogene paled. This could not be happening. Surely the Dark Lord would not try to capture her again. He knew what the consequences would be as Ziah had made it very clear to him what would unfold if he ever came near their family again.

'Might I suggest that if Aislinn sent a letter home to keep your suspicions at bay that maybe Drew was also forced to write a letter to his father. Perhaps we should go and see Dr. Williams and find out what he knows,' Aedan said.

So much for dinner being a social event – now it had turned into another crusade, Imogene thought.

She longed for the day that they could all live without the fear of their past catching up with them. She prayed silently to the Great One to keep Aislinn and Drew safe. She watched the men as they gathered their coats and mounted their horses. The feeling of déjà vu had a gnawing familiarity that made her stomach turn.

Dr. Williams was surprised to find five men at his door so late at night. He invited them in and listened to their suspicions about Drew and Aislinn.

'I'm sorry,' he said at last, shocked. 'I should have told you this as soon as Falstaff sent his messenger. The patient is Gwendolyn, the Dark Lord's wife. Drew and Aislinn are at the castle in Griswold. If I had known that Aislinn was in danger, or of her past dealings with them I would never have kept this from you. I only kept quiet to protect my son from learning the truth from that cruel man. He deserves to hear it from me, but now I may have cost them their lives.'

'What truth?' Mac asked the old man.

Dr. Williams hesitated momentarily. He did not want to tell them about Drew's twin just yet – he wanted to tell his own son first before everyone else knew. Still he had to tell them something.

'There is more to Drew's mother's death than I have told him. Let's just say that Falstaff knows this and he has threatened to tell Drew if I do not keep quiet, but I won't put their lives in danger despite his threats. If he has harmed them I will kill him myself.'

'No, they are still alive,' Ziah stated. 'The Dark Lord needs them, but once that baby is born there will be no need to keep them around. If Falstaff wants to keep his evil plot a secret then Drew's life will be in as much danger as Aislinn's. We must go and rescue them. If we leave in the morning we can be there in a few days.'

CHAPTER 11

FACE TO FACE

"In life you will journey into certain challenges, and also come face to face with heartache just remember to keep strong no matter what happens"
- Jeremy Limn

GWENDOLYN drank her herbal tea as instructed and soon the bleeding stopped and she felt more like her old self. She enjoyed Aislinn's daily visits as it was company for her. It would not be too long now till the babe arrived and she looked forward to holding the child in her arms. She had made Daemon promise that he would get Aislinn to safety once the child came. She could not bear the thought of anything happening to this new friend she had made.

'I will let you rest now,' Aislinn said as she packed away her supplies.

The door to Gwen's chambers opened and Legion stepped over the threshold stopping dead in his tracks when he saw her. He had hoped they would not come face to face while she was here in his castle. He had played this moment over in his head time after time over the last four years, imagining every possible scenario of how he would react and what he would say to her when he saw her again. None of them came to mind now – his body felt numb, shocked to see her standing just a few paces away. She was just as he remembered her, only a little older and even more beautiful if that was possible - her hair a mass of auburn waves and her eyes piercing blue. His heart lurched then anger started to creep in as his senses returned.

Control Legion, you need her right now.

'I'm sorry,' he said curtly, 'I didn't realize you were still busy. I will come back when you are done.'

'No, please stay, I was just about to leave,' Aislinn replied, her heart hammering in her chest. This was the moment she had dreaded. She picked up her bag and left the room as fast as her shaky legs would carry her.

Gwendolyn could see how much the encounter had shaken them both. He pretended everything was fine but she could tell he was wrestling with unresolved feelings and anger. He was harder than usual and very businesslike in his manner toward her.

What kind of marriage was this? Clearly not one of tenderness and love.

⌘

Aislinn felt sick after her encounter with the Dark Lord. The only comfort she could take, was knowing that he appeared equally shocked and shaken when they had come face to face. She hoped it wouldn't happen again. She picked at her lunch, distracted, and thought about Drew, touching her lip with her index finger. It was still a little swollen from his bite. He had hurt her – something she would never have believed possible. Her only hope was for her parents to decode her message about the ribbon and for them to realize where she was.

'Great One,' she called. 'You once told me that I could call for the keys of freedom anytime I recognized that I needed them. Well I need them now. Please send Ziah to get me out of here.'

⌘

Lionsgate

The Great One smiled – she hadn't forgotten.

'They are coming Aislinn. Just be patient child.'

⌘

Daemon could not get Aislinn out of his head. That kiss had affected him more than he believed possible. Now he had something else to worry about. Gwendolyn feared for Aislinn's life once the baby was born. She had begged him to get her new friend to safety and to keep her away from their father and her husband. Truth be told, he did not want to see such a beautiful woman go to waste. He would get her away from here when Gwen's baby was born – he would help her to forget all about Drew Williams. She would realize what a real man was like – he would make sure of that.

⌘

Drew was tired of being caged. This was the most bizarre set of circumstances he had ever experienced – consulting for a patient he had never met. It certainly gave medical practice a new definition. He wondered if Gwendolyn actually existed. Maybe this was the story they were weaving to keep him prisoner here. His use for luring Aislinn back to the castle was over. He had no idea whether she were alive or dead. He had to get out of this room and find out how she was doing. He scratched in his doctor's bag and pulled out a small vial. He would have to be very careful using the liquid – too much and he would die an agonizing death. If he were careful though, it should make him just sick enough. He prayed silently that Aislinn was still alive as without her his actions could have fatal consequences. Still, he was willing to take the risk as he had no desire to live without her.

He took just a very small amount of the herb and dissolved it in a goblet of water. He looked at it, afraid at what he was about to do, but then thought of Aislinn and how helpless he was locked up here in the tower. Falstaff was due to come for their daily consultation. He would wait to hear his key in the lock then he would drink the potion. It would take about ten minutes to begin working and hopefully all would go according to plan. If not, then his life would be over.

⌘

Falstaff smiled, pleased with the way things were progressing. Legion had no idea what he was plotting behind the scenes. He unlocked the door to Drew's chamber and found the doctor reading one of his medical journals.

'How are we this morning Dr. Williams?'

'I'm afraid I haven't been feeling very well.' My stomach is cramping and I feel a little nauseous. Was the food from the kitchen all right? Has anyone else been feeling sick?'

'Not that I'm aware of. We all eat from the same kitchen and I've been feeling fine. Let's get to business shall we?' Falstaff said. "Gwen's bleeding has stopped and Aislinn says that the baby seems to be in the right position.

He continued to give Drew a run down on Gwendolyn's health. The young doctor tried to listen to the old wizard's ramblings but he started to sweat, clutching his stomach, as he fell to the floor as the herb began to take effect. Falstaff stopped, alarmed at his sudden change in pallor and condition.

'What's wrong with you?' he asked worried.

'Help me please, I feel like my insides are burning,' he begged as he retched and heaved.

'What must I do?' Falstaff panicked. The doctor could not die – he needed him to complete his plan and for Gwendolyn to be safe. It couldn't possibly all fall apart now.

'Get Aislinn,' he pleaded. 'She'll know what to do.'

Falstaff hesitated momentarily. He did not want Aislinn and Drew face to face but he did not know what else to do. The castle physician was away in the villages doing his rounds for the next few days. It may be too late for him by then if he didn't get treatment now, besides the doctor didn't look in any state to collude with Aislinn.

'I'll be back,' he said as he rushed out the door leaving Drew curled up in an agonizing heap on the floor.

This had better be worth it, Drew thought as his stomach cramped and nausea overwhelmed him again.

⌘

Mac, Nuada, Ziah, Regent and Aedan prepared their horses to leave for Griswold. As they climbed into their saddles another horseman joined them.

'I'm coming too,' he said.

'Are you sure?' Mac asked surprised at this change of heart. Eion nodded his head.

'Surer than anything Mac. I owe Aislinn for what she did for Rozanne and me. If it weren't for her my family would not be here.'

Eion thought back to the day Rozanne was in labour and the sheer terror he had felt. Martha, the midwife, had not given him much comfort or hope when she told him the baby was breech. She had not been able to turn the baby despite her best efforts and Roz had been in excruciating agony. Eion remembered the terror and helplessness he had felt. When Rozanne had passed out he thought it was all over and that their baby and his wife would surely die. Martha had yelled at him to find someone with small hands to help her. The only person close enough that he could think of was Aislinn. The poor girl looked terrified when he begged her to help, but she had been brilliant. Martha had instructed her to put her hands inside Rozanne and try to gently coax the baby down the birth canal. Slowly and working with her contractions Aislinn brought their beautiful son into the world. He had her to thank for Rozanne and their child's life. Without her, his wife would have haemorrhaged and their baby would have been born with brain damage due to lack of oxygen. She had been the miracle they needed in their moment of need. He would be eternally grateful to her forever. Aislinn had appeared radiant after the experience and her future path and dreams born the same day as their first child. Rozanne and Eion named their baby in her honour – Asher – as close as they could get to her name for a little boy.

Now he would face the Dark Lord to save her – she saved his child once and now he would help Mac save her. It was time to put aside his fear of the Dark Lord and become the man he always wanted to be.

'Thank you Eion,' Mac smiled. This would change his friend's life forever.

Things do always happen for a reason, he thought as they rode out to invade the kingdom of Griswold. Sometimes bad things brought out the best in people and made them realize they had a strength they didn't know existed. Eion had just discovered his strength.

⌘

'Drew,' Aislinn gasped when she saw him doubled over, sweat dripping from his brow. 'What's the matter with you?'

Drew smiled weakly at her. He had never been so glad to see her.

'Get me some fresh water,' she yelled to Falstaff who was hovering in the doorway like a lost child. He quickly disappeared to find some.

'I had to see you Aislinn, to make sure you are all right. Please forgive me for putting you in danger – I love you more than anything. I've taken some Monkshood because I needed to see you and they wouldn't let me. You need to get me some charcoal to drink – it's the only thing that will work.'

'It's okay Drew, don't talk.' Clearly the drug was giving him delusions, believing he had not seen her, forgetting how he had treated her recently. She did not understand why he would poison himself. His mental state worried her.

She found charcoal in the hearth and ground it underfoot while she waited for Falstaff to bring the water.

What was taking him so long?

After what seemed an eternity he returned with the water pitcher and she mixed the inky concoction. She tilted his head as she poured the vile black liquid down his throat.

She prayed he would not vomit. Charcoal can prevent absorption if it is given quickly after the poison is consumed, but he had to keep it down or it wouldn't work. She had read that in one of Drew's many medical journals she had borrowed. She hoped it was not too late. She helped him onto his bed and mopped his brow. He closed his eyes holding her hand.

'Thank you for coming. I've missed you so much. I needed to know you were safe. I love you - you must know that.'

'I'm fine Drew, really I am. Stop worrying now and sleep,' she murmured surprised that he was still confused. This man was the complete opposite of the man who roughly pushed her up against the door and threatened to take what he wanted from her. This was the Drew she loved. She best get over her infatuation – this relationship would never work. She never knew what to expect from him. Every time they came together he showed a different side of his personality. It was confusing.

His breathing evened out and she realized that he was asleep. She watched him, stroking his hair gently, her heart aching at a love that would never be – a love that could never be.

CHAPTER 12

A QUESTION OF TRUST

"Have enough courage to trust love one more time and always one more time" — Maya Angelou

THE MEN made good time. They rode hard to get to Griswold stopping only to water and feed their horses and catch a few hours of sleep before they rode again. Now they found themselves at the secret tunnel that made its way into the castle through the stables.

'What is our plan Ziah,' Mac asked.

'We don't have one, but I think the element of surprise will work well for us. I did warn Sephtis that if he ever messed with your family again that there would be trouble. I think he will back down when we confront him.'

They made their way into the castle grounds and no one questioned their presence as each subject went about their own daily chores. At their arrival in the great hall they joined the throngs of village peasants who waited for the Lord of their lands to hear their disputes for the day. Legion listened daily to his subject's disputes and ruled accordingly. Most days it was simple things like neighbourly disputes or a request for an extension to pay their dues for the land they lived on.

'Next,' Legion shouted, after ruling a villager to return the pig he claimed he found wandering on his property to his angry neighbor who swore it had been stolen.

Ziah stepped forward, sending whispers through the people who recognized him. Legion looked shocked and fear flickered momentarily over his face before he covered it up.

'Ziah, what a surprise! What brings you here to Griswold?'

'I think you know the answer to that already Sephtis.'

'Please, call me Legion – Sephtis died a long time ago.' His smile was fixed to his face, his eyes wary.

'Very well Legion. We are here to get Aislinn Hamilton. It seems that you have imprisoned her against her will once more. I warned you about that and what the consequences would be.'

'Now don't be so hasty Ziah. She is not here against her will – the young doctor and Aislinn chose to come here and care for my wife during her confinement. She certainly is not a prisoner, I can assure you. Besides our history is just that – history! A lot has happened since then, I am a married man with a child on the way. If anything I am truly grateful to Dr. Williams and Aislinn for their help in what has been a very difficult time for Gwen.'

'Where is she then? We need to talk to her ourselves. You'll excuse my reluctance to take your word.'

'Master, Aislinn is attending to your wife at this very moment. Perhaps the gentlemen would like to talk to Dr. Williams in the meantime,' Falstaff cunningly offered.

'Yes that is fine Falstaff. Would that satisfy you in the meantime?' Legion asked.

'Certainly,' Ziah replied.

Falstaff left to find Daemon. He would have to play the role of Drew once again. It was vital for him to convince Ziah and his men of his authenticity. He knew this would be the true test as Ziah was very astute.

'I see that you have a new addition to your band of merry men,' Legion said sarcasm lacing his words. He looked straight at Eion. 'Morelock, I never expected you to have the courage to return here?'

'Just like you Legion, I too have changed my name I am known as Eion now. Morelock is dead and buried.'

'Well it seems things are going well for you. I should really make a deal with Ziah for your exchange for Aislinn – after all you did betray me and should pay for that.

'There will be no exchanges this time Legion,' Ziah stated firmly. 'You forget that Eion has quite a powerful way with magic. It wouldn't do for him to cast a curse upon your family – say a spell against the firstborn child perhaps.'

Legion smiled but underneath seething anger was brewing. They had him and they knew it.

'You're right Ziah,' he said. 'This is not the time or the place for dredging up old memories.'

Falstaff returned with Daemon on his heel before the surprised men could respond. Legion certainly seemed cooperative.

'Drew,' Mac said and hugged the young man. 'Are you all right?'

'Yes, fine thank you. Falstaff here tells me that you are concerned for Aislinn and my well-being. I can assure you that we are both fine and being treated very comfortably.'

'Yes but did you agree to come here? I can't imagine Aislinn would ever agree to it,' Regent asked. 'She was very worried when we travelled to Trenton.'

'Yes, she was worried and I assured her that she would be safe with me as did Legion. As physicians of the afflicted it is our duty to care for everyone. Aislinn agrees with this and would never turn away a woman in need. She can be quite stubborn your daughter.'

Mac laughed only too well aware of her stubborn streak. No one could change Aislinn's mind when it was made up.

'I trust you will do as you promised Drew – that you will take care of her and bring her safely home if she chooses to stay, but first I want her to tell me that herself. I'm not leaving here until she does,' Mac stated.

'You will hear from her as soon as she is finished with Gwendolyn,' Falstaff assured him.

He planned to get her cooperation by threatening to kill her precious Drew. She would never jeopardize his life.

'Falstaff, go and see if she is finished her consultation and in the meantime Ziah you and your travelers are welcome to join me for refreshments.'

It was bizarre – sitting down amicably with the arch enemy for drinks. Still Legion seemed to be quite pleasant. They hoped it wasn't too good to be true - a plot to let their guard slip.

Falstaff left the room, urging Daemon to go with him. 'Come Dr. Williams, you can take over the consultation with Gwen so that Aislinn can see her family.'

Daemon smiled knowingly – his father was certainly a cunning old fox. He knew that he could not be in the same room as Aislinn or she would know he was not Drew. Drew still lay recovering upstairs and until he was well Daemon had to stay away from Aislinn.

⌘

Aislinn felt real fear for the first time since she arrived. Her father was here with Ziah to rescue her and yet now she knew she could not go with them. If she even gave them inkling that she was a prisoner then Falstaff would kill Drew. The old wizard had made it perfectly clear what would happen if she did not give the performance of a lifetime. Drew was on the mend thanks to the charcoal but he was completely unaware of the drama unfolding. She would not be responsible for his death even after all he had put her through

– she would not betray him – it was not in her nature. She would have to find another way to let them know her plight.

She followed Falstaff down to the great hall. She could not contain her delight to see her father and friends and ran to them embracing them.

'Aislinn are you all right,' her father asked concerned.

'Yes Papa, I am fine. It's so good to see you all.'

'You don't have to stay here if you don't want to Aislinn,' Ziah said.

'I'm here to help Gwendolyn. Drew and I will assist her with the birth. It won't be too long till the babe is born – another moon and the wee one should be here,' she added. Hopefully giving them a time frame would make them come back for her soon.

'Aislinn do you still have the ribbon I gave you,' Regent asked cryptically.

'Yes Regent and thank you for it. I will use it the way you asked me to.' She smiled hoping he would understand her message. He nodded.

'Enough small talk,' Legion said. 'I trust you are satisfied that Aislinn is not being mistreated while she stays with us. I will ensure she is safe while in these castle walls Ziah. I give you my word.'

'I recall your word not meaning much Legion.'

'You forget that I have a son waiting to be born and that Aislinn is crucial to that happening without incident. She will be safe.'

'What happens when the child is born?' Mac asked 'She won't be any use to you then. How can we be sure you won't harm her then?'

'I will swear on my son's life that she and Dr. Williams will leave here safely. If I don't keep that promise then you can take my son's life in return.'

Ziah nodded satisfied. He had noticed small changes in Legion – having a son was giving him hope and dreams for the future - something else to focus on besides revenge and power. This was not the same man he met four years ago.

'So be it,' Ziah said.

⌘

'How are you feeling Drew?' Aislinn asked.

Falstaff had allowed her to come and see the doctor daily to ensure his full recovery. This would be the last day she would see him, although she would not know it. Neither of them realized that Daemon would impersonate Drew again now that he was well enough. It was time to separate them before his little ruse was discovered and before they started talking about deeper things that may arouse suspicion. Already Aislinn was confused by why Drew behaved a certain way. She had put it down to the poison giving him hallucinations but that wouldn't wash for long. Soon she would begin to question the things he said.

'I'm feeling good Aislinn, thank you. You saved my life.'

'Yes, well we won't go there – I still don't understand why you did it Drew.'

'I needed some time with you, to know you were all right and to ask you to forgive me for not protecting you. I couldn't bear it if you hated me Aislinn.'

'I don't hate you Drew. I just don't understand you.'

'Things will be better when we get out of here, you'll see. This place makes one crazy.'

'Drew, we can never go back to where we were at the pond in Trenton. Too much has happened since then, what with Gabrielle and Cillian and now this.'

'What do you mean Aislinn?' She could see fear in his eyes.

'I don't trust you anymore – at least not the way I should if I am going to be your wife one day. That trust was taken in Trenton. We can be friends but that is all.'

'You can't be serious Aislinn. I love you. What can I do to make it right?'

'Nothing Drew – don't make this harder than it has to be. We still have to work together for a little while and I would prefer it not to become awkward.'

'Look me in the eye Aislinn and tell me that you don't love me, that you want me to leave you alone and I will respect your wishes.'

'That's not what you said to me the other day when you hurt me and told me you would take whatever you wanted from me whenever you wanted it,' she challenged.

'What are you talking about Aislinn – I never said those things, did I?' He was trying to remember whether he said things when he was overcome with Monkshood poison. Perhaps the drug had made him behave in a manner most unlike himself.

'This is what I'm talking about Drew. I can't deal with the double personality you display all the time. You won't take responsibility for your actions.'

Drew had no comprehension of Aislinn's accusation.

'Tell me you don't love me,' he said encircling her waist with his arms and drawing her in close. She tried to push him away and she could feel his heart hammering in his chest and his breath on her neck as he hugged her.

'Aislinn, I love you. Nothing will change that ever. Tell me you don't love me and I'll let you go.

'Don't, Drew please. I can't love you – it won't work ....'

He silenced her with a kiss, gentle and loving, teasing which left her breathless and weak. Why was he so tender sometimes and yet so brutal at other times? It was confusing.

He let her go gently and looked into her blue eyes.

'You don't need to say anything Aislinn – I know you love me by the way you respond to me. I will wait for you as long as it takes because I'm not giving up on us even if you are. I love you too much.'

Aislinn said nothing – her body had given him the answer he needed and she despised her own weakness. She turned on her heel and left the room before she made a complete fool of herself yet again.

CHAPTER 13

REVOLUTIONARY

"Man cannot discover new oceans unless he has the courage to lose sight of the shore" — André Gide

FALSTAFF was delighted with the interaction that had occurred between his Master and Ziah. Legion had promised his son in return for Aislinn's safety. He didn't realize the double-edged sword he had placed in Falstaff's hands – the very weapon that would take down his Master and Aislinn Hamilton at once and give him the power and prestige he so craved. Gwendolyn would blame Legion for the death of her only child and he would get favour with the local villagers and druids when he put his plan into action. Things were working out better than he ever anticipated.

⌘

LIONSGATE

The Great One watched Falstaff and his brow furrowed. He suspected that the wizard was up to no good - well he would have to keep an eye on him. Aislinn was still in that castle because this man had threatened someone she truly loved. He had seen how true love sacrifices for others and she had done the same once again.

'Stay strong Aislinn, I will be watching you – call when you need us.'

⌘

Daemon felt restless. He had not seen Aislinn for over two weeks due to the doctor's illness and he was frustrated. He couldn't stop thinking about her beautiful face and how she tilted her chin in defiance, the flash of passion in her eyes when she was angry, the full lips that begged to be kissed and the curve of her breast as her chest heaved in indignation. She was some woman he had to admit. The more she tried to reject him the more he desired her. He wanted her more than anything. He would woo her – he didn't want her against her will – he wanted her to choose him.

'Aislinn, would you like to get out of the castle for a ride this afternoon? Falstaff has given us permission if we take two guards with us,' he asked her.

'Oh that would be wonderful Drew. I feel so cooped up here – just getting out in the fresh air would make me so happy and would probably do you the world of good too.'

For now they would have a truce – it was easier than constantly trying to figure out what mood he was in – some days he would be loving and gentle and other days a sheer brute. She was tired of the game and had decided to be friendly and amicable no matter what.

'Good, I'll ask if the kitchen can pack us a picnic lunch.'

Aislinn felt excited at the prospect of getting away from this morbid castle for a few hours. She quickly paid Gwen a visit to check on her and ensure that she was all right.

'Oh I am so envious,' Gwen said when Aislinn told her of her plans to go for a ride. 'There are times I wish I could escape these walls and just be free to roam the countryside. Have a good time Aislinn. Lord knows, you deserve a break from this place.'

They rode out into the fields, Aislinn enjoying the wind blowing through her hair as she cantered behind Daemon. The sun shone and the sky was azure blue. It was a perfect day and for the first time she felt free and happy. She had to admit that being with Drew was also the reason for her happiness.

Daemon looked over at her and smiled. She was beautiful.

'Come on let's stop here and have some lunch.'

He tied up the horses and helped her down, holding onto her waist lingeringly and letting his fingers caress her ever so gently. Then he let her go. He would not force himself on her because he wanted to drive her crazy till her passion could no longer be denied.

He set out the blanket and helped her to find a seat. Then they ate their lunch and sipped on some wine the cook had given them. Aislinn was not used to drinking and felt her head lighten as she sipped the rich, red liquid. She lay back and covered her eyes with her hand, soaking up the sun's warmth. He watched her etching her face into his memory – oh lord, how he wanted her. He leaned over her and touched his lips to hers ever so gently so she could almost barely feel his touch. She opened her eyes and came face to face with his deep violet eyes that reflected his passion. She moaned and he kissed her deeper, discovering her very soul. She wound her hand around his neck into the dark curls at the nape of his neck.

Her senses returned suddenly as she remembered they were not alone. The two guards would be watching them. She did not want to become castle gossip, her reputation ruined and held up for scrutiny. She pulled away.

'Drew, stop. We aren't alone and I have a reputation to keep. Anyway I thought we discussed our relationship the other day. You've forgotten what I said about just being friends,' she said trying to sound teasing and light-hearted. In reality her heart was pounding – that kiss was deep and tender. It totally revealed her heart. He was not going to make this easy for her.

'Sorry, I couldn't help myself,' he said huskily. 'You drive me crazy Aislinn. I want you so much it sends my reason out the window.'

She laughed and stood up, straightening her skirts. '

'Well you will have to work on that. I will not give myself to anyone but my husband.'

'I would gladly fill that position if you would have me Aislinn.'

'We better get back. It's getting late,' she evaded.

⌘

The next few weeks flew by and Daemon made every effort to woo Aislinn. He picked some heather and flowers from the fields and brought them to her. He took her for walks and made her laugh. He was by her side at every opportunity and he could see her walls of resistance and indifference beginning to crumble. She looked at him differently. There was love in her eyes and the last trace of suspicion and wariness was disappearing every day. He had restrained from kissing her although every part of him wanted to consume her. Daemon felt confident that she was in love with him. He was correct in that thought, however it was Drew Aislinn was in love with. She had no idea that Daemon even existed and that would become an obstacle he would have to face.

⌘

Gwendolyn woke – something was wrong. She felt a searing pain in her abdomen. She put her hand between her legs. Then when she lifted the coverlet she screamed in fear. Her fingers were streaked with blood, her nightdress turning red.

'Wake up Aislinn,' Falstaff banged on her door. 'Gwen needs help now – she's bleeding out. You have to do something.

Aislinn sat up and pulled on her gown as fast as she could. She followed Falstaff down the dimly lit halls to Gwen's chambers. Legion was there when she arrived looking worried and helpless.

'Where is Dr. Williams?' Aislinn asked Falstaff. 'I need his help now.'

This was messing with Falstaff's carefully laid plans. Aislinn had to deliver this child – bringing the doctor in here would reveal everything.

'I'll be back,' he said rushing out the door. He could not have Drew in the room with Gwen – she would question everything. He had to think fast. His Master would question why the physician wasn't present at the birth.

Gwen was crying with the pain. Legion held her hand but was silent. He did not know how to be loving; how to support and encourage his wife. It went against his complete nature – all the years of hatred, anger and bitterness left him unable to know where to begin.

Aislinn padded the bleeding and gave Gwen another dose of the False Unicorn Root and Lobelia. She was not hopeful it would work – obviously there was hemorrhaging taking place although she wasn't bleeding furiously. Still they needed to get the child out quickly before she became too weak and died from loss of blood. Aislinn suspected that the placenta had separated from her uterine wall – something that could have dire consequences for mother and child. She gave Gwen a herbal sedative to make her drowsy. She needed the young mother to be awake but to relax as any further stress or worry would affect the baby.

Falstaff arrived back with Drew. He had told the doctor to give Aislinn instructions on what to do. He also warned Drew that Gwen was hallucinating and may think he was her brother as they looked similar. It was the only explanation he could give the doctor under the circumstances. He prayed that she would be in too much pain to care who Drew was.

'Thank goodness you are here,' Aislinn said when Drew entered. 'I think it's the placenta.'

'Drew nodded and felt Gwen's stomach. Aislinn was right – they needed to get the baby out immediately.

'Daemon,' Gwen smiled half drugged. 'You've come to be with me.'

'Of course Gwen, just relax and listen to Aislinn.' Falstaff was right – she was delirious. 'I need you to do an internal examination Aislinn, but you will need to be very careful – any mistake could see her bleed out.'

'Is that necessary?' Legion asked.

'Yes, I'm afraid so – if the placenta is covering the cervix then there will be no way to save either your wife or the baby.'

Legion paled at this news.

'All right,' he said. 'Do what you must.'

Aislinn prepared to do the exam. She was afraid – this was the Dark Lord's child. What would he do to them if the child died? There would be no need to keep his word of ensuring their safety if his child were dead. He would blame them for this. She gently started her examination, all the while talking to Gwen to keep her calm.

Aislinn washed her hands, the exam complete, her brow furrowing with worry.

'I need to talk to Dr. Williams alone,' Aislinn said to Legion.

'No, you need to tell me what you found,' he said.

'We don't have time to play games. Your wife and child are in great danger. Now let me talk to the doctor so we can work this out,' Aislinn countered. 'I promise I will let you know what is going on after we talk,' she reassured him.

'All right,' Legion relented. Falstaff paled but said nothing.

Aislinn and Drew exited the room to talk.

'It's bad Drew. The cervix is covered by the placenta. She can't deliver this baby and will die. I am afraid if that happens then we are in great danger.

Aislinn quickly filled Drew in on the deal Legion had made with Ziah.

'There is one other option Aislinn, but it is very risky and I have never performed it myself. I heard about it when I studied overseas. A century ago a farmer got permission from the local authorities to cut the baby out from his wife's womb when the midwives could no longer help her. Both mother and child lived to tell the tale.'

'Is that true? Well it's not a great option but I guess we don't have any choice Drew. If this baby dies then we die – it's as simple as that. Do you think you can do it?'

'I guess we'll find out.'

They returned the room and filled Legion in on the situation.

'Have you ever done this before?' he asked. 'I've never heard of it.'

'We have to be honest with you. Neither of us has ever attempted it but it is their only chance. If we don't do it Gwen will hemorrhage and the baby will die too - that I can assure you of. At least this way the baby stands a chance of surviving.'

'What about Gwen?'

'I can't make any promises – we'll do our best,' Drew replied. 'Get me some opium soaked sponges Aislinn, some boiling water and towels.'

She did as she was told and then proceeded to clean the instruments he would use. That was the one thing Drew had taught her well. He had seen many people die from septicemia due to unclean instruments and hygiene. Cleanliness was imperative for a successful operation.

Aislinn helped Gwen breathe in the fumes from the sponges. The opium would help her to cope with the pain that would come with the incision. Then she gave her a piece of leather strap to bite on.

Drew took a deep breath.

'Legion I need you to leave the room while we do this. It will not be pleasant for you to watch. Falstaff can assist us and as soon as the baby is born we will call you. '

Legion was about to refuse but then thought better of it. They were right – he did not want to see them cut open his wife and possibly witness the death of his child. They waited as he left the room.

'Aislinn you hold her shoulders while I make the cut.'

He readied his hand to begin cutting but stopped. He could not do it. The after effects of the poison had left his hands shaky and unsteady. No physician should ever operate under those circumstances. He focused and tried again. One mistake could mean the end of all their lives.

'Is everything all right Drew?' Aislinn asked concerned.

'No, I can't make the cut. My sickness has given me the shakes and until it is completely out my system I am going to be useless as a surgeon. You will have to do it Aislinn.'

He looked apologetic, as though he had let her down once again.

'You'll have to tell me exactly what to do.'

Great One, help me please – I can't mess this up!

⌘

LIONSGATE

The Great One watched Aislinn as she prepared to cut Gwendolyn's bulging abdomen. He saw the look of concentration on her face. There was something else there too – fear and uncertainty.

'You can do this my girl – I believe in you,' he encouraged.

She was courageous this young woman. She never shied away from a challenge and he was proud of who she had become.

'It will be all right,' he whispered 'Follow your instincts.'

⌘

Aislinn took the sharp instrument and willed herself to be brave. She looked at her hand holding the knife.

Was that gold dust shimmering on her hand?

She remembered Regent giving her that gift years ago – a reminder of who she was – he said it came from within.

Was this the Great One's way of telling her he was with her?

She smiled, feeling calmer. If he was with her everything would be okay. She had always imagined delivering babies the way nature intended, seeing joy on the parent's faces when they met their new babe; she had never imagined cutting a woman's belly open. She had never imagined this. Steeling herself she made the incision exactly as Drew told her. Gwen screamed in pain as the men held her down. Aislinn felt sick.

Not now. Focus, you can do this Aislinn. Your life and Drew's depend on it.

CHAPTER 14

BIRTH

"The two most important days in your life are the day you are born and the day you find out why" — Mark Twain

GRISWOLD - EARLY SUMMER 1624

LEGION stood looking out the window. He was pale and smelled of fear. He had never been so terrified in all his life. Hearing Falstaff's account of Aislinn cutting open his wife made him feel sick yet at the same time he admired the young woman for her fearlessness. The cry of his son when he was pulled from her belly was a welcome noise and sent him rushing back into the room. They all smiled at his lusty and indignant yells at being pulled from his warm cocoon Drew took the baby, cut the cord, wrapped him in swaddling and handed him to Legion who looked extremely afraid of this newborn flesh. He had to pinch himself – he was a father. Gwen seemed to be doing well and Aislinn had done a good job of stitching her wound under Drew's instructions. He owed his family's life to the same girl he hated so deeply for all these years. For the first time he disliked the person he had become. She had showed him what love and compassion was. She had helped them, her enemies because her heart was good. He was grateful for that and he would make sure he kept this promise to Ziah – to get her home safely.

⌘

Falstaff was furious. He was glad Gwen was safe although he had been willing to sacrifice her for the power he plotted to gain. His anger was directed at Aislinn Hamilton. She had saved the day and ruined his plans. He wanted that baby to die – for Legion to blame her and the doctor, to have them killed. He wanted his Master to have no heir and to be distracted with hatred and vengeance. Instead the child would live and become the heir to Griswold. Griswold should be his inheritance – he had helped the Dark Lord all these years to keep it through his spells and magic. Now it was his time to get something in return. It was no longer good enough to just be chief wizard. He wanted it all. That girl had ruined it. He paced like a caged animal, waiting impatiently for the one person who could help him.

'Come in Cillian,' he said to the young man when he finally arrived at his door.

'You said it was urgent Falstaff.'

'I have a little problem that needs taking care of. I need it done discreetly without the Dark Lord knowing I was behind the plan.'

'I'm not sure I can help you then,' Cillian replied. 'The Dark Lord would kill us if he even knew we were having this conversation.'

'I understand your reservations Cillian, but there is reward in this for you too. Not to mention the revenge you never really had.'

'What do you mean?'

'I'm talking about Mackenzie Hamilton. You never really did crush him did you? He landed on his feet and is happier than ever – in fact he's even grateful for what they went through but what about you? You ended up taking over as leader to some disgruntled people. You thought they would love you and that it would be easy to fill Mac's shoes but from what I've heard they never really trusted you or followed you.'

This was a brutal reminder to Cillian. Falstaff was telling the truth. Mac had found freedom and a new life while he had ended up feeling miserable and alone. It wasn't right that Mackenzie Hamilton had such favour. He wished with all his heart that his sword had killed him four years ago.

'So what does this have to do with Mac?' Cillian asked.

'Not Mac, but something that will crush him and bring him years of pain and suffering. I'm talking about Aislinn. I want her killed but in such a way that it looks like we had nothing to do with it. Then you can sit back and watch her father's grief.'

'What do you have in mind?'

⌘

Legion held his son in his arms. He had never experienced this rush of love for another person ever in his life. His heart had always been hard and cold. Looking at the sleeping face of his child he wondered how his own mother could have hated him so much when he was born. Babies looked so pure and innocent. The realization that one is not born evil slowly sunk into his consciousness. He had not been born evil – his mother's hatred and disdain had made him that way – had infiltrated his entire personality and festered until whatever came out was ugly and cruel. He would not let his son grow up that way. He felt ashamed at how he had treated his wife – he had pushed her away and allowed his rejection to affect his whole life.

'He's perfect, isn't he Gwen?'

'Yes, he has your eyes,' she said.

Gwendolyn had been surprised at Legion's tenderness since the baby had been born. It was as though they had both been born that day. When Aislinn cut the child out, bitterness, anger and hatred had been cut out of Legion's heart at the same time. He appeared to be a different man – a man she could love again.

'What should we call him?' Legion asked. 'I know how important a name is Gwen. My mother cursed me when she called me Sephtis. Every day she used that name, was her way of speaking eternal death over me. This child's name must speak life and hope – of rebirth because he has saved my soul.'

'I had a name in mind. I like the name Beathan which means life. What do you think?'

'Yes I like it, but we need more than that. What about Phoenix – the bird that regenerates from the ashes? I feel that his birth has regenerated my soul."

'It's perfect Legion. Phoenix Beathan it will be,' she said happy for the first time in years. Maybe they would be a real family yet.

'Aislinn says my wound is healing nicely. She has made up a salve from herbs to put on it to prevent infection and scarring. I know she is anxious to get home to her family. Would it be possible for them to travel home soon, Legion?'

'I gave Ziah my word that she would get home and she will. The past is the past Gwen. I understand now why she did everything in her power to protect her family, why she tried to save her brother. I would do the same for you and Phoenix.

I will get cook to pack some provisions for their journey and get some horses ready. They are free to leave whenever they choose.'

⌘

Aislinn could not believe their good fortune. They were free to leave and return home. It would be a long journey but the sooner they got out of this castle the better. She packed her few belongings, delighted that she would never have to stay in the south tower at the castle again. She couldn't wait to see her family and to tell them of all the adventures they had had. This journey was terrifying but at the same time she learned so much. They had discovered a new method of birthing babies when a mother could not do it naturally. This would change the face of medicine forever. It meant that when a mother died there was still the possibility of saving the unborn child. She was grateful that they had the opportunity to discover this. Granted they would have had their heads on a pike if they had failed but there was nothing like incentive to get the process right. She still could not believe that she had performed the surgery. Drew was a great teacher. She also had to admit that she did trust him implicitly – she would not have been able to do as he instructed if she did not. That was the last excuse she had used for telling him that they could not be together – trust. Well she had shown him that she did indeed trust him. What would happen with their relationship now? She still loved him desperately. He was feeling so much better now. His shaking had stopped and it seemed that almost every drop of poison had worked its way out of his system.

'Are you ready Aislinn,' he interrupted her dreaming.

'More than ready Drew– let's go home.'

Falstaff watched them from his spell chamber window as they mounted their horses. He had not told Daemon they were leaving as he feared the young man was becoming too attached to Aislinn Hamilton. He could not have him interfering in his plans now. Drew and Aislinn needed to be seen leaving the castle in one piece, together. They rode out of the castle to make their way to Trenton where they would spend the night before riding on to Sherbrooke. That was where the adventure had started and they had come full circle.

Watching them from a thicket outside the castle a group of four men discreetly followed the pair as they left.

CHAPTER 15

CAPTIVES

"Captivity can't be overcome with inactivity"
— Constance Chuks Friday

DREW and Aislinn rode side by side chatting about their stay at the castle.

'I still don't understand why you poisoned yourself Drew,' Aislinn said.

'I told you why.'

'Yes but it doesn't make sense to me because we saw each other almost every day when we discussed Gwen's treatment.'

'What are you talking about Aislinn? We were deliberately kept apart. I was not allowed to see you or Gwendolyn for weeks after I was kidnapped out of my bed at Trenton and brought to the castle. I even began to doubt that Gwendolyn existed.'

'That's impossible Drew because it was you who took me to that house out of town where Cillian captured me.'

'You really believe that I would hand you over to Cillian?' he asked horrified at her accusation. 'Aislinn I would never do that to you. I love you. I told you I would never put you in danger. I was taken by two men from my room the night before we were due to leave.'

'No you weren't Drew, because I had breakfast with you the next morning. Stop lying to me – you are just making things worse. If you wanted me out of your life so that you could pursue Gabrielle you just had to say so.'

'Is that what you think – that I was trying to get rid of you to be with her?' He laughed sardonically.

'Aislinn I have never been with her in the sense of a relationship. She has done nothing but trick me since I met her and now she even has you believing we were ever a couple. She took advantage of me when I was drunk one night and I woke up beside her the next morning. I don't know what happened and if I could prove it to you I would, but I have no way of doing that. She says we were intimate but I don't remember any of it.'

'Well I know how to get the answer,' Aislinn said fed up with his lies. 'I will ask my ring for the truth.'

She looked down at her hand at the gleaming neutral stone. This ring would settle it once and for all.

'Was Drew taken by two men from his room in Trenton?'

The ring became hazy and then shone deep purple.

'You're telling the truth Aislinn gasped. How is that possible?'

'Did Drew lead me to Cillian and betray me?'

The stone changed colour, becoming a deep yellow.

'I told you Aislinn it wasn't me – I would never betray you to that man. All I can assume is that Falstaff must have used a spell to deceive us or an impersonation spell to make you believe it was me when in fact it was someone else.'

'You're right Drew – it could only have been magic – he looked and sounded exactly like you. I'm sorry, really I am. All this time I have been angry with you for something you have never done. I'm so embarrassed – I should have known better.'

'It's all in the past now – let's not dwell on it. My feelings for you haven't changed. I love you more today than ever before – I meant what I said at the pond Aislinn – every word.'

'And I love you Drew. I never stopped even when I was angry with you, or rather your imposter,' she smiled, relieved that he was so forgiving.

'Don't you want to know the truth about Gabrielle?' he asked. 'Your ring will tell you if you ask it.'

'No, I don't,' she smiled. 'I believe you Drew – I don't need the ring to confirm it for me – as you said, it's all in the past.'

'Are you sure, my love – I don't want any secrets between us.'

'I'm sure.'

The riders watched the pair as they travelled, completely wrapped up in one another and oblivious to their tail. They would make their move when they entered Grimwood Forest – these two would never know what had hit them.

⌘

Cillian stood before the Elders of their clan. He shuffled his feet, slightly afraid of the outcome of his visit. He had shared the information with them and hoped that they would respond accordingly and would lend their support to his and Falstaff's cause. The success of their plan depended on their help.

He thought back to when they had attacked the Hamilton family years ago and how afraid he had been that the Elders would favour Mac and Imogene Hamilton. It had surprised him that they had washed their hands of the whole Hamilton debacle and feigned ignorance by not getting involved. Well this time he would ensure that they played a part in ruining that family once and for all.

He waited patiently while they discussed the issue at hand, throwing their opinions and supposed wisdom back and forth to reach a decision.

⌘

Mac and Imogene looked forward to Aislinn's return – they had missed her and especially Mitchell who doted on his older sister. They were also relieved that Legion had kept his word. In fact they had been extremely surprised when a Monwing had come from the castle with a note telling them that Aislinn and Drew were on their way home. Was it possible Legion had changed that much?

Eion had been a different man ever since he had faced the Dark Lord and stood his ground. Now he wondered why he had ever been so afraid of the man.

'The mind does strange things when it is afraid,' he said to Mac.

'Yes, you're right Eion. Half the battle of life takes place in the mind and if we allow people to intimidate us or scare us then our belief in ourselves becomes distorted and then we can never achieve greatness.'

'I looked at Legion and realized how much he swayed and manipulated my thoughts and actions. I am so grateful we met you and the Great One. You've changed our lives. Even then, I let him keep us prisoners for four years by being fearful of him. It is so good to feel free at last. I have decided to start working on some of my spells and remedies again, nothing that will ever be used to harm folk, but remedies and potions that will strengthen and help people.'

'I think that's wonderful Eion – that is where your gift lies.'

'I was too afraid to dabble in spells after I left Griswold. I was afraid that my heart and soul were contaminated by that place. Now I know that it is a choice to become evil, one is not born into it.'

'Not everyone would agree with you on that Eion. When we were sent to Griswold by the Elders of the Clan all those years ago, it was because we believed that all are born evil and that we needed to be saved from our evil nature by the Great One. It took meeting the Great One face to face to show us that mankind is not inherently evil and that he is not full of wrath toward us. His love changed us too, from being so blinded by the Clan's prophecies and rules, to becoming free to be who we are. We may both have come from opposite sides of the fence but we have both learned about his goodness. Sherbrooke will welcome your talents Eion – I'm sure of it. You should chat to Dr. Williams about adding some of your remedies to his practice. He would be delighted to have an apothecary making up some of the herbs he needs.'

'I think that's a splendid idea Mac. Thank you for being so patient with me and for being a real friend.'

⌘

Drew and Aislinn headed deeper into Grimwood Forest. The light shone through the trees and danced in slivers along the mossy ground. It was beautiful in an eerie way. The footfall of their horses was muffled by the moss and bracken.

'Stay close to me Aislinn. We need to get through here as quickly as possible.'

Aislinn had told Drew some of the stories she had heard about Grimwood Forest when they had lived in Griswold all those years ago. No one knew if there was any truth to them or whether they were simply legend but neither of them wanted to find out. They made their way with as much speed as they could, neither of them speaking. This was always the worst part of the journey to Trenton.

'Oh no,' Drew groaned as he noticed the fallen tree lying across the path. 'We can't get through, we'll have to try and cut into the brush to get back on the path.'

They only became aware of the four men hedging them in when they turned their horses. They both knew this was not a good omen.

'What do you want?' Drew asked concern in his voice. 'We have no money or anything of worth.'

'If we deliver you safely to Cillian then we will receive our reward.'

'What does he want now?' Aislinn asked. 'I knew it was too good to be true to be let go by the Dark Lord. He just wanted us to think he had changed. He always gets Cillian to do his dirty work.'

'It ain't the Dark Lord Miss who wants you captured,' one of the men volunteered.

'Shut up you fool,' the other man barked. 'Don't say another word or you won't get your share of the bounty.' The man instantly closed his mouth.

'Why would Cillian want us then?' Aislinn asked Drew.

'I have no idea, but I guess we are about to find out.'

CHAPTER 16

CONFRONTATION

"Not speaking up against pure evil is equal to co-operating with it"
— Constance Chuks Friday

DAEMON had just received word from Gwendolyn that Aislinn and Drew had left the castle. He had hoped to whisk her away before they departed and to reveal the truth to her. He would have to go after her now – he could not lose her. She did something to him – he was not quite sure what, but his senses felt heightened and his desire out of control whenever he was around her. He headed to his father's chambers to seek a spell or potion that would make her fall in love with him and forget his twin brother. He must not let his father know he was there – wizards tended to be very protective of their own spells as they viewed them as an extension of their personality, and more importantly as an indication of their power. Daemon had excelled at wizardry school but he still had a lot to learn. It would be much easier to use one of his father's tried and tested spells. This was usually the time when his father would be attending to disputes with the Dark Lord down in the great hall – his only opportunity to get into the spell chamber and look for what he needed. He entered the chamber and pulled out a volume of spells. The book was heavy and dusty. He browsed through the pages searching for the spell. Finding nothing he replaced the big book and took down another volume. He had just started reading when he heard his father's voice out in the hall. He was coming and someone was with him. Daemon shut the book, hastily replaced it and hid inside the armoire that housed his father's wizardry apparel.

'It went better than we imagined Falstaff.' The voice said. 'We have the girl and the doctor – they were captured in Grimwood Forest as planned.'

'Wonderful, and the rest of our plan? Is it coming together?' Falstaff asked.

'Yes splendidly. I was worried the Elders wouldn't want anything to do with it, but once they heard what I told them, they felt they could not look the other way. To do so would be a gross sin.'

'You are to be commended Cillian. The Dark Lord will never know we were behind the death of Aislinn Hamilton.'

Daemon inhaled deeply. Why did his father want Aislinn dead? Gwen was right worrying about the girl's safety but the threat was not from her husband. It was from their father. What could he possibly gain by Aislinn's death? He would not allow it to happen.

⌘

Aislinn and Drew were confused. What did Cillian want from them now? Aislinn had a sick feeling in the pit of her stomach. Nothing good ever came of her encounters with Cillian. She gasped when she saw where they were headed.

Was this some kind of sick joke - his way of gloating and dredging up the past?

'Drew I know where we are going but I just don't why,' she whispered to him.

'Where are they taking us?'

'We are going back to our old home in Griswold – the one that Cillian and his men burned down four years ago. That is where it all started – where our lives were changed forever.'

'Why would we be going there?'

"I have no idea, but I have a horrible feeling they are trying to make a point,' she said.

⌘

'Where is she father?' Daemon yelled his anger rising. 'What have you done?'

Falstaff looked shocked. How did Daemon know that he had Aislinn?

'Yes I know you have her. I overheard you and Cillian talking earlier. If you hurt one hair on her head you will regret it.'

Daemon had not expected his father to laugh at this – loud and scornful.

'I pity you, you fool. The witch has turned your head and you have fallen under her spell. Well I guess you are not the first man to do so. Even my Master fell for her four years ago and look where it landed him. He lost the respect of everyone in this castle, not to mention Griswold. She will use her wiles to make men weak and useless, but not for long. She will be tried for the witch she is and punished accordingly.'

'What do you mean father?'

'That is all I am prepared to say – get out of here Daemon and stop acting like a lovesick puppy. If you mention this to anyone I will destroy you.'

'Don't walk away from me father,' Daemon said coldly as Falstaff turned his back.

'You are weak – just like that brother of yours. Your blood is not mine clearly. You don't have the backbone to follow in my shoes as a wizard. Get out of my sight Daemon and don't come back here. You are not my son and never will be.'

The hurtful words cut Daemon's heart. He had idolized his father as a child – wanted to be just like him and follow in his footsteps. His anger rose as he drew his sword.

'Don't be ridiculous Daemon, we both know you don't have it in you to kill me.'

'Tell me what you are planning or I will cut you open from navel to throat.'

Falstaff was surprised by the steely resolution in his eyes.

'Fine, I will humour you, but this is the last time,' Falstaff relented. He would take care of the young man later. He was becoming a problem.

⌘

Aislinn and Drew arrived with their captors at the old farmhouse she had called home once before. The burnt ruins were an ugly reminder of the past, grass and moss now growing over the blackened stones. There was nothing but rubble left. The willow tree to the side of the house was green with summer leaves and its branches swayed in the wind without a care in the world. This was the tree her mother had been left hanging from – the weeping willow – an appropriate name. She thought again of Ziah and how he had saved more than one of her family.

'Ziah we need your help and those keys of freedom you carry. Something is not right here. Please come and save us,' she whispered under her breath.

⌘

LIONSGATE

The Great One let out a whoop of joy.

'Get Ziah, Nuada, we have a mission to complete, 'and tell him to bring his keys.'

CHAPTER 17

THE TRIAL

"Today's trial is tomorrow's testimony" - Unknown

DAEMON rode as fast as his horse would carry him. He kicked the beast in the sides urging it on faster and faster. His father was evil, mad – he really believed that he would have the power of Griswold soon. He had to get to Sherbrooke and find Aislinn's family – he had to get help before they tried her. His father had squealed like a pig when he was threatened with a sword to his throat. He would have gone straight to the burned down ruins of Aislinn's old home had he known where they were. It would take longer but he needed Mac to show him where to go and he would need them to fight alongside him. He prayed they would be in time.

⌘

Falstaff paced up and down his chambers. His son was on the verge of betraying him. He would have to speed up his plans in the castle before Daemon ruined it all. He plotted all the while dreaming of his rise to power. He would be the next lord of Griswold. Nothing and no one would stop him – not even his son.

⌘

'Where are you taking him,' Aislinn screamed as Drew was hauled away from her and caged in a wooden cart with iron bars. 'What do you want from us?'

She noticed a group of men staring at her with cold eyes.

Who were they?

'Bring the girl here,' one of the Elders instructed to Cillian. Aislinn fought him as he pushed her toward the group of eight men seated in a circle. They all looked at her, their expressions emotionless. Then it dawned on her. Were these the Elders her father had once trusted with their lives? They were dressed in simple robes and they all looked the same.

'You are Aislinn Hamilton, daughter of Mackenzie and Imogene Hamilton?' they asked.

'Yes.'

'It has been brought to our attention that your family has deviated from the path of righteousness and that you have forsaken the Prophecies spoken over your lives. Is that correct?'

Aislinn did not respond.

'If you choose not to speak we will take your answer to be affirming what we say.'

'We have forsaken nothing,' Aislinn declared defiantly. 'If that is a crime then you should all be looking at yourselves. I recall you forsaking our family when Cillian burned down our home and attacked my parents. Where were you then?'

The Elders glared at Aislinn, shocked by her blatant challenge.

'I see you have no respect for spiritual authority. This appears to be another form of heresy I would say,' the chief

Elder declared. The others all nodded their heads vigorously in agreement.

'You will address me as Elder Merek. It is your parent's deviation from the Prophecies that has led you to this moment Aislinn. They did not train you in our beliefs the way they should have and now you have no idea of the Great One and how to be an obedient follower.'

Aislinn tried to contain the laughter that was threatening to bubble over.

Were these archaic old men really serious?

'Actually Elder Merek, they have done much better than just training me to obey the Great One. They have brought me to him face to face. I have spoken to him recently and know him to be loving and kind and a wonderful friend. I have a relationship with him and I'm like a daughter to him. Can you say the same thing about your relationship with him?'

The other Elders looked on disbelieving. Did she know who she was challenging?

'You speak heresy Aislinn. No-one sees the Great One face to face unless they have passed over. You look very much alive to us. The Great One is also pure – he does not tolerate evil or sin in any form. In fact he demands justice and judgement for evil.'

'You are wrong about him,'Aislinn interjected. 'He is not full of wrath as you suppose. He is light and love and everything good.'

'How dare you insinuate young lady that we do not know the Great One. We are his chosen ones, the harbingers and ordained to teach truth. Your ramblings are evidence that an evil spirit has consumed you and taken over your soul. We have had claims made to us that you have been practicing witchcraft.'

'That is ridiculous,' Aislinn spluttered. 'Who has made these claims?'

'We have witnesses to a brutal ritual where you cut open a woman and removed the child from her womb. Do you deny that?'

'No, but I was saving her and the child from death. They would have both died if I had not operated. It was not a ritual as you put it but a medical procedure.'

'Ritual or not, life is decided by the Great One Aislinn. It was not your place to perform the act and change the course of history. Only evil could have made you do that. If the woman and child died it would have been the Great One's will. Those who mess with his will work against him.'

Aislinn could not believe what she was hearing. Their logic was ridiculous. These men had no idea who the Great One even was and yet they considered themselves the spiritual leaders of their clan. No wonder her parents had broken away and found freedom.

'Again, you are wrong about the Great One. He allows us to choose our own destiny – to make a difference to people around us – to love everyone no matter who they are.'

'Choose your own destiny – good lord child whoever taught you that. As for loving everyone that is equally ridiculous. We are called to teach people the right way to live but should they not comply then we are to have nothing to do with them. Their sin will contaminate us and be our downfall? We cannot be a part of those who forsake the way – surely you know that?' Merek scoffed. 'Aislinn it is clear to us that you have committed witchcraft by the act of saving the Dark Lord's child. The Great One wanted that woman and child dead and you chose to save them. You chose to save the bloodline of darkness and that pure act of evil has to be punished. Do you admit to your transgression and are you willing to repent for it?'

'I have done nothing wrong. I am a midwife and my job is to help pregnant women no matter who they are. I saved that woman and her child because they are worthy of being saved – they are loved by the Great One too. I do not believe a baby is born with evil as you clearly do. I will not apologize for doing my job well or for choosing compassion over judgement.'

The Elders whispered among themselves, angry and frustrated at her defiance.

'You leave us no choice then. If you will not repent for the evil you have done then you will be burned at the stake for witchcraft. Do you understand the punishment Aislinn? The hour is late and we are all weary. We will commence with the punishment tomorrow when the moon is high and full. You can still save yourself Aislinn. Search your soul and humble yourself to repent of your evil ways. We will talk again tomorrow.'

Aislinn could not believe this was happening to her. She was going to be burned for saving lives – for medically advancing childbirth. They dragged her to the cart and threw her in with Drew, locking the door behind her.

'I'm sorry Aislinn, I've failed to protect you again,' Drew said.

'Don't say that, it's not true,' she said falling into his arms, his embrace welcome after the onslaught she had been through. She had stood her ground and defied them but now her body shook, shock setting in.

'How can they accuse me of being a witch Drew?'

'I've heard stories overseas of midwives who have been called witches. When a baby of an infidel is saved and the spiritual leaders don't like it they say it was evil that kept the child alive and the midwife is punished. When a baby of a believer dies the midwife is accused of causing the baby's death and is equally punished. These spiritual leaders have no concept of medical advancement – they are ignorant fools who pass on their traditions and illogical beliefs from generation to generation. We can't just sit here Aislinn. We have to try and get out of here. I won't lose you now – not when we've just found each other again.'

'There is no way out of this cage Drew, but I believe the Great One will rescue us. I know you don't know him the way I do, but what I told those men was true – he does care for us and the one truth I have learned from him is that everything is possible for those who believe.'

'I don't understand how you can be so calm Aislinn. They have threatened to kill you and yet you sit here and talk about this Great One rescuing us. How does he even know we are in trouble or where we are?'

'He knows everything Drew. I've called for him and Ziah and they will come. I'm sure of it. They have never let me down yet.'

She leaned against his broad chest and he smelled the lavender water she used in her hair. He wrapped his arms around her and hoped that she was right. He admired her unwavering faith. One of the things he loved most about her was her strength and sense of justice. She had stood up to these men who tried to beat her down and make her feel small, she had stood up for what she believed in – and it would mean her death.

Why did she have to be so noble?

⌘

Daemon went straight to Dr. William's rooms when he arrived in Sherbrooke. This wasn't the reunion he had in mind with his real father but he did not have time to dwell on that. He had to find out where Mac and Imogene lived. He entered the rooms and called for the doctor.

'I'll be with you soon,' the doctor called back. He was with a patient and Daemon paced restlessly up and down the little waiting room. Eventually a woman and a child exited his room, followed by the doctor.

'Drew,' he exclaimed when he saw the young man. 'You're home at last.'

'I'm not Drew Dr. Williams – I am Daemon, Drew's twin brother.'

The old man looked shocked then embarrassed. What could he say to the child he gave up?

'Good lord, you are the spitting image. Why are you here young man. Drew doesn't know about you does he? Your father promised me he would not tell him till I had a chance to.'

Daemon felt hurt momentarily.

He isn't even pleased to see me.

He pushed down the disappointment. Now wasn't the time to allow his hurt feelings to get in the way.

'My father is the reason I am here. Drew and Aislinn are in great danger. I need to see Mackenzie Hamilton immediately.'

*Well I guess my secret will be let out of the bag now. I guess
it was a matter of time before people found out that Drew had
a twin. I just wish I had been able to tell Drew before all this
happened,* the old man thought to himself.

As they rode out to Mac and Imogene's thatched cottage.
Daemon filled the doctor in on Falstaff's conspiracy.

'My father has gone mad I fear,' Daemon said. 'He is so set
on getting power that he is willing to murder anyone who
stands in his way. Although Drew is not their target I fear he
will defend Aislinn and in so doing will end up being killed.'

They arrived at the cottage and could see smoke curling
up from the chimney. It seemed awfully quiet – perhaps Mac
was out thatching with Eion.

Imogene came to the door of the cottage when she heard
the riders approaching. She was not expecting anyone and felt
a little alarmed at who might be calling.

'Dr. Williams, what are you doing here?' she asked
surprised. She looked over at the young man travelling with
him and paled.

'Drew, how did you get here? Is Aislinn with you?'

'This is not Drew Imogene. It is his twin brother Daemon
I'm sure Mac mentioned to you that there were other
circumstances surrounding my wife's death.'

'Yes,' he did mention it after they visited you, but I didn't
realize the complications were twins.'

'I can't explain it now Imogene other than to say I could
not raise both boys. That is not the problem though. It
appears Aislinn and Drew are in grave danger and Daemon
has come to warn us.'

'Yes we know. The Great One was called by Aislinn and
he's sent Ziah, Aedan, Mac and some others to rescue them.

'Do they know where to find them?' Daemon asked.

'Yes, the Great One saw them heading for our old homestead in his Mirror of Time. Do you have any idea what this is all about? Ziah did not have time to tell me anything before they left except to promise me they would find them. I have been out of my mind with worry.'

Daemon breathed a sigh of relief. Someone would rescue them.

'Yes, I can tell you what I know,' he said.

'Why don't you come in and have some tea?' Imogene offered.

Dr. Williams and Daemon gratefully accepted the refreshments and Daemon explained everything that had happened to Drew and Aislinn since leaving the castle and of his link to Falstaff and Griswold. He omitted to tell them of his involvement in deceiving everyone and of his plan to win over Aislinn. That was his secret and one he still hoped to put into action when she was safe and sound.

'So Legion had nothing to do with Aislinn's capture then?' Imogene asked surprised.

'No, he knows nothing about it. I know it's hard to believe but he is a changed man.'

'I'm sorry, I know I keep staring at you but your resemblance to Drew is uncanny. I would not be able to tell you apart. Do you plan to stay on and meet him when he returns?' Imogene asked Daemon.

'No, I need to get back to the castle before my father does anything else he may regret.'

That was not the complete truth. He had no choice but to honour the doctor's wishes not to tell Drew about him. He did not feel he owed it to the old man – after all he had abandoned him, but he did not want to cause trouble between his brother and his father. It was better they not meet under these circumstances. The time would come for them to meet one day. Besides it would be easier to win Aislinn over if his brother did not know who he was just yet.

CHAPTER 18

TRUTH UNVEILED

"In a time of deceit telling the truth is a revolutionary act."
— George Orwell

AISLINN and Drew woke feeling stiff and sore. Aislinn laughed at the irony of it all. The last time she had been here she was a captive and yet again here she was in the same circumstances. She rubbed her eyes and yawned. Sleeping in the hard, cold cart had not been very comfortable but at least she had Drew with her and they had kept warm by wrapping themselves together in his cloak. Her first night spent with him – not quite what she had imagined it would be and she only hoped it would not be her last. She wanted to live life to the full – to be wed to the love of her life, to feel his touch and bear his children. She looked at his sleeping face, listening to his even breathing and her heart exploded with love for him. She kissed him gently on the lips.

'Wake up sleepy head.'

He smiled before he opened his eyes.

'I could get used to waking up this way, although I promise you sweetheart that I will definitely make sure we have a more comfortable bed than this when we are married.'

She laughed and he pulled her closer kissing her passionately as though this moment would be their last.

'Whatever happens today Aislinn, know that I love you.'

'And I you,' she replied.

⌘

Ziah and his men camped around the farmstead in Griswold. Four year earlier Mac's attackers had lain in wait in these same trees waiting for an opportunity to destroy the family. Now they lay in wait to save Aislinn and Drew from the destroyers. It seemed strange they had come full circle. Mac looked at the burnt rubble that was once his home and reminisced over the memories they had made there. Mitchell had been born in this cottage. Mac thought of the bed he had made when they arrived from the Highlands. Imogene had loved that bed and all the love he had put into crafting it. Those things were gone now and the black stones were all that remained of their life here – that and the willow tree.

They could see Aislinn and Drew in the cart and Mac smiled when he saw Drew tilt his head and kiss his daughter. He had guessed she was in love with him even though there had been times that she had come home and called the young doctor insufferable. Seems they had worked it out. Mac liked the young man immensely. In previous years he would have disapproved of Aislinn's choice as Drew would be considered an infidel – an unbeliever by the Elders of the Clan they used to belong to. Now Mac believed that everyone belonged to the Great One and that nothing was required to be loved by him – no sacrifice – not even acknowledgement. He chuckled to himself. If the Elders could hear him now he would be thrown into that cart alongside his daughter and burned with her for heresy.

'What's the plan Ziah?' Mac asked.

'We will wait till they are taken out of the cart. We cannot break into it because of the iron bars and it is chained to the willow tree so we can't move it without being discovered. But once they are out the Elders will be distracted and that is when we will make our move.'

'That's cutting it a bit fine Ziah,' Aedan said 'but you are right. It is the only way – the element of surprise is our best chance and for that we need to be patient.'

'Let's make ourselves comfortable boys – we have a long wait. They'll wait for nightfall – it's something about believing that burning the evil out of them at night returns the evil spirits back to the realms of darkness,' Ziah said chuckling.

'Do they really believe that hocus-pocus?' Nuada laughed.

'In the meantime we will take turns to keep watch while the rest of us get some rest. They will be coming into the forest to gather wood for their fire and they must not see us,' Ziah instructed.

'Eion and I will take first watch,' Nuada said.

⌘

Daemon had a lot of time to think on his way home. He had listened to Dr. William's story and felt sorry for the old man. He did not have the capacity to care for both him and Drew when his biological mother had died. Nonetheless, he still felt angry at having his brother kept from him all these years. Now he understood why he always felt a part of him was missing. He had assumed it was because his mother had died leaving him and Gwen but now he realized it was because he shared a womb for nine moons with another – a brother who looked just like him. He was torn in two. He wanted to meet this brother and build a relationship with him, but he also desired the same woman as his twin. Which would become more important to him, he had yet to work out.

He arrived back at the castle and went to see Gwen. He had no desire to see his father. Knocking at her chamber doors he entered surprised to find Legion with his sister.

'Daemon, I don't think you've ever actually met Legion, have you? Legion this is my brother Daemon.'

Legion's brow furrowed and he looked confused.

'Dr. Williams, I was under the impression your name was Drew. I had no idea you were Gwen's brother. Falstaff never mentioned it to me.'

'What do you mean Legion? This is Daemon – he's not a doctor – he's a wizard like my father and a very good one I might add,' Gwen clarified.

'Why would you pretend to be a doctor then? Was this your father's idea?'

Legion was furious and tried to conceal his simmering anger.

Typical Falstaff. He had not been able to find a physician so he got Daemon to impersonate one. No wonder Daemon had been unable to perform the operation. He was just damn lucky that Aislinn Hamilton knew what she was doing. He would pay for his deceit.

'You're right to be confused Legion. It's time Gwen knew the truth anyway. This deception has gone on too long in our family and has caused more problems than anything. I am not Gwen's biological brother. I was taken into Falstaff's family as a newborn when my birth mother died. I have a twin brother whose name is Dr. Drew Williams.'

Legions eyebrows raised, the information sinking in.

'Yes, the very same doctor. My father kept Dr. Williams from seeing Gwen as he did not want her to make the connection. She was in too much pain during labour and the opium kept her from putting two and two together when Drew was giving Aislinn instructions for surgery.'

'I just thought that it was you,' Gwen said astounded by this new revelation.

'But how is that possible? If Dr. Williams did not see Gwen then how did he give me daily reports on her progress?' Legion said.

'That was me I'm afraid. I impersonated Dr. Williams so the truth could remain a secret. The truth is that Dr. Williams never actually ever consulted with Gwen. Only Aislinn saw her. I'm sorry we deceived you but it was also because my father made a promise to Drew's father that we would not let him find out he has a twin this way. It was sheer coincidence that the best physician in the country happened to be my brother.'

'You mean he still doesn't know that he has a twin?' Gwen asked.

'Not yet Gwen, but I guess Dr. Williams will tell him now that I have made contact after all these years. Now where is this nephew of mine? I've been dying to see him.'

Legion picked up the chubby baby and handed him to Daemon. This was something Daemon wanted beyond anything – a family of his own. He had seen the power this child had yielded with his birth – by simply being, he had changed the Dark Lord from a cruel hard man into someone who cared about something other than his own needs and wants. Daemon thought of Aislinn as he looked at the child. He loved her, he was sure of it, and he wanted a child with her. He made up his mind as he gazed at the contented child.

He had lived twenty-six years without his brother and he had survived. He wanted Aislinn more than anything and he would have her, even if it cost him his brother.

⌘

The men gathered sticks and firewood for the bonfire that would burn Aislinn Hamilton – an evil they believed would contaminate them. They cut down a tree which they made into a stake and then buried it deep in the ground forming a mound of sand at the base. Then they began to build brush and sticks around the base ready to be burned. The men sweated and toiled to ready the bonfire before nightfall.

'Good,' Aislinn said watching them working in the hot summer sun. 'At least they have to work hard to carry out their evil deeds. I hope they get sun sickness.'

Drew smiled but his heart ached. It was late in the day and she did not have too many hours left in this world. What they planned to do with him he did not know. He did not wish to live without her though. She was the sunshine in his life, his reason for living. She still believed that the Great One and Ziah would rescue them but he was not holding out much hope for that to happen. He believed in things that could be seen and proven, not in hope and blind faith – it was the one difference between them. She believed before it came into being and he only ever believed once there was irrefutable evidence. For the first time he hoped that she was right.

'Don't be afraid Drew,' she said seeing his worried expression. 'Even if I do die tonight I know where I am going. I have been to Lionsgate before and it is the most beautiful place. There is no fear there and I will be with those who love me so greatly. I will miss you though, but we will be together again one day.'

At the bravery of her words he could no longer bear it. Tears slid from his lashes as he growled huskily, 'how can the Great One let this happen if he loves you so much Aislinn? Where is his goodness in seeing you burned to death for being honest and brave and beautiful to people who hate you and are trying to have you killed? How does that show his great love?'

'I know it doesn't make sense to you Drew, but promise me you will not blame him for the evil in this world – for the spiritual leaders who misrepresent who he really is – they are the ones who do this evil in his name – it is not him. Mankind is cruel at times – that is why there is horror in this world. It is up to us to stand up for truth and goodness. The Great One would never allow his people to die this way – I know him and I believe he will come. Promise me that you will open your heart to find his great love.'

She wiped his eyes and kissed his cheeks.

'Promise me Drew.'

'I promise I will try Aislinn,' he sobbed burying his face in her neck as she embraced him, trying to give him strength and not let her own sadness and fear show. The truth was that she was terrified. She had seen firsthand how these men had turned their backs on her family years ago.

The sun began to sink and orange streaks covered the sky turning pink and then purple as the last rays made their way to bed. Time was running out.

Don't let me down Great One, Ziah, she thought.

⌘

Daemon felt relieved – he had made a decision. He couldn't stop thinking of Aislinn. Was she safe or had they been too late to save her? He promised himself that if she survived he would do everything to make her his wife.

Gwen and Legion had other things on their mind. They were planning a ball in honour of their new son. He would be declared heir and firstborn in Griswold and it would an auspicious occasion. His father had been furious when he discovered that Daemon had told Gwen and Legion the truth about Drew, especially since Gwen refused to talk to her father and Legion had banished him from attending the ball. They were going to make his life difficult. Daemon was afraid that when his father found out that Legion had offered him the position of chief wizard that he would do something drastic. They had agreed to wait till after the ball so that nothing would distract from Phoenix's introduction to court.

CHAPTER 19

FIRE AND SALVATION

"I am he who will sustain you. I have made you and I will carry you;
I will sustain you and I will rescue you." - The Bible

'GET THEM OUT,' Elder Merek ordered the two men guarding the prisoners.

Drew and Aislinn were pulled from the cart, their hands bound as they were seated on two of the burned stones.

'Again I ask you Aislinn Hamilton, if you are ready to repent of your evil ways. You may receive forgiveness and be restored should you admit to being overcome by the darkness. We will ensure that every evil thing is driven from you and that we put you back on the road to goodness – to following the Prophecies over your life if you confess,' Merek droned on.

'And who decides what the Prophecies over my life shall be?' Aislinn asked.

'The Elders do of course. We have the gift to be harbingers. You can trust us Aislinn, to do what is best for you.'

'I don't believe any man should speak destiny over another man's life, Elder Merek. Each man should follow his heart. I believe love is greater than destiny, that the Great One desires us to love more than to serve. Service and obedience without love is not love at all.'

'There is nothing greater than service and obedience Aislinn – you have been blinded to this truth. You still have not answered my question. Are you ready to repent?'

'I have nothing to repent for Elder Merek. I would do the same in a heartbeat. An innocent baby's life should not be decided by fate or fear when there is something that can be done to save it.'

So be it Aislinn – you have sealed your own destiny.'

He turned to Drew. 'Young man, what do you have to say about this? Were you a part of this abomination?'

'I am a physician Elder Merek and my job is to help the afflicted and to bring them healing. To neglect to do that would be a gross misconduct of my duty as it would be should Aislinn turn from a baby in distress. I assisted her in the surgery – in fact it was I who instructed her on what to do. I don't know about your spiritual laws – all I know and trust is science and it was science that enabled us to save that woman and her child, not evil.'

'It was the darkness Dr. Williams but you would not know any better as you are clearly an infidel. Science is the magic of the darkness. We have seen the way you and Aislinn Hamilton look at each other and the love she has for you. Your unbelief has caused this darkness to enter her soul and now you will both burn for it. We will make sure there will never be any offspring to come from either of you.'

'No,' Aislinn cried. 'Kill me if you must but Drew has done nothing wrong. He is seeking the Great One, I assure you, and I was the one who cut the baby out. Don't punish him for my sin.'

'So you admit at last that you sinned.'

Aislinn kept quiet. Of course she did not believe that, but they were determined to kill her anyway and if her admission could save Drew then she would have confessed to being the devil himself.

'Aislinn, I know what you are trying to do and I love you even more for it,' Drew said looking into her desperate face. He looked back at their accusers.

'The truth is that I fully supported what Aislinn did and I wouldn't want to live without her anyway so if you are going to set that pyre alight you damn well better make sure I am on it with her.'

'No Drew...'

Cillian smirked – the stupid girl's pride had sealed her fate and her lovesick doctor was going to join her – all the better if there were no witnesses alive to tell this tale. Mac Hamilton would hate the Elders for what they had done to his daughter – he would never forgive them and his soul would be destroyed. At last he would feel the pain that Cillian felt years ago. Losing his father had left an ugly wound and every time he thought of Mac's insensitivity during that painful time the scab of that wound would be ripped open yet again. Finally Mac would know what it was like to lose something you dearly loved.

'Tie them to the post,' Elder Merek instructed.

⌘

Falstaff was furious. Daemon had ruined it all. His favour with the Master had diminished and now Legion had nothing but disgust and disdain for the wizard. After all he had done for his Master he deserved more respect. This was not going to get in his way. He pulled out the spell book, searching for a stone spell. He would turn his Master into a statue after he had poisoned him – one that the whole of Griswold could look at when they came to the castle. It would be a reminder to the people of his magical powers. Many still feared the Master but he had seen firsthand what a sop he had become since that child had been born. Once the Master and Gwen were dead he would kill the child followed by Daemon. They would all pay for their treachery.

⌘

Mac watched as his daughter was tied to the post with Drew next to her. Their hands touched and their fingers entwined. He was proud of her – how she had stood up for her beliefs. Right to the end she had been her loving self, ready to sacrifice herself for the man she loved. She was a remarkable young woman.

'Great One,' he whispered into the dusk air, 'please don't let her die.'

Mixed with his pride was a terrible fear that things could go horribly wrong. He felt responsible for her predicament.

Why did I encourage her to go to Trenton!

'Eion do you think you could use some of that magic if necessary?' Aedan asked.

'What do you have in mind?'

'If they should get that fire lit before we get to them I need you to put it out. Can you do that?'

'Not a problem – a snuffing spell is one of the first we learned at wizardry school – although I never ever imagined myself using magic for the Great One,' he smiled.

"Nuada, you and Regent come with me. We will waylay the Elders. Mac you get Aislinn and Drew out of there while Aedan causes a distraction.'

Ziah made sure everyone knew what to do as they readied themselves for the great rescue.

⌘

'I love you Drew,' Aislinn whispered as they lit the torches ready to fuel the pyre.

'I will always love you Aislinn. Do you think I will see you in Lionsgate or am I really just an infidel as they said?'

'Do you want to see me in Lionsgate?'

'I want nothing more my love.'

'Then you will see me Drew – the Great One is very gracious and loving to all. We will be together even if it is not in this world we know.'

The men advanced, burning torches in hand and Aislinn shut her eyes. She waited for the smell of the burning brush, for the acrid smoke to clog her nasal passages; a reminder of the event four years previously. It was ironic - she should have died in that burning house years ago and now she stood on the very same spot to be burned again. This was Cillian's cruel punishment. She waited, the anticipation killing her. Then she felt a rush of wind past her face and she and opened her eyes.

What was that?

She shrieked in delight as she recognized the whirlwind that tore around the pyre. She had seen it before at Griswold castle when Aedan had defeated the dragon Zantorian.

'Drew, I knew they would come for us,' she laughed as she saw her friends running from the forest, the fierceness of their approach causing confusion. Mac jumped over the brush barricade and hugged his daughter.

'You didn't think we would let them get away with this did you?' he beamed.

'I knew you would come, Papa – I knew you would all come.'

Ziah, Regent and Nuada rounded up the Elders and put them into the little cart, the men complaining and cursing them as they did so.

Mac busied himself untying Aislinn's ropes. He did not notice Cillian silently creeping up, holding two of the lit torches and setting the brush alight. It hissed and crackled fiercely as the dry kindle caught alight, bright orange flames hungrily devouring the brushwood like a starving man.

'Watch out Papa,' Aislinn screamed as the fire leapt up almost catching on Mac's tunic.

Mac leaned back against the post protecting his daughter from the licking flames and the thick black smoke – they were trapped.

'Papa, untie Drew please,' Aislinn begged. 'I'll be all right. Just get him free.'

Mac heard her desperation and fear. He edged sideways around the pyre and quickly untied Drew. The young man slapped his shoulder gratefully. It was no good; the flames were too high to jump over. They would have to run through it and roll on the ground, praying that they didn't catch alight.

Through the flickering flames Mac saw him – Cillian watching and waiting to see them burn.

He was the one who set it alight. Was his hatred so deep?

Anger flared up afresh inside of Mac.

Eion rushed forward - the pyre had gone up in flames so quickly – he had to do something or they would all burn to death? He stood legs apart, hands raised up over the flames.

'Fire bright, fire alight, I wish that you would die tonight.'

Chanting the words he had used so often as a wizardry student he commanded the fire to die. The flames spluttered in defiance and then went out as quickly as they started. Eion sighed in relief – for a second he thought he had the spell wrong. Drew scooped Aislinn into his arms and jumped over the burning embers, followed by Mac. Cillian cursed and turned to flee, coming face to face with Aedan, his red hair flashing as it always did when he was angry. He backed up almost running into the sword in Mac's hand.

'I should cut your evil heart out Cillian,' Mac spat furiously. 'It's one thing to face me like a man if you have issues, but to try and kill my daughter who has done nothing to you, that is despicable and cowardly.'

'Do it then Mac. You have done nothing but ruin my life. Even after all these years you continue to destroy it. I would be better off dead,' Cillian goaded.

'Papa, don't' Aislinn said gently touching his arm. 'If you cross this line there will be no going back – you will lose your soul. Vengeance is an ugly thing.'

Mac's anger evaporated as he remembered his daughter.

'No Cillian, Aislinn's right. I am better than that. Killing you would destroy my life. I have chosen a better way now.

You have chosen to let me ruin your life because you are unwilling to forget what is behind and live for today. Don't waste the next years of your life on hatred and bitterness. Move on and enjoy life. I am truly sorry that Imogene and I were not there for you when you needed us most. We never meant to hurt you, but we did – we can't change that now except to say that we realize how much we hurt you and for that we wish we could turn back the clock.'

Mac lowered the sword. He could not read Cillian''s expression and he had no idea what the man was thinking. Still, he could do no more than he had. It was up to Cillian now, to choose the path he would take.

Aedan took Cillian by the arm and locked him up with the Elders who were still complaining bitterly.

'You won't get away with this,' Elder Merek said. 'The Great One will judge you for this evil – for saving the devil from that fire.'

'I'm afraid you are wrong Merek, I won't be judging anyone – at least not the way you expect me to.'

They all spun around at the voice – the Great One had arrived.

'You weren't expecting me to turn up were you?' he laughed seeing their surprised faces.

Aislinn ran and hugged the old man.

'Thank you,' she said 'for saving me yet again.'

'Well I couldn't let them burn you at the stake Aislinn. After all you did say some rather flattering things about my character – a rather refreshing change from the usual things that are said about me by the so-called gifted ones.'

Merek and the other Elders glared at the old man.

'Who are you? How dare you impersonate the Great One – this is the evil we spoke of,' Merek shouted angrily.

The Great One laughed.

'See I told you – they don't even recognize me. It will always be this way as long as their interpretation of who I am is passed from one generation to the next. Maybe one day, one of them will actually think about what they are taught and realize that much of it just doesn't make sense. That's when change can happen, but I wouldn't hold my breath,' he whispered mischievously. 'Let's go home everyone – it's been fun but I think it's enough adventure to last me for aeons. We'll let someone know where to find you,' he informed the Elders, 'but if you ever attempt to do this again I will leave you to the dark forces,' he winked at us as he made the threat. 'That should keep them at bay for a while since they are so fearful of actually living.'

CHAPTER 20

POISON

"When did a dragon ever die from the poison of a snake" - Nietzsche

THE PLANS for the ball were coming on nicely. Gwen looked at herself in the mirror wishing her waist were as slim as it used to be. She would have to be careful not to pull her corset too tight as her scar was still healing. She wished Aislinn could be at the ball to see how wonderfully both she and Phoenix were doing. The little boy was a delight – he was almost two moons old now. He had dark eyes like Legions, but Gwen had a feeling they would become greener as he got older, just like hers. His hair was thick and dark like his fathers. She could tell he was going to be a very handsome young man one day. She made a mental note to check with cook that she had everything she needed for the menu. Since the baby had been born the staff treated her with greater respect and affection – it was as though she had earned her place in the castle. Perhaps it was because Legion had really been making an effort to mend their marriage. He had become very protective over her and Phoenix. She smiled as she remembered how he nervously asked her whether she would be willing to try sharing chambers again. She had been dumbfounded. Her heart felt content and happy – her husband wanted her as a woman again. He would make it known at the ball that anyone referring to him as the Dark Lord would not be in his good graces. He was not proud of his past and the hatred that fueled his ambition. Now his only task was to raise an heir worthy of Griswold. He wanted more than anything to have the people love and respect his son. To do that, they would first have to love and respect him. He had a lot of work to do to change people's perceptions of him as a ruler. This ball would not only be Phoenix' introduction to Griswold, but his as well in a sense.

Legion came up behind Gwen as she dreamed and kissed her on the neck as he encircled her waist.

'How are the plans coming on?'

'Everything is as it should be. I wish Aislinn could see our boy.'

'I know,' he answered but we have not mended fences well enough to be at that point – maybe one day they will feel safe to be around us again.'

He let go of his wife and picked up the gurgling baby from his bassinet.

'Phoenix, you will be a great man,' he said smiling at the bonny child.

⌘

Aislinn was delighted to be home with her family. She slept for fourteen hours straight the first night she was home in her bed. She only stirred when Mitchell could wait no longer to see his sister and bounced on her bed waking her.

'Mitchell,' she growled, 'you're making me seasick.'

"Wake up Aislinn, I've missed you.'

How could she be angry with him? She had missed them all and she would be grateful for every day that she woke up. She nearly lost the chance to enjoy another morning.

'All right, I'm coming. What has Mama made for breakfast? – I'm famished.'

Aislinn wolfed down the scones her mother had baked. They tasted better than she remembered.

'Where's Papa?' she asked, her mouth full as she licked the dripping butter from her fingers.

'Drew came over very early this morning to see your father. You wouldn't happen to know what that is about?' Imogene asked noticing the deepening hue of her daughter's face.

'No,' she evaded, 'can I have another scone please?'

Imogene smiled. She knew very well why Drew had come to see Mac. He had told her about the kiss he had witnessed. It was good that he wanted to do the right thing. They would be perfect for one another. She and Mac had never pressured Aislinn to marry any of the young suitors who had asked for her hand in marriage because they wanted her to be sure she loved the man she married, but deep down Imogene was glad that her daughter had found someone and that she would know love and companionship. It was an added bonus that Drew was a physician and understood Aislinn's passion for her work.

⌘

Daemon received news that Aislinn was safe. He felt so relieved although his father was furious with Cillian for failing in what he called a foolproof plan and even more so with his son for meddling .His anger and bitterness toward Daemon mounted daily as did his hunger for greater power.

The young man did not plan to stay around for too long after the ball. He had Legion's permission to leave for a full moon once his father was deposed as chief wizard. Then when things settled he would return and take up his father's position in the castle. For now it was better they were kept apart.

'It will be a good thing that you leave for a while,' Legion had said. 'Your father is going to be very angry. Still I will be fair to him – I'll offer him a cottage bond free on my lands to live out his days. That way he can come and visit Phoenix and Gwen whenever he chooses and he can help the local villagers with ailments. He once was a very good apothecary so I believe.'

'Thank you Legion, I have some personal business to attend to before I can begin my work for you and I don't want to be around when father moves out of his spell chambers.'

'I understand Daemon – take care of your business and when you return to us it will be a fresh start for you.'

Daemon planned to use the time away from the castle to woo Aislinn. She had to know that not all her kisses had been reserved for the man she thought she loved. He needed to remind her of the times they spent together when she was at the castle. If he could sow a seed of doubt then he could use the love spell to change her heart's affection. That was one of the requirements for the spell to work – a measure of doubt - without it he would never sway her heart. Once the ball was over tonight he could leave and set his plan into motion. He packed his saddlebags ready to leave at first light.

The castle was abuzz with activity for the ball. The lanterns were lit throughout creating a magical feel as the light danced off the stone walls casting a soft ethereal glow. Gwendolyn looked beautiful in a golden silk dress with fine golden flowers embroidered along the neckline and sleeves. Little pearls were stitched to the bodice making it even more magnificent. It had been a gift from Legion to her, especially for the ball, and she had been so touched by his generosity and thoughtfulness. She dressed Phoenix in the special little outfit they had for him. He was none the wiser as to what all the fuss was about. He was content as long as he had his mother's milk and a warm bed to sleep in.

The guests arrived and filled the great hall. The musicians played, the wine flowed and tasty morsels were brought from the kitchen. Everyone enjoyed the hospitality of Legion and Gwendolyn – Lord and Lady of Griswold. They had yet to make their entrance and everyone waited for them, keen to meet the new heir to Griswold. Finally they entered the great hall carrying their son. The women clucked and fussed over the baby and the men slapped Legion on the back and wished him well. After a while Gwendolyn took Phoenix back to their chambers to put him to bed – all the excitement had tired him out. She fed him, offering her breast and he sucked hungrily, gulping the milk as it dribbled down his chin.

'Slow down Phoenix,' she smiled, 'it's not going anywhere.'

Once she had him settled into his crib she returned to the great hall leaving her lady in waiting caring for the youngster. She took her place beside her husband and he smiled at her kissing her hand.

'Has he settled for the night?' he asked

'Sleeping like a log,' she replied.

Legion lifted the jug to fill her goblet. It was empty.

'I'll send for some more.'

'That sounds good, thank you.'

Legion waved to his valet and ordered another jug of wine. The young man scurried off to the kitchen to do his Master's bidding. He opened a new vat and poured it from the Master's special reserve – the wine that was given as a gift to him and Gwendolyn for the ball. He wondered what it would be like to be in the Master's shoes. He bet life was a lot greener on their side of the fence. Well he would never know, he was simply the valet and waiting on the rich would be his lot in life. Still, there was no reason why he could not enjoy some of the Master's pleasures every now and again. What he didn't know wouldn't hurt him. He nipped into an alcove and took a sip from the jug. It was good wine, better than the stuff they served to the other guests. He took another sip and then made his way to the great hall to serve the Master and his wife.

'Thank you,' Gwen said as he poured wine into her goblet.

She smiled at him and he blushed. She was one of the Master's pleasures he wished he could savour. Fearing she could read his mind, he quickly moved over to fill Legion's goblet. Her husband would have his hide if he knew the lecherous thoughts going through his head. Suddenly the room began to sway and he lost all control. The jug crashed to the floor clanging noisily, followed closely by the valet as he clutched his stomach convulsing and screaming in agony. His eyes rolled back eerily and froth poured from the corners of his mouth as he gagged and choked.

'What's wrong with him? Is he having a seizure?' Gwen shrieked terrified.

'No, I believe he's been poisoned.' Legion leaned over the young man and asked him urgently, 'what did you eat or drink?'

The young man pointed to the empty jug he dropped on the floor next to him before breathing his last.

'Gwen, do not touch that wine in your goblet. Someone has tried to poison us tonight. He must have drunk some of it before bringing it to our table.'

Gwen was horrified. 'Who would do such a thing Legion?'

'I don't know yet, but I will get to the bottom of this,' he replied. 'I think you should go and check on Phoenix. If someone wanted us dead then he may be in danger. Take a guard with you and don't be alone at any time. I need to allay our guest's fears before chaos breaks out,' he said seeing the fear written all over the people's faces.

Gwen rushed out the hall, fear gripping her heart. She had almost drunk that wine – she should be dead now. Who hated them so much? She prayed that Phoenix would be fast asleep in his crib where she left him. The guard almost had to run to keep up with her as she raced down the passageways. Entering her chambers she searched frantically for her lady in waiting. She was not there.

Oh dear Lord please let him be all right.

She looked into the crib, her worst fears confirmed. The empty bassinet stared back at her.

'Legion...' she screamed.

CHAPTER 21

LOVE AND HATE

"No one is born hating another person because of the colour of his skin, or his background, or his religion. People must learn to hate, and if they can learn to hate, they can be taught to love, for love comes more naturally to the human heart than its opposite."

— Nelson Mandela

MILES away in another kingdom, a different celebration was taking place in Sherbrooke. Drew and Aislinn were celebrating their betrothal. It had happened so suddenly and Aislinn could hardly believe it. She thought back to her father and Drew returning from that early morning walk. Mac had given nothing away as Aislinn tried to read his expression.

Oh he could be so infuriating.

He simply came into the house, kissed her on the head and asked whether she had left them any scones for breakfast. They all sat at the table and ate together as though nothing had happened and the tension was tangible. Eventually she could take it no more.

'Well, is either of you going to share anything with us? What were you and Drew talking about?'

'Oh, just the weather and the harvest we will get at the end of summer, the thatching business and some medical things,' Mac teased.

'Papa! You know what I mean.'

Drew could not keep a straight face a moment longer and burst out laughing at her frustration.

'Drew it's not funny,' then she laughed too.

'Drew was very forthcoming Aislinn, regarding his feelings toward you and his intentions. Now I will leave the rest for him to tell you – I have to get to work.'

'Papa!' What does that mean? What did you say about it all?'

Her father kissed her mother then strode out of the house leaving her with no answers. She looked at Drew and he smiled secretively as he finished the last mouthful of scone.

'Would you like to take a walk with me Aislinn?' he asked when the last crumb had been eaten.

'May I Mama?' Aislinn asked. Now that they were back home again courting took on a whole new meaning – she had to get permission from her parents to be alone with Drew. It almost seemed ridiculous considering they had travelled together the last few months but she wanted to do this the right way.

'Of course,' Imogene smiled. She remembered what young love felt like – the dizzy, heart pounding, weak-kneed feeling.

They had walked out into the meadow where they found a tree to sit under.

'Well, what happened?'

'I told your father that I was madly, crazily in love with you and that I wanted his blessing to make you my wife.'

She gasped.

'I thought you wanted to court for a while before getting married?'

'Aislinn Hamilton, you seem to get yourself into all sorts of scrapes and considering we were nearly burned at the stake, I don't think I want to waste any more time. I love you and want you as my wife. Will you marry me sweetheart?'

'Yes, oh definitely yes,' she said as he pulled her into his arms kissing her on the mouth, teasing a response from her as she wound her arms around his neck.

'I love you,' she smiled up into his violet eyes.

Now here they were, a few weeks later, celebrating their betrothal with the people who mattered to them the most. Drew had been concerned that he did not have a ring with a stone for her. His father had given him his mother's wedding ring to give to Aislinn on their wedding day. It was a beautiful gesture as she would have something that was special to his mother. Aislinn had asked whether he minded if she wore the truth ring as her betrothal ring – it was a reminder that there would always be honesty between them, plus it had the stone Drew wanted her to have.

'That is a brilliant idea Aislinn,' he said. 'Then you will have a ring that is precious to you and one from my side of the family when we are wed – it is a perfect symbol of two families becoming one.'

Aislinn looked again at the beautiful stone on her ring finger. She could not believe how happy she felt. She looked at Drew who was dancing with Maddy at the celebration of their upcoming marriage. They had wanted a simple affair at the farmhouse. Everyone had contributed to the evening by bringing eats and there was a succulent pig roasting over the hot coals. She would be a married woman before the next moon. They had decided they would not have a long betrothal. They loved each other and wanted to begin their life together and she could not wait. Besides, they were often called to nearby villages to care for the sick or birth babies and it would not be good for her reputation if people knew they were staying at the village Inn together, even though they had separate quarters. People loved to gossip and speculate, so it would be easier if they were married. They just needed enough time for Imogene to make a dress for her. Everything was perfect and her happiness complete.

⌘

Gwen sank to her knees as she continued to sob. Where was her baby? Daemon rushed into her chambers with Legion.

'Look after her Legion,' he instructed. 'I will find your child. I promise that whoever did this, will not get away with it.'

He left the chambers and headed down to the servants quarters.

Where was Maeve, Gwen's lady in waiting and why did she leave the child?

He needed some answers.

Maeve was not in her room so Daemon headed to the kitchen to see if she were there. No one seemed to know anything. As he left the kitchen a young girl followed him.

'Master Daemon, I don't want to get Maeve into any trouble,' she said, 'but I saw her go into the stable with Robbie.'

Thank you Daemon said.

The stables seemed deserted and a little eerie in the darkness. They were fuller than usual with extra horses from the visitors who were attending the ball. Daemon walked through the stalls listening to the horses as they settled for the night. Then he heard it, – low moans and giggles coming from the end stall, easy to miss with the other noises happening in the castle that night.

So she was here with Robbie.

He stood at the stable door peering over at the entwined couple, clearing his throat loudly. His presence sent them scattering, Maeve pulling down her skirts while the young man fumbled awkwardly with his trousers.

'Master, it is not what it looks like,' Robbie explained as Maeve blushed furiously.

'I think it is exactly what it looks like,' Daemon responded, 'however, if Maeve can give me a few answers then perhaps I could consider forgetting that I ever saw anything here tonight.'

'What do you want to know?' she asked guarded.

'You were supposed to be caring for the baby tonight Maeve – why did you leave the child alone?'

'Master, I would never leave the baby alone,' she said horrified. 'I only left because he said that it would be all right if he cared for the young one while the ball was on. In fact he told me that Gwen said it was a fine idea.'

'Who told you that?' Daemon asked.

'It was your father Master, the baby's grandfather.'

Falstaff!

Daemon should have known he would be behind this – his father was so angry that all reason had left him, especially after Gwen and Legion banned him from attending the ball and this was how he would punish them.

Surely he wouldn't hurt the child though – his own flesh and blood.

'Thank you Maeve,' Daemon said turning on his heel. 'Your secret tryst is safe with me.'

He raced to his father's chambers.

Had he been the one to try and poison his sister and Legion?

He would not put it past the old man. He burst into the chamber only to find it empty.

Where had he taken the child?

He looked at the big spell book that lay open on the wooden slab and his eyes scanned the content. His blood froze. It was open to the spell 'FEAR NUA'- a ritual that was considered pure evil amongst the wizardry fraternity. It had been a hot debate amongst the apprentice wizards at the school as to whether this ritual actually worked, but they had never discovered the answer as none of them had ever heard of it being performed. It was widely believed that once a wizard crossed this line their soul would be eternally dark.

Daemon read through the ritual quickly. It was specific and had to be followed to the letter for it to work. His father had to take the baby outside in the moonlight to a place where the dead lived. There was only one place that he could be. He had taken the child to Skull Hill, the burial grounds behind the castle. Daemon grabbed a sword as he left the chambers and made his way to the hill.

Don't let me be too late!

⌘

Aislinn and Drew danced, their fingers entwined.

'You look beautiful Aislinn,' he whispered into her ear.

'Only because you make me so happy,' she replied.

'I am going to look at a cottage this week. It is small but it is on a good sized piece of land near the stream and has some vegetables growing and a beautiful small garden with wild flowers. Would you like to come and see if it is suitable for my new wife to move into after our wedding?

She squealed delighted. 'I would love to – it sounds perfect Drew. You do know that I don't require a castle to be happy. I would live in a stable with you if I had to.'

'Well thank the lord you don't need a castle to be happy but I think we can do a little better than a stable.'

'I can't wait to make a home for us.'

'I have another surprise,' he added. 'My father has a special gift for us both when we marry.'

He smiled seeing the curiosity on her face at his cryptic news. He pulled her away from the other dancers so they could avoid being run over and gently sat her on a tree stump surrounding the folk that danced.

'Wait here, I'll be back in a moment.'

She waited while he disappeared to fetch the surprise. She watched her parents dancing; saw the love they had for each other after all their years together. She hoped she and Drew would be the same.

He returned with a large piece of wood that was beautifully planed. On it were letters that had been burned into the wood.

Dr. Drew Williams and Mrs. Aislinn Williams (midwife), she read on the wood. She looked at him a question in her eyes.

'He has decided to retire and is leaving the practice to us. He will stay on in the little cottage attached to the consulting rooms but the rest is ours to work side by side caring for Sherbrooke's people What do you think?'

'I think I like the sound of Mrs. Aislinn Williams,' she smiled tracing her index finger across her name on the wood.

He kissed her quickly and she giggled.

'Drew, behave yourself; there are people watching – we don't want to give them means for gossip.'

'Certainly Madam, I will try very hard to keep my hands to myself but I have to confess it is going to be very difficult for the next few weeks,' he said as he saw her mock shocked expression.

CHAPTER 22

FATHERS

"It is a wise father that knows his own child" – William Shakespeare

DAEMON was out of breath as he climbed Skull Hill. He had to be quiet – he did not want to alert his father to his presence. He hoped fervently that Phoenix was safe. He peered between the crude tombstones searching for his father. This place gave him the creeps. He thought back to the FEAR NUA ritual described in the spell book. It was believed that the grave of a person who had lived many years would yield incredible power when the blood of a new baby was poured over it. As the blood of the baby mingled with the soil that housed the old bones, the new life and energy of the baby would join with the experience and wisdom of the departed soul. Then the person who wanted to harness this power would cut themselves and add their blood to the mix. They would then lie face down upon the bloody soil whereupon they would draw in this new strength and wisdom.

Daemon hoped that it would take his father a while to find an old grave. He searched looking for the ones that appeared to be the oldest. Then he saw him. He had a long blade in his hand and was reaching down for Phoenix who lay on the ground whimpering and shivering in his thin wrap.

He was going to kill the child.

'Don't father,' he said coldly. 'If you move another muscle toward my nephew I will kill you.'

'Daemon,' Falstaff said sarcastically. 'I should have known you would try to thwart my plans once again.'

'Let me take Phoenix back to Gwen and they need not know what you planned here tonight. Legion has promised me that you will be well provided for.'

'Yes, I heard that you have stolen my position as chief wizard – my own flesh and blood betraying me. You really think I want to live out my days in a little cottage pottering around with potions and sick people asking for help every five minutes. I have devoted my life to Griswold and to that man in the castle, and for what? He has become weak and easily swayed. I have done everything he ever asked me – I have given him his success – my magic is what has kept him in power and he can't even see that. I am not ready to be relegated to a menial position. I have a little something grander in mind Daemon – I deserve it after all I've done for him. Now leave me - neither you nor Legion will stop me. I am taking what is mine.'

'You would do that at the expense of your grandchild, your own children? Mother would be ashamed of you father if she could see what you have become.'

'Don't you dare mention your mother to me, Daemon.'

He had hit a raw nerve.

The wizard chanted something and in an instant vanished.

Of course it would not be that simple Daemon thought as he rushed over to pick up Phoenix.

As he bent over to lift the infant he felt an arm clench around his throat squeezing the life out of him. So his father had not disappeared, simply made himself invisible. Well the old man forgot that he knew magic too. He jabbed his elbow backward into the invisible ribs of Falstaff. He heard the old man grunt and felt him release his grip, the impact causing the spell to wear off, his form becoming visible once again. He grabbed the knife lunging at his son who dodged the blow. Daemon drew his sword, holding it out in front of him.

'Father, I beg you, please don't do this.'

'You, begging me,' he scoffed. 'What makes you think I would listen to you? Besides, if all has gone according to plan then neither Gwen nor Legion will be around to raise this child. I'm doing them a favour.'

'So it was you who tried to poison them? Well father, even that plan went awry. Legion's valet stole some of their wine before he served them which alerted the whole court to your plot. They did not touch your wine and are in good health even as we speak.'

'You are lying.'

'Really? What do you think Legion will do to you if he suspects you? I can make this all go away for you if you just surrender. They do not have to know it was you.'

'Never. You are the only person who knows that I am behind this all and I plan to rectify that.'

Falstaff raised his arms, ready to cast a spell. Daemon knew it would be a spell that would cause his death– his father hated him that much. Before the old wizard uttered a single chant Daemon mustered all his strength, throwing his sword, hitting him squarely in the chest. He fell to his knees clutching the protruding blade, his eyes registering surprise at the fatal blow. Daemon ran to him catching him in his arms as he lowered him to the ground.

'I'm sorry father, you left me no choice,' he said, his tears dripping onto the face of the old wizard as he held him, his life slipping away.

⌘

The celebration for the young couple was coming to an end. All their friends had come –Ziah, Regent, Nuada, Aedan and Serena had travelled from Lionsgate to Sherbrooke to give their best wishes to Drew and Aislinn.

'My father sends his congratulations to you both. He wishes you both long life and a blessed union. He really wanted to be here but unfortunately he had a crisis to deal with. However he will not miss the wedding for anything,' Ziah said.

'Thank you for coming all this way. I know it is a long journey from Lionsgate.'

'We wouldn't have missed it for the world,' Serena said hugging Aislinn. 'Now there is just one more thing we need to discuss but it is woman's business so I am going to whisk you away for a while.'

'Ooh sounds exciting and mysterious,' Aislinn giggled.

The two women entered the little cottage and sat at the table. Aislinn poured them some cider and they sipped it beside the fire.

'The Great One asked me to do something for him. He has sent a gift for your wedding day He knows how special it is when a couple pledge their love to one another and he wants you to remember your special day forever. She leaned over and opened a silk bag she had carried into the house. Carefully she pulled out a dress. Aislinn gasped. It was the most beautiful dress she had ever seen.

'Oh, it's beautiful,' she breathed huskily, emotion overcoming her.

Serena held up the dress for her to admire. Its fitted bodice would hug her petite figure perfectly. The ivory silk fabric flared out to the floor leaving a train of soft fabric flowing behind. The sleeves were off the shoulder and flowed in a translucent fabric down her arms. The bodice was laced at the back and the front was embroidered with tiny silver butterflies and little diamond-like jewels. The hem of her gown was adorned with more silver thread that looked like climbing ivy. There was also a sheer cape of the same translucent fabric that she could wear if it got cold. It was simple and yet exquisite. Aislinn could not believe that is was hers.

'I don't know what to say Serena. It truly is more than I ever dreamed of.'

'It has symbolism Aislinn. The Great One wanted you to have a dress that reflects your personality. The sheer cape is a symbol of your transparency and vulnerability. The dress is silk because it is so beautiful and valuable as you are. The silver thread represents your ability to heal and help. The butterflies are a symbol of new life that you will see many times in your own life but also as a midwife and the diamonds reflect your heart – pure and strong and unlike any other person. You are unique Aislinn and you must never let anyone change that about you.'

A tear escaped and slid down Aislinn's cheek. She felt speechless. She wiped it away quickly.

The Great One had not just given her a gown – he had designed it especially for her – to affirm her and make her feel special.

'No tears sweet girl. Every woman should feel special on her wedding day. In case you are worried we haven't forgotten Drew either. He has been given a handsome ensemble to wear on your special day. It wouldn't do to have him in attire that doesn't match your own in grandeur.'

'Thank you so much. I can never repay you all.'

'That's the joy of it though – you don't have to,' she smiled.

⌘

Daemon carried Phoenix back to the castle. The babe shivered and he tried to keep the child warm with his own body heat. He hoped the infant would not get ill from being exposed to the elements. He felt sick at heart and struggled to come to terms with the fact that he had killed his own father.

Why did you do it father? Why couldn't you just let it all go and end your days peacefully?

He had already decided not to expose the evil in their father's heart. He wanted Gwen to remember the old man with love and affection, not as someone who tried to murder her and her family. He also did not want his sister to hate him for what he had done. He could not bear it if she could not look at him because of his deed. He felt guilty enough without her accusing eyes.

'Daemon,' Gwen said as he carried the child into her chambers. 'You found him – oh thank the lord.'

She pulled the child into her arms and hugged him fiercely causing the infant to cry. She settled on her bed and offered him her breast which he gratefully took.

'Who had him and where was he?' she fired questions at him.

Daemon had to come up with a plausible story.

'Someone from the north heard about his birth and wanted him dead, as did he you and Legion. He tried to poison you and take the child. Father and I went after him. There was a battle Gwen, and I would have been killed had it not been for our father. I was about to be struck down by his sword when father stepped in. I'm afraid he's dead Gwen – he sacrificed himself for me.'

'Oh no, Daemon it can't be true. I was so mean to him the last few days. Now I will never get to tell him how sorry I am. Did the man get away?'

'I'm afraid so. Father spoke to me before he died Gwen. He told me to tell you that he loved you and wanted you to be happy – that saving your son was the last gift he could give you that would ensure this happiness. He wants you to remember him that way and not as the crazy man he has been the last few weeks.'

'He said that?' she asked.

'Yes,' Daemon lied.

CHAPTER 23

PREPARATIONS

"The best way to predict the future is to create it" - Peter Drucker

THE COTTAGE was perfect. Aislinn loved it, especially the wild flowers that grew in abundance around the house. It had whitewashed stone walls and a thatch roof. The inside had a hearth with a big wooden mantel, and a big wood stove to cook on. Wooden shutters kept the cold and draught out at night but let in the sweet scent of the meadow during the day. There were two small rooms for sleeping and a small loft to store things. The furniture was very basic but comfortable enough for them.

'I love it,' she said to Drew as they stood in the garden.

'Then it's ours,' he said as she squealed in delight.

He lifted her hand and kissed it.

'I can't believe we will be moving here in a few weeks,' Aislinn said.

'It does seem a bit surreal, doesn't it?' he replied. 'It's hard to believe that just eight moons ago we did not even know each other.'

'Yes,' she giggled, 'and I thought you were an arrogant pig when we met.'

'Good thing my charming side came out then.'

'Mmm, and charming it is, and handsome too and...'

He silenced her with a kiss, teasing as he probed her sweet mouth. She responded and he groaned pushing her away.

'You drive me wild Aislinn. If I am to make good on my promise to your father to court you the right way then we need to keep these kisses to a minimum or I may lose all reason.'

'Just giving you a foretaste of what's to come,' she quipped as he smacked her playfully on the bottom.

'Right, back to work we go – we've patients to see.'

⌘

Phoenix shivered in his crib, his little body on fire. He cried non-stop and not even his mother's breast would calm him. Gwendolyn and Legion were at their wits end at what to do for the young child.

'He needs help Legion. Can't the castle physician do something for him?'

'He says the child has a fever from being out in the cold air the other night. All he suggests is keeping him cool to get his temperature down. Other than that there is not much he can do.'

'I think we need another opinion. Can't we get Dr. Williams to come and see him? I have faith in what he says and think he may have some way to help Phoenix.'

'It's a long journey for him Gwen – it will take him days to get here.'

'Please Legion, all the more reason to dispatch a Monwing immediately. I have just lost my father – I couldn't bear it if anything happened to our child.'

'All right Gwen, I will send a message but I can't promise he will come.'

'He will, I'm sure of it,' she said. 'We must let Daemon know he is coming – we wouldn't want to shock the doctor by having them come face to face.'

Daemon had put his plans on hold to leave the castle and find Aislinn. After his father's death there was a lot to organize. They had to bury him and Daemon felt he could not leave without seeming cold and insensitive to his sister. Besides, his father's anger at being ousted as chief wizard was his reason for going away and that reason was gone. For now he would wait it out – he would have to come up with a reason to get away from this place soon. He missed Aislinn and desperately wanted to see her again. His longing grew every day they were apart.

⌘

Drew made the decision to move into the little cottage a few weeks before the wedding. He wanted to get the little home comfortable and ready for Aislinn and get a start on the vegetable patch that would sustain them. He whitewashed walls that were looking drab and in need of care and planted and weeded in his spare time. The little cottage slowly changed from drab and overrun with weeds to a sweet, fresh home covered with honeysuckle on the one side. It looked inviting and cosy and Drew couldn't wait to share it with Aislinn.

He had just finished whitewashing the front of the home and was covered in lime solution, speckles of the white mixture in his hair, on his hands and face. He pulled off his shirt, throwing it down on the floor and poured water into the basin on the washstand. Then he began to scrub his hands – it wouldn't do for the local; doctor to have white hands when doing a consultation. He smiled – for the moment he was a Jack-of-all-trades. He washed his face and dried it with a cotton cloth. He was so engrossed in his task he did not hear Aislinn enter the cottage behind him. She stood, dumbstruck at his half naked form, his trousers riding on his hips, his strong broad back and muscular arms flexing as he washed himself. She had never seen a man this naked before and she watched him, curiosity keeping her silent. She did not want him to see her as she felt a mixture of intrigue and desire. He certainly was desirable and she flushed at her thoughts. As Drew looked up he saw her reflection in the little mirror. He spun around surprised to see her.

'Aislinn, when did you get here?'

She blushed and stammered, 'I... I just arrived now but I didn't realize you were changing,' she said apologetically.

He did not seem fazed by her embarrassment or his own semi-nakedness. She could not help but let her eyes wander down his chest and abdomen. He was well-toned and he obviously took care of himself. She noticed that just below his bottom left rib was a birthmark. It was not overly big or dark but visible enough for her to see. She decided that she liked it – he would have been too perfect without it. She tore her eyes away from his body looking at his amused face. He had caught her admiring his form and she felt mortified.

'I'm sorry Drew, I'll let you get dressed,' she said, finally gathering her senses and walking out the cottage, embarrassment engulfing her. She heard him chuckle as she left.

She inspected all the work he had done while she waited for him. He had made their home so pretty and she loved him even more for that. It was so considerate of him to care about the little things that would be important to her. She had been working on something equally important every night after work. Mama had given her some fabric and she had painstakingly sewed all the little squares together to make them a quilt for their bed. Finally it was finished and she hoped he would love it. Drew joined her out in the garden, finally dressed, wrapping his arms around her waist. She felt his strength but now she also had a mental picture of his body that held hers close. She blushed again fearing that he could read her mind.

'What brings you here, my sweet,' he murmured brushing his lips against her ear.

'You of course,' she smiled. 'I've brought some lunch for all your hard work.'

'My heroine,' he smiled. 'You certainly know a way to a man's heart.'

'My Mama taught me well,' she laughed.

As they sat and ate their lunch they dreamed about their future. Their musings were cut short by the arrival of an ugly creature. Drew leapt to his feet, startled by the ugly beast.

'Get behind me Aislinn,' he shouted. 'What the devil is that?' Drew asked looking at the half monkey, half bird-like creature that edged its way toward them.

'I know this creature Drew, don't be alarmed,' she said. 'It's a Monwing from Griswold. Legion uses them to send messages.'

'What does it want?' Drew asked, still suspicious of the strange creature.

The Monwing hopped forward, its eagle-like claws scratching the ground and dropped a pouch in front of them.

Aislinn retrieved it and pulled it open. Inside she found a handwritten note. She read it quickly then passed it to Drew.

'It's from Legion, Drew. Phoenix is gravely ill and he and Gwen are urging you to come. They feel you will be able to help more than their own physician as you have studied overseas and have more experience. You must go at once. I will go with you if you want.'

'But it will take days to get there Aislinn. What if the child dies before then and what about our wedding? I may not get back in time.'

'We can send instructions on what treatment to give until we arrive,' she said. 'We can't abandon that baby – not after all we did to see him safely delivered.'

'All right,' Drew said, 'but you are not coming with me. Sherbrooke needs you here as there are women about to give birth and it will be quicker if I go alone. Besides, you have a wedding to get ready for sweetheart. I can't have my bride looking exhausted on our wedding day after travelling halfway across the countryside. I will make sure I am back in time. I would not miss it for anything.'

They drafted a note with instructions on how to reduce Phoenix's temperature and what herbs to give him to strengthen him and tucked it into the pouch. Then they dispatched the Monwing back to the castle in Griswold. Aislinn helped Drew saddle his horse and packed some provisions for his journey.

'Please let my father know where I have gone – he will have to take care of the patients till I get back.'

He kissed her lingeringly, loathe to leave, but duty called.

'Take care,' she said as he kicked his horse into motion.

She watched him ride off down the road, a feeling of apprehension in the pit of her stomach. She had no idea why she felt that way.

CHAPTER 24

THE PLAGUE

"Even if you're on the right track, you'll get run over if you just sit there"
— Mother Teresa

DREW arrived at the castle in Griswold tired and hungry. He had ridden virtually non-stop to get there in time to save Phoenix's life. Now he looked down at the fretful child. He clearly had a raging fever. Gwen had been giving him the medicine he suggested to no avail. Drew looked at the child, listened to his breathing and felt concerned. This was more than a simple chill he wagered. He asked Gwen to undress the child so that he could look at his body. It was as he feared – the child had a rash that glared angrily at them – red welts and spots that covered his torso front and back.

'What is that?' she asked alarmed. 'That wasn't there this morning when I dressed him.'

'It is as I thought Gwen,' Drew said. 'Phoenix has the red plague – this isn't from being out on Skull Hill as you thought – he must have caught it from someone who was contagious.'

Gwen thought of all the people at the ball who held her son and cuddled him. Any one of them could have brought the sickness to the castle.

'It is important to find out if anyone else has shown any symptoms in the castle – fever and vomiting followed by this rash. They need to be isolated as do those who have been in close proximity to them. If we don't contain this it could become an epidemic. In the meantime I can try to make Phoenix as comfortable as possible. I need you to bind his hands with cotton strips so that he cannot scratch at the sores as this will cause scarring. I have also seen cases overseas where the red plague has caused blindness. You need to keep this room darkened and we need to make a cloth patch to cover his eyes. His fever should come down now that the welts have appeared. I will mix some herbal water that will help the itching. Bathe him four times a day in it. Other than that there is nothing more I can do for him. Keep him isolated with minimal contact with people outside these chambers.'

'Thank you Dr. Williams. How is Aislinn doing?'

'She is well Gwen. In fact we have some news of our own. Aislinn and I are going to be married before the next moon.'

'Oh that is wonderful news. I hope you will both be very happy. Please send her my very best wishes.'

'I certainly will. Now I think I will get something to eat and have a rest before I go and assess the damage this red plague may or may not have caused.'

Drew retired to the room that Aislinn had previously stayed in in the south tower. He hoped fervently that the plague had not spread. Hopefully most of the adults at court had been exposed to it as youngsters and would not catch the infection. It did not take him long to fall into an exhausted sleep.

⌘

The Elders convened to discuss their failed attempt at burning Aislinn Hamilton. The Hamilton family had been a thorn in their flesh the last four years and they had to be stopped. They were spreading rumours and false truth all over the kingdom about the Great One. It seemed that The Lord of Griswold wasn't too concerned about it, not that they expected him to be, since Aislinn Hamilton and Dr. Drew Williams had saved his child. Rumours abounded that The Dark Lord, or Legion as he now insisted on being called, had changed his cruel and evil ways. Now people were saying he was trying to be fair and make up for all the wrong he had done in the past. If that were true then perhaps there was hope for his soul after all. They would send a note to the castle extending their good wishes and desires to offer spiritual guidance. Perhaps Legion would be willing to be cleansed from the evil spirits that hounded him all those years. If they could gain the trust and favour of the Lord of Griswold it would give them the much needed funds for their sanctuary they were planning to build. For many moons they had this deep desire to build a place that people could go to for spiritual guidance and cleansing, but it had only been a dream up to this point. Now that Legion was being more gracious perhaps he would tolerate a place of worship in his kingdom.

⌘

Daemon felt sick at the conversation he had just had with Gwendolyn. She eagerly told him of Aislinn and Drew's plans to marry before the next moon. He could not allow that to happen - Aislinn was to be his – it was destiny. Drew was staying at the castle but he would be anxious to get back home as soon as possible and Daemon had a plan. It was time for his brother to meet him.

⌘

Aislinn missed Drew. Daily she went by the cottage and watered the vegetables he had planted. She also cleaned the cottage and added homely touches to it ready for the day they would be there as man and wife. Drew had sent her a message telling her of the red plague and fortunately it had not spread. It seemed that if there were any other sick they had not stayed in the castle but moved on after the ball. Aislinn was grateful that Drew did not have a full blown epidemic on his hands or he would never have gotten home in time for the wedding. Now he let her know that he would be home the day before the wedding – only ten days away. Secretly she tried on her wedding gown almost daily and each day she fell more and more in love with the beautiful dress. She couldn't wait to see his face when he saw her in it. Planning their wedding had not been simple - there had been many issues facing their marriage. Usually the Elders gave permission for a local priest to marry couples, but in their case this was not an option. The Elders had tried to kill them – they certainly would never bless their union. Aislinn recalled Elder Merek's words that they would ensure no offspring was ever born from them.

No, the less they know about our wedding, the better.

They had decided upon a small ceremony at her parent's farm where her father would marry them. He was once ordained by the Elders themselves and told to carry out his spiritual duty and since they never revoked this authority they would use it to their benefit. Besides, the Great One himself would be there and since he was the one they needed a blessing from that was all that counted. It was going to be a great day.

⌘

Phoenix continued to get sicker by the day. Drew found this very confusing as the red plague was working through his system and his fever should have been coming down. Instead it continued to escalate, causing the poor child to convulse. Drew looked for all the medical answers but he could find none. He hoped the sickness would break soon as he really wanted to get back home to Aislinn.

'Why is he not getting any better?' Gwendolyn asked.

'I am not sure Gwen, but we have done everything we can for the moment. Aislinn always tells me that nothing is impossible for those who believe. My problem is the simply believing part – I guess my brain is just too scientifically wired although I have seen her faith in action and it saved our lives.'

He recounted their close escape from the fiery pyre and how they were being burned for saving Phoenix.

'I can't believe they wanted to kill you for saving a child. Legion is meeting with those Elders today. They sent him word saying they wanted to bless our child. What if they have come here to kill him?'

'I don't know, but you can use his contagious illness as an excuse to keep them at bay. I would prefer it if you do not mention my presence in the castle for obvious reasons.'

Gwendolyn hurried off to find Legion. They must be careful with the Elders in the castle. She found him and relayed her conversation with Drew.

⌘

'Welcome to Griswold Castle,' Legion smiled at the eight Elders standing before him. 'What can we do for you?'

'It has come to our attention that you have a new son and we thought it only fitting that we come and pay our respects to the Lord and Lady of Griswold and their new heir. We were wondering if we could give the child a blessing and whether you would consider us asking the Great One for favour over your household.'

Legion kept his face blank. Gwen looked alarmed. She knew how her husband hated the Great One. Would he explode with rage at their suggestion?

'That is a most gracious offer,' he said, 'but what would you expect in return for this blessing? I've learned as Lord of Griswold that people don't usually offer something unless they want something in return. What are you hoping to receive?'

Elder Merek looked a little uncomfortable. The Dark Lord had read him perfectly.

'As Elders and spiritual leaders of Griswold we hoped that we could work together instead of against one another as we have all these years. We hope to gain a truce and peace in the land. We also hoped that you would endorse and encourage the building of a sanctuary for all people to worship.'

There, it was out in the open. The real truth of what they wanted. Legion had to hold back his disgust. They had no intention of blessing his family – they simply were playing a political game to get money to build their sanctuary.

'I'm afraid you may not see the child – he is sick with the red plague but I am sure you are able to bless him when you next pray. As for the sanctuary, I am not opposed to one being built. I have come to see that freedom for all to worship the way they choose is one's right. However I feel that I need to address the issues of poverty and hunger within Griswold before I give money to put up a sanctuary. You will need to raise the funds for that yourself. I believe in taking care of my subjects needs first.

'Surely spiritual needs are first and foremost? If a man loses his soul then hunger and poverty is just a natural reflection of the poverty within. When we take care of the spiritual side of a man then his natural life follows suit and everything becomes better.'

'That sounds truly philosophical Elder Merek, but I don't agree. I am fully convinced that you believe what you are saying, but really a man needs his family cared for and his children fed. Only then his spirit is unburdened and he can be thankful. You expect men to give coin out of their pockets when their children are starving and sick. That is not the kind of love the Great One would expect I imagine. How do I know this? - because I have lived it. I used to exploit my subjects and they had to pay me more than their dues. I watched families suffer and I didn't care – till my own son was born. That is not what I want for my people anymore.'

'Those extra dues they paid can be put to good use then,' Elder Merek persisted. 'Let us take that blood money off your hands and build our sanctuary. That way your conscience will be appeased and the people will have their place of worship.'

'I do not need my conscience appeased Elder Merek. I have already distributed that wealth back to the families it came from, as a goodwill gesture in the name of my son. There will be no sanctuary funded from this court. If indeed you care about the people of Griswold why don't you go and visit them in their homes instead of expecting them to come to your sanctuary? Maybe then you will really understand their struggles and pain.'

Elder Merek blushed at this accusation.

'Very well my lord. I am sorry that this has ended this way. Clearly we cannot come to a truce. I have understood something today. The Great One has seen that your heart cannot truly be turned and he will remove all blessing and protection from you for this. Mark my words, there will be a reckoning if you don't support his people. You wait and see, great judgement and wrath will be unleashed on Griswold and it has clearly already begun with the sickness of your son. I warn you it is only just the beginning. You will see his anger come in the skies – his displeasure will be displayed for all to see – a sign of his coming judgement.'

'What, no blessing now that there is no coin from this court?' Legion asked sarcastically. 'Get out of here Elder Merek. You and your greedy men are not welcome here any longer.'

As they left the hall Gwen leaned over to Legion and whispered, 'Is it true – will there be a reckoning? Will the Great One rain down fire on us and did he make Phoenix sick? Is that why Drew can't help him?'

⌘

The Great One looked in his Mirror of Time, annoyed. He had been misrepresented again. Even Legion who fought against him all those years knew his character better than the men who claimed to represent his spiritual truths. Yes, there was a plague in Griswold castle but it wasn't the red plague that was the thing to be fearful of. It was a plague of manipulation and spiritual deceit that would try to invade and eat away at the people of Griswold like maggots eating the flesh of a newly dead corpse. Elder Merek and his fellow maggots would not get away with their plan to trick people into building his sanctuary. The Great One always wanted people to know that he could be found anywhere and everywhere – that he was available to them at any time. He would not allow them to dictate to people where and how he could be found. The Great One felt a sense of pride at Legion's defiance to their request. He knew that deep with Legion's heart was the man he always believed in way back when he lived in Lionsgate. That man had made himself known today. Legion just needed to feel love and acceptance for that man to come out. Phoenix and Gwen had done that for him and his real character was clawing its way out little by little.

CHAPTER 25

THE SIGN

GWEN could not shake the Elder's words. Would the Great One punish Legion for his hatred by hurting their child? After all, Legion had tried to kill Ziah all those years ago. What if this was payback? She looked in on the child and bathed him again with the cool water to soothe his itchy red skin. He still fretted and felt clammy to the touch.

'Great One, I don't know you but please don't take my child from me. I know that Legion has done some horrible things in his time, but he is not that man anymore. He has changed and wants to do good for the people of Griswold. I fear that if he loses his son he will lose his soul and never return from that again.'

She had no idea if the Great One could even hear her plea but it was all she could do in the moment. She stood at the window and looked out at the evening sky. It was a beautiful clear evening, a star shooting across the inky blue night. The moon hung in the sky, full and bright like a giant yellow ball. She marveled at the shimmering beams it threw across the stony walls below her window. Griswold castle was quite beautiful in this light. Everything seemed still and peaceful and even Phoenix was finally sleeping. Maybe it would be all right after all.

⌘

Elder Merek met with Cillian. They had a problem and Cillian had helped them in the past to deal with it. Granted not all the plans had gone off without incident, but this time he hoped all would work out in their favour. They met at the edge of Grimwood Forest. Both knew that no one would venture into the forest at night for fear of being attacked and mauled by the legendary creatures that lived there. This meeting was one of those clandestine affairs that both men would deny ever took place if asked about it. The moon shone brightly and lit the way for them.

'It is imperative that this plan work,' Elder Merek stated. 'Our only hope for getting any coin from Legion is to make him believe that the Reckoning has started and that the Great One is angry. We have to help that process along. It is our duty to the people of Griswold to save their souls.'

'How do you propose to do that?' Cillian asked.

'A few years ago you and some men went to the home of Mac and Imogene Hamilton and burned it down. You brought fear and uncertainty to their world.'

'Yes, and it got me nowhere. It didn't affect their lives in the long run.'

'Oh but it did. Their souls are eternally damned – there is no path back from the place they have gone.'

'You really believe that don't you? Cillian asked.

'Now I need you to scare a few of the villagers of Griswold. Make them believe that the darkness is closing in and that because of their lord's denial to build a sanctuary the Great One's wrath is being rained down upon them.'

'What if I am not willing to do that? These are innocent people.'

'The Elders and I are the only people besides Legion who are able to tie you to the burning of the Hamilton homestead. That is still a crime as far as I am aware.'

'Are you threatening me?' Cillian asked.

'Nothing like that Cillian, I am simply reminding you of your hunger to stop spiritual corruption. That is why you accused the Hamilton family if I remember correctly. This is no different. To save the many from the darkness we have to allow a few to suffer for the cause. That is the only way to enforce change.

'What do I need to do,' Cillian said resigned.

⌘

As Gwen watched the moon she felt the night air change. It became cooler and a breeze began to blow gently. She pulled her shawl tighter around her shoulders and sighed. The last few months had taken their toll on her both physically and emotionally. On one hand things were so much better than before Phoenix was born. She had a husband now who was willing to engage and allow her to be part of his life and she had a beautiful baby she adored. That had come with a price though as she remembered the Elder's words that the Great One would judge them for their past deeds. She had no answers – she did not know the Great One or how he operated. Her thoughts were far away and she did not hear Legion come up behind her. He draped his arm over her shoulder and pulled her in to his body.

'Don't worry Gwen, it will be all right. He is a strong child.'

'I know, I have to believe that it will all be fine.'

'Dr. Williams is doing all he can. If anyone can bring him through it is him. He is a fine physician.'

They stood silently looking into the peaceful night sky each deep in thought.

'No, oh Legion no,' Gwen exclaimed in horror.

'What is it?' he asked alarmed.

She extended her arm and pointed at the night sky.

'It's begun,' she said. 'The reckoning he spoke of – it has begun.'

⌘

Drew entered Gwen and Legion's chamber to check on Phoenix. His mother was there, sobbing quietly, inconsolable.

'What is wrong with Gwendolyn?' he asked as Legion paced up and down the room like a caged animal.

'The Elders came and warned us that if we did not give them money to build a sanctuary that a reckoning would take place. I just laughed them off but they said it had begun with Phoenix's sickness and would then become evident in the skies. Come with me,' he said heading to the balcony.

Drew followed him and looked up to where Legion pointed. The beautiful yellow moon had changed and was deep red, filling the sky like an eerie omen.

'That is a blood moon,' Drew said. 'Why are you so afraid of it?'

'Have you ever seen the moon that colour?' Legion asked amazed at Drew's nonchalance.

'Actually, yes I have,' Drew smiled. 'When I studied overseas I had the opportunity to meet with some great philosophers and discuss the meaning of life. I learned a lot more than I bargained for. One of my good friends was studying the stars and he showed me a moon just like this one. They call it a blood moon because it turns red. Even then spiritual groups referred to it as an evil omen or a sign of impending doom, but I never ever saw any indication of that being true. Legion it is not judgement coming but a simple occurrence that happens every few years and has everything to do with the moon aligning with the sun.'

'I have never heard such things.' Legion marveled. 'Why have I never noticed this moon before if it occurs every few years?'

'Unless you know it is happening, or you regularly look up into the night skies it can be easy to miss,' Drew explained. 'Legion it is purely coincidental that this is taking place now after Elder Merek has threatened you. For all we know he may be well aware that this phenomenon is due to occur and is using it to his advantage to terrify you into doing what he wants. Trust me, he is not a nice man and he uses his spiritual influence and power to manipulate people. I have experienced his judgement firsthand.'

'How am I going to convince Gwen this is not a sign?'

'I will explain it to her,' Drew offered.

'It does seem quite a coincidence though doesn't it?' Legion murmured.

'Belief is powerful thing,' Drew said. 'If you believe something fervently enough then it will take place. If you choose to believe that bad things are going to happen to your family they will because your thoughts and speech create the reality you live in. I have always believed that our hearts and minds change our atmosphere and build our reality. I have yet to prove that scientifically but one day I will, I'm sure. Aislinn just calls it faith and it's probably the same thing. You need to believe that Phoenix will get well every time you hold him. Positive energy will flow to him and the more you believe the sooner it will become a reality. Medicine can only do so much – now it is touch and belief that will do the rest.'

'That makes sense to me,' Legion said. 'When I was angry and bitter the atmosphere in this castle was one of tension and fear, but it has changed because I have changed. I see what you mean Drew. I am living proof that this is true.'

The men wandered back in to the room where Gwen was drying her tears.

'No more crying Gwen,' Legion said gently. 'This baby will get well, you'll see.'

⌘

The Great One smiled. Drew Williams may be called an infidel by the Elders, but he had a better understanding of things than most who called themselves believers. He was right about people's ability to change the atmosphere and create realities. Too many people just moaned about their lot in life instead of believing that life was a beautiful gift and could be wonderful or as miserable as one chose. The doctor had a remarkable insight – he and Aislinn would make a great team.

CHAPTER 26

THE REVEAL

"There are no secrets that time does not reveal" - Jean Racine

DREW prepared himself to leave the castle. Phoenix had turned the corner and was on the mend. His rash was fading and his fever was gone. His appetite had also returned and the weight he had lost was being quickly gained again. Drew could not wait to get back home. In a few days he would be facing Aislinn and declaring his love for her in front of all their friends and family – he would pledge to love and care for her as long as he breathed. He had missed her terribly – being without her left an empty ache in the pit of his stomach. He packed his few items and put them at the door.

He was surprised by the knock on his door and assumed that Gwendolyn had sent someone to call him. He opened the door and came face to face with himself.

'Dr. Williams, I am Daemon, Gwen's brother.' He could see the shock on Drew's face.

Drew did not say anything – he just gazed at the man in front of him looking him up and down. A thousand thoughts ran through his mind.

'Yes, I know this must come as a huge shock to you – after all we do look identical.'

'How is this possible,' Drew asked even though medically he knew the answer screaming itself at his brain.

'I am your twin brother, Drew. Your father never told you the real story, did he? Our mother died giving birth to us – maybe if there had been just one of us things would have been different, but her body could not take delivering two babies. I was shipped off to live with Falstaff and his wife and your father decided to keep you. Imagine having to choose which child to keep. I see you are still speechless – well I guess it's no wonder since the father you believed always loved you and cared for you has kept such a deep, dark secret all these years.'

'It's unbelievable and yet it must be true – we are identical. Why didn't father say anything?'

'You must be wondering why I have chosen to reveal myself to you now and not when you were here for Gwen's delivery. The truth is my father wanted to keep this secret out of loyalty to your father. My father is dead now and there is no reason to keep this secret anymore. I felt you needed to know the truth, that you deserved to know the truth.'

'Come in,' Drew stood aside and let his twin in.

'There is something else you need to know. Aislinn and I spent a lot of time together when she was in the castle. We grew very close if you know what I mean,' he said.

'What are you insinuating Daemon?' Drew replied coldly.

'Let's just say that Aislinn and I shared some intimate moments together. I have developed very strong feelings for her as I know you have. My question is this –which one of us is she really in love with?'

'That's a ridiculous question. She doesn't even know you exist Daemon. She told me that she was confused by why I behaved so differently toward her when she was here. We assumed it was a deception or impersonation spell created by your father but it seems it was just you pretending to be me.

That should answer your question about who she really loves. Why don't we ask her – give her the choice.'

'I'm surprised you are so quick in jumping to her defense. What if I told you that she gave away more of herself to me than is decent for an unwed woman.'

Drew flushed angry at this man's accusations.

'I don't believe you,' he said.

'She is rather irresistible when she teases with those kisses. I'm afraid I found it hard to keep my hands off her and she seemed to enjoy the caresses. She's quite passionate when you get her in the mood.'

Drew could not help himself, he punched his identical twin hard in the face, causing Daemon to reel backward and hold his hands over his bleeding nose.

'Touché,' he laughed. His words had the desired effect – they had caused doubt in Drew's mind which is what he needed for his plan to work.

'Get out,' Drew spat. 'I don't care if you are my brother I want nothing to do with you – stay away from me and Aislinn.'

Drew felt like he was the one who had been punched in the stomach. Aislinn could easily have been deceived into giving herself freely to this man. He had to remember that she would never have intended to hurt him as she would have believed it was him. Still it hurt to know she was intimate with someone other than himself. He could not tell her of Daemon's insinuation. It would ruin their wedding and embarrass her terribly. He hated it even more that they would be beginning their marriage with a secret.

⌘

Imogene and Aislinn prepared for the wedding day. Maddy helped, excited to be part of the celebrations. She was at the age where she was becoming conscious of boys and how she looked. She continually asked Imogene and Aislinn if they thought she was pretty enough. Imogene smiled when she saw her youngest daughter out in the garden carrying some flowers she had picked from the meadow and wearing a piece of fabric draped over her as a veil, pledging herself to the imaginary suitor she was marrying.

It would be strange without Aislinn living at home but Imogene was grateful their cottage was not too far away and that her daughter was marrying someone she loved deeply. Something had been bothering her since Aislinn and Drew were rescued from the witch hunters. Old Dr. Williams had begged her to keep Daemon's identity a secret until after the wedding when he would break the news to Drew about his brother. Imogene recalled how shocked she had been when they arrived at the farmhouse and she had discovered Daemon's existence. She hated keeping secrets from people, especially Mac whom she usually shared everything with. However she had promised to keep quiet till after the wedding. She would be glad to be honest again – nothing good ever came of secrecy.

⌘

Drew rode fast – desperate to get away from the thoughts that haunted him. No matter how fast he urged his steed on he could not outride the images that played in his mind – images of Aislinn in Daemon's arms. He shook his head – he had to get rid of them or it would destroy their relationship.

Stop it Drew, you know Aislinn. She would not do those things Daemon said.

He had to get home and see her – feel her arms around him. That would surely wipe away any doubt he had?

Drew had another fear he dared not entertain. Daemon claimed to have feelings for Aislinn. What if he came to Sherbrooke and ruined everything? Logically Drew knew that Aislinn would be angry at his deception, but what if it didn't turn out that way? What if she actually chose Daemon over him? The sooner they were wed the better. He would deal with Daemon if and when he became a problem. For now he would let nothing ruin his day with the woman he loved.

CHAPTER 27

THE WEDDING

"Union is strength" - American Proverb

THE MORNING dawned, beautiful and clear, dewdrops glistening like jewels on the grass. Aislinn stretched in her bed and then remembered it was her day – the day she and Drew were getting married. She had waited with anticipation for this day and now it had finally come. Drew had returned from Griswold only two days previously – earlier than she had expected. He had held her so tight and close that she had scolded him.

'Drew you are squeezing the life out of me. I can't breathe.'

'I'm sorry sweetheart. I missed you so much. I don't ever want to be without you. Promise me we'll always be together.'

'Drew, you're scaring me. Is everything all right?'

'It's all fine now that I'm back with you.'

Aislinn did not know what had happened but clearly something had frightened Drew. He was far more introspective and guarded than he was before he left. She did not want to push him – he would share his concerns with her when he was ready.

'Rise and shine,' her mother said interrupting her thoughts as she carried a breakfast tray, a beautiful red rose with the feast she brought.

'Mama, this is so sweet. Thank you.'

'Well it is the last time I'll ever be able to bring you breakfast in bed and every girl should feel pampered on her wedding day.'

'I love you Mama. I'm going to miss you all.'

'We love you too Aislinn, but this is not a day to be sad – you are beginning a new adventure. We will always be here for you – that will never change.' Imogene kissed her daughter on the forehead.

'Now, how about a bath? I have heated up some water for you to have a good long soak.'

⌘

In the little cottage Drew also readied himself for his day. He pulled out the dark trousers and tunic that the Great One had given him to wear for the ceremony. He looked at the ring that had been his mothers. It was a beautiful silver ring that had patterns engraved into the wide band which gave it a delicate and ornate look. Aislinn had tried it on to find that it was a perfect fit and the truth ring looked as though it were made for the band. Drew wished his mother could be there to see him wed Aislinn. Still she would be a part of their day in the ring. He thought about his father and the betrayal that still stung. He had believed his father had never lied to him and now he discovered that his whole childhood had been a lie. He had chosen not to confront his father – it would have to wait till after the wedding. He did not want there to be any animosity on this day. For now he would pretend that everything was fine. He placed the ring next to his trousers and tunic which lay ready for him after his bath.

He bathed enjoying the peace and thought of his beloved. Tonight she would become wholly his in every sense of the word. He pushed the accusation Daemon had brought away and determined not to let it dominate his day. She loved him – he was sure of it. That was all that mattered. In a few hours they would begin their lives together.

He pulled himself out the bath and shaved his face. He smiled remembering Aislinn's embarrassment at catching him without his shirt a few weeks previously. Her desire had been obvious as had been her curiosity and sweet naivety. He could not believe Daemon's claims simply because it was obvious she had not seen a man semi-naked before. Remembering this reassured him and he felt a new confidence grow. He would be her first and only love.

A loud rap brought him back to reality. He hastily pulled on a shirt and opened the door. He felt the pain before he registered that he had been hit. He grunted as the wind was knocked out of him, his nose beginning to bleed. The last thing he remembered before inky blackness swallowed him was Daemon's face looking down at him, smirking.

⌘

Imogene helped Aislinn into her dress and laced the back tightly. It fitted like a glove and accentuated her curves. Aislinn pulled on the silver slippers and admired herself in the little mirror in the thatched cottage. She looked like a dream, her thick dark curls falling in perfect ringlets down her back. Imogene pulled the front of her hair back, securing it with a jeweled pin Serena had given her. Then they attached a wreath of sweet scented roses to her head which finished off the dress with a romantic flourish.

'You look beautiful,' Imogene breathed in wonder.

'Oh Mama, I can't believe this dress. It's a dream come true. Do you think Drew will like it?'

'He will love it because you are wearing it.'

Mac knocked gently on the door. 'Are you nearly ready Aislinn? The guests are arriving and it won't be long till we start.'

'Almost ready Papa. Is Drew here yet?'

'No but I'm guessing he will arrive soon.'

⌘

Drew felt nauseous and his head throbbed. He tried to remember where he was and what had happened.

'Awake at last. I was beginning to think you would never come around.'

Drew looked at the voice and remembered.

'Daemon, what do you want?'

'Only what is rightfully mine brother. For years you have had the silver spoon in your mouth now it is my turn. I think it is time I received my dues. Anyway I can't chat now as I'm going to be late for my wedding. My bride awaits in eager anticipation and I mustn't keep her waiting now must I?

'You bastard, you can't do this – its deceit.'

'Well I guess in a way I am the bastard of the family since father disowned me. Nonetheless I did warn you that Aislinn would be mine.'

'You won't get away with this – when she finds out who you are she will leave you.'

'She won't find out Drew – you see I am going to become you, and you dear brother are going to be found dead in a tragic accident – your body will be returned to Griswold and Gwen will mourn the death of her dearly beloved brother Daemon. No one will ever know the truth, except the two of us. I managed to convince everyone that I was you once before, so there is no reason why I could not do it again – to become you and live your life with Aislinn. It is an easier alternative than trying to get her to fall in love with me through magic. This way she'll never know the truth.'

'Daemon please... I know you hate what our father did but we are brothers. You can't do this. You don't give Aislinn enough credit. She will know that you are not me.'

'I love her Drew – don't take this personally. This is the only way I can have her and I do want her more than anything.'

'So where am I?' He noticed that he was no longer in the little cottage but in a strange place.

'Somewhere where no-one will find you, dear brother.'

Daemon took some opium and held it to Drew's nose rendering the young man unconscious again.

'Sorry brother, all's fair in love and war. Now I have a wedding to get ready for,' he said as he left an unconscious Drew.

⌘

Mac looked at his daughter, speechless. This was the first time he had seen her in her dress and she was a vision. He got a lump in his throat and he swallowed hard. Here was his firstborn and now she was a grown woman about to begin her own family. This would be her last moment as a Hamilton. He remembered how she loved to climb into his lap as a little girl and listen to stories of his adventures and encounters with the Great One, of how she would always give him butterfly kisses on his cheek and then beg him to do the same to her.

'I love you more than rainbows,' he blurted out. They always used to say that to one another. He couldn't remember why it had started but it became their special saying. Aislinn giggled.

'I haven't heard that in a very long time. I love you more than rainbows too Papa,' she said.

'You look beautiful Aislinn. I am so proud of you – you have turned into an amazing young woman. Drew is a lucky man. Now let's get you married,' he said leading his daughter to the cottage door.

Imogene and Maddy had made it beautiful. Eion had made wooden benches for everyone to sit on and they had thrown rose petals on the floor which led to a wooden canopy covered with ivy and flowers. Mac took his daughter by the arm and walked her down the makeshift aisle. Gasps of admiration could be heard as Aislinn moved through their family and friends. She smiled at people but she really only had eyes for one person – her husband to be. Drew looked immaculate in his attire and her heart skipped a beat at how handsome he was. His violet eyes sparkled and when he smiled his dimple deepened. She felt blissfully happy.

Daemon watched her walk down the path toward him. She was so magnificently beautiful and after today he would take on a new life with her – have the family again that should always have been his. He was sure he could learn everything he needed to know about medicine from Drew's numerous journals. It couldn't be that difficult looking after a few sick villagers. His father had been right about one thing – a person did need to take what they wanted in their life because nothing ever just landed in your lap. He was making his own destiny now.

⌘

Drew came to his senses. It was dark and his head ached. It felt like nothing compared to the ache in his heart. Aislinn would be married to Daemon by now. They would be celebrating their union and she would be none the wiser to his deception. She would never know that he had been murdered by his own brother. He shifted position trying to get more comfortable. Where the hell was he? He was in some kind of barn chained to a horse stall. He had to get out of there – it was his only chance to save himself and Aislinn from this mess. At that moment in time he really resented his father for keeping such a monumental secret.

CHAPTER 28

EXPECTATIONS

'Expectation is the root of all heartache" – William Shakespeare

Everyone waved goodbye to the newly-wed couple. It had been a magnificent celebration and much wine had flowed. Even the Great One had joined in the celebration dancing with Aislinn and Maddy much to Imogene and Mac's delight. Daemon lifted Aislinn onto his horse and climbed up behind her pulling her tight against his broad chest.

'Ready my love,' he whispered in her ear.

He urged the horse forward and they waved goodbye as they headed down the road to their new cottage.

'Did you have a good day?' he asked her.

'The best – I'll always remember it,' she replied.

'This is just the beginning for us.' He nuzzled her neck, desire for her increasing.

It did not take them long to get to the cottage and Daemon took the horse and tethered it to the post. He lifted his wife down then led her up the path.

'Welcome home Mrs. Williams.'

Aislinn giggled.

'I really like the sound of that,' she said looking at the silver band on her finger.

'Let me do the honours,' he said, swooping her off her feet and carrying her indoors.

He placed her down gently and bent his head to kiss her soft, sweet lips. She willingly responded tangling her fingers in his dark hair that curled at the nape of his neck. He groaned, eager for more.

'You're so beautiful,' he whispered huskily. He pulled away and spun her around. Slowly he began to unlace her dress.

'I'm scared Drew,' she whispered, surprised at her own honesty. She had looked forward to this moment but now that it had come she was also a little afraid.

'Will it hurt?' she asked.

'Only for a moment. I'll be gentle Aislinn I promise,' he said touched at her vulnerability.

He finished unlacing her bodice and prepared to help her remove the heavy dress. An urgent knock on the door interrupted them.

'Who is it?' Daemon called out trying not to sound ungracious.

'It's Master Finn. My mother sent me to get Miss Aislinn – the baby is coming and she needs her now.'

Aislinn could not help but let out a laugh when she saw the frustration on Daemon's face.

'Sorry darling, babies wait for no one – they never arrive at a convenient time as you well know. I will have to go,' she said pulling off her beautiful dress and replacing it with a simple one. Drew could see the curve of her breast and her hips through the sheer undergarments and mentally he cursed the child who was making his entrance into the world that night of all nights.

'Do you want me to come with you?' he asked.

'No, you stay here and get some sleep. It could be quick but it may take all night. I'll see you in the morning.' She kissed him quickly and rushed out the door to the waiting lad.

Sleep was the last thing on Daemon's mind. He had to get rid of Drew soon, but not just yet. He still had to plan his accident carefully and ensure that everyone believed it was he that was dead. They must never make the connection to Drew. He was worried about one other thing – a mistake he had made and one he would have to rectify soon. When he left Griswold he had been in such a hurry to stop the wedding that he had forgotten to bring his journal. If anyone found it his plan would be ruined. For now, he needed to be the attentive husband to his new bride, but once things settled he would return to the castle and retrieve it when everyone was sleeping. Nothing must spoil his plans. In the meantime, Drew was safely locked away at the old forge that was on their property. Aislinn had no idea the place existed as it was overgrown with brambles and weeds. He had only discovered it by accident when he followed Drew back to the homestead. He had looked for a place to camp that would not reveal his presence in Sherbrooke. Then he had found the forge. It was perfect for what he had in mind.

⌘

Drew felt cold. It was dark and insects bit him. He struggled against the chain one more time. It was no use. There was nothing around him to help him break it. He decided to wait till daylight and then try again. He had no idea where he was but he knew time was running out. Daemon would be back soon to get rid of him and he had to have a plan before that happened. He worried about Aislinn. Was she all right? He did not want to think about their wedding night and what was happening but his mind would not allow him to block out the images of them together. He let out a growl of anger and pain. His brother was taking her virginity – the thing she had saved for him. Drew swore that if he ever got out of his predicament that he would kill his brother with his bare hands.

I don't care if I am a doctor and sworn to protect and help all life – I will kill him.

⌘

Things were progressing slowly and Aislinn worried about the baby. The child was not moving down the birth canal as it should have and the mother was getting weary. Aislinn rubbed her back as she moaned with another contraction.

Aislinn did an examination to assess the progress.

'I want you to push on the next contraction,' she instructed the exhausted woman.

As the next wave of pain came she pushed as hard as she could, sweat breaking out on her forehead.

'Good, you're doing well – I can see baby's head. Just a few more pushes like that and it will all be over,' she encouraged.

It took another forty minutes for the baby to enter the world. Aislinn knew immediately that something was wrong. The child looked limp and blue. The usual lusty wail of a newborn ripped from its warm water cocoon did not happen. Aislinn wrapped the child and rubbed its body vigorously. Then she gently cleared its mouth of mucous and finally she smacked its bottom. She had to shock the child into breathing. Nothing happened.

Breathe child she willed.

Another sharp smack and the babe let out a wail in indignation at its introduction to life in the big wide world. Aislinn let out a sigh of relief. This was the first baby she had birthed alone. She should have had Drew with her but he was so tired after his trip to Griswold and she wanted him to have time to rest tonight. The mother who looked panicked at her child's lack of response let out a sob of relief.

'Congratulations,' Aislinn said, her heart still pounding furiously in her chest. 'You have a beautiful daughter.'

Aislinn helped mother and child to clean up and established the babe on the breast before gathering her things together to make her way home. The sun was just coming through the shutters – another beautiful day and another life brought into the world. Aislinn smiled. Drew would still be sleeping as it was only just sunrise. She would surprise him with hotcakes for breakfast. Her first morning as a wife – the beginning of many to come.

⌘

Daemon woke to the smell of hotcakes wafting through the little cottage. He could smell coffee too. He jumped out of the bed and pulled on his trousers and shirt.

'Good morning,' he said kissing her neck as she leaned over the woodstove. 'It smells almost as good as you do. How about we leave the hotcakes for a while and go back to bed?' he murmured.

Aislinn felt panic engulf her. She did want to make love to him but not this way, when she was dead tired.

'Drew, I've had a really long night and I'm pretty exhausted. Would you mind very much if we waited till tonight. I want to be rested and I want the first time to be special and memorable.'

She hoped he would understand and not be offended. A fleeting look of annoyance crossed his brow but was wiped away as quickly.

'Of course my love, I just missed you. After breakfast go and catch up on some sleep. I have a few things I need to attend to anyway.'

'You're the best she said kissing him squarely on the mouth before handing him a plate of hotcakes. Then she headed for bed to get some much needed rest.

CHAPTER 29

THE HEART'S CONDITION

"You can close your eyes to the things you don't want to see, but you can't close your heart to the things you don't want to feel."
— Johnny Depp.

IMOGENE had a large hamper of left-over food from the wedding. She rode over to Drew and Aislinn's little home to give them the surplus food. She also wanted to ensure her daughter was all right. A wedding night could be a terrifying experience if you were unsure or afraid. She arrived at the cottage and was surprised to find it so quiet. Maybe they had gone into Sherbrooke for a meal. She knocked on the door waiting to see if there would be a response. There were no sounds from the cottage. She knocked again a little louder. As she prepared to leave the food on the doorstep the door was pulled open. Aislinn stood there half asleep rubbing her eyes and yawning. Imogene laughed.

'Looks like it was quite a night,' she said.

'You'd be right about that Mama, but not in the way you think. Come in and have some tea with me.'

Aislinn told her mother all about her night.

'So we still haven't consummated the marriage Mama,' she finished.

'You have a whole lifetime of loving Aislinn. It was wise not to feel pressured to have intimacy the moment you returned from birthing. You will feel more relaxed if you can take it slowly. I'm sure Drew understands that and wouldn't want it any other way.'

'I'm not sure Mama – he looked really disappointed and even a little annoyed when I asked him to wait.'

Imogene laughed loudly.

'That would be about right. When a man is aroused it's like trying to douse a raging fire. He'll be fine Aislinn – waiting a little longer won't kill him – in fact it might just make it even more special for both of you.'

Aislinn thanked her mother for the food – at least she wouldn't have to worry about feeding them for the next couple of days. She waved goodbye, grateful that she had the chance to talk to her mother about these things. She had a lot to learn about how a man thought and behaved. They were not as easy to understand as she imagined.

⌘

While Aislinn slept Daemon took the time to go and check on Drew. He took some leftover hotcakes from breakfast. It wouldn't do to have Drew looking wasted away from starvation when they found his body.

'How long do you plan to keep me chained here like a dog?' Drew asked.

'Just long enough to set my plans in motion. 'I've sent a message back to my sister at Griswold castle letting her know of my plans to return. In a few days my body will be found in Grimwood Forest and it will look like thieves attacked and killed me. Of course I'll have to tell Aislinn of my dear twin brother and it will all make sense to her once I put her in the picture why your personality seemed to change like the wind when you stayed at the castle.'

'If you hurt Aislinn I swear Daemon I will kill you,' Drew spat.

'Well, I would be trembling in my boots if you actually could do anything about it Drew; but since you can't I'll just assume that it's your passion for the girl talking. On that subject though, I have to tell you she is certainly passionate between the sheets. Don't worry I was as gentle and considerate as possible – after all I am meant to be you now. She pleased me very well. I thought you should know since you will never get the chance to make love to her yourself.'

Drew bit his lip hard trying not to let his hatred show. He would not let Daemon get away with this – he would not let him ruin their lives.

⌘

'You're back at last,' Aislinn said when her husband entered the cottage. "Mama brought us some of the leftover food,' she said indicating the hamper.

Daemon took an apple and bit into the sweet juicy flesh.

'I'm going to ask my father to cover for us for a few days at the practice. I think we deserve a few days to get to really know each other and have time to be together before we rush back to work,' he said with his mouth full.

'That will be lovely,' she smiled.

He pulled her close and breathed in her sweet scent – she always smelled like lavender and honeysuckle.

'I love you,' she whispered standing on her tiptoes to reach around his neck. He was so tall – he towered a full head above her.

'And I love you Mrs. Williams.'

He really wanted her, but not like this. He was not going to take any more chances of being interrupted during their lovemaking and since it was not even dusk yet there was always the possibility of that.

'Let's go fishing,' he said spontaneously.

Aislinn laughed.

'You like fishing? I did not know that about you.'

'There's a lot you don't know about me, my love, but we have plenty of time to discover everything about each other. Come on I'll teach you how to catch a fish.'

They ran through the meadow hand in hand while Daemon carried the fishing gear in his other hand. She squealed when he gave her a worm to tie onto the fishing pole. She squealed even louder when a fish tugged on her line.

'You're a natural,' he said his arms around her waist as she leaned back on him.

'I think it's time to get home,' he said shifting his body. He could not bear being near her and not being able to have her.

⌘

'Daemon will be back soon,' Gwen said to Legion. 'I've had word from him. I have missed him.'

'That's good to hear. I could use his opinion on some issues that have come up in court. Your father used to advise me occasionally, but mostly he worked on spells and potions to keep me powerful. I don't rule that way any longer. Daemon will still work on potions but they will be available to help people. I don't want dark magic in this castle anymore.'

'That is wonderful Legion. I think Daemon will enjoy working here at the castle. Finding out that he was adopted has been very hard for him. He puts on a brave face but I know that it has hurt him deeply. Feeling part of our family will be good for him.'

'Feeling part of our family has been good for me too,' he added. 'I can't believe that I missed out on this for so long in my life.'

'Well you never really had a parent to look up to. Your mother certainly never showed you any love. No child should ever have to grow up that way Legion.'

'You're right about my parents. Father did not want me and mother hated me, but I did know love and acceptance at one point in my life.'

'You did?' she asked intrigued. 'What happened?'

'When I was sixteen my mother threw me out of the house when I refused to be her whipping boy any longer. I had nowhere to go and no money. I slept under a bridge near Trenton and at night I would go to the Inn and forage for food and scraps when the revelers had gone home.'

'I'm so sorry Legion – I had no idea.'

'One night after I had been scavenging for scraps I heard the innkeeper coming and I panicked. I ran out of the alley and into a horse. I frightened the poor animal and it knocked me to the ground. I would have been trampled to death had it not been for its rider. Still, I was knocked unconscious. The rider paid for a room at the inn and nursed me back to health. When I was well enough to leave he insisted on getting me home safely. I explained that my mother did not want me but he still insisted on taking me home. When we arrived home he asked my mother whether she had been worried about my absence. Do you know what she said?'

'What?'

'I would have worried if I actually cared, but I don't. I don't have a son and I never did.'

'How can any mother ever say such a thing to her child?' Gwen said horrified at his mother's cruelty.

'This man was the first person to ever stand up for me. He looked her in the eye and told her that she should be grateful to have such a wonderful son and then he took out some money and gave it to her. He told her that he was giving her the money to buy my freedom, so that I would never feel indebted to her ever again. Then he took me home with him and made me a part of his family.'

'Why have you never mentioned this before and why have I never met this wonderful man Legion? He should be part of Phoenix's life now that his grandfather is dead.'

'You have never met him because I had a hard heart Gwen. I never realized how much he cared for me even when he did all in his power to show me. I was broken and wouldn't allow myself to be fixed. Even his love couldn't fix me because deep down I hated myself so much and I was so emotionally scarred that I could never believe someone could love me without an agenda. I pushed him away and ruined my chance to be loved.'

'Could you ever restore the relationship?'

'I don't think so. How could he forgive me for the evil I have committed against his family? I killed his son Gwen to hurt him after all he had done for me.'

'The man you're talking about is the Great One?' she asked incredulous.

'Yes,' he looked ashamed. 'The Great One rescued me from my own mother.'

Legion had been doing a lot of thinking since his son had been born. He had made right with the tenants on his land, paying back the extra money he had charged them. There was still one deed he had committed that bothered him and he could not make it right no matter how much he wanted to. Still, he was determined to do the best he could. He had sent a Monwing to Lionsgate with a letter inviting Nuada to Griswold.

CHAPTER 30

TRUTH AND CONSEQUENCES

"Sometimes when things are falling apart, they may actually be falling into place." - Unknown

IT WAS a cool evening considering it was summer and rain fell gently outside watering their newly planted garden. Daemon lit a fire and it crackled and spluttered in the hearth. He poured himself and Aislinn a goblet of wine each. Old Dr. Williams had agreed to take over their medical emergencies for the next week and so they could relax and have a drink. They settled on the quilt Aislinn had made in front of the fire, snacking on food from the hamper. Aislinn loved how the firelight cast soft shadows on his handsome face. It accentuated his manliness and made his eyes seem deeper and darker. She could see desire smouldering in them and she felt her stomach leap in anticipation. She was quite shocked by how much she actually desired him in return. He bent his head to hers, just brushing her lips gently, teasing her and daring her to pretend she did not want more. She tilted her head up to him indicating her eagerness for his mouth to claim hers wholly. He waited. He wanted her to forget her fears and be ready to become one with him. She moaned and pulled his head to hers showing her eagerness and passion. They kissed and held one another till they both felt giddy and breathless. Daemon began to untie her dress and pushed it off her shoulder, her milky skin perfect. He moaned as his mouth brushed her shoulder moving lower as he enjoyed her. She knew about sex and making babies – that was her job, but she never imagined it would be so sensory and delightful.

'Drew...' she whispered his name.

Daemon froze for just an instant. He had forgotten that she was responding to the man she thought he was. He wiped away his conscience kissing her again so that she could say no more. He was Drew now – he had no reason to feel guilty.

Aislinn lifted his shirt and pulled it over his head. She wanted to see him, to engrave his form into her memory. He had a magnificent body – his muscles strong and toned. She felt safe in his arms. She ran her fingertips over his bicep and up to his shoulder then traced it down over his chest and around his nipple. He watched her, amused, enjoying her delight at discovering his body. She ran her finger down the side of his body to his birthmark. She stopped dead. It was not there. Aislinn felt confused. Had she imagined the birthmark on him? No she distinctly remembered it – it was on the left hand side just below the bottom rib. There was definitely no birthmark on this man. She felt suddenly cold, sick.

'Is everything all right?' he asked seeing her guarded expression.

'I'm sorry she said, 'I just got distracted for a moment. Could I have some more wine please?'

What was going on, who was this man?

'I think you are trying to procrastinate or drive me insane, Aislinn,' he laughed getting up to pour her more wine.

Aislinn looked at his torso again. No birthmark. Whoever this man was he wasn't Drew and she felt terrified and angry. Maybe there was no birthmark – perhaps it had been a trick of the light. Still she had to be sure.

Don't panic Aislinn, think straight, she urged herself.

'Drew I know I said I didn't want to know the truth about Gabrielle, but I have to know. What really happened with her?'

She saw the alarm in his eyes as he quickly recovered from the question. He had no idea what she was talking about.

'Aislinn, why are you bringing this up now? You said you were happy not knowing.'

'I know, and I really thought it wouldn't be a problem but it has been at the back of my mind all this time and I need to know the truth if this marriage is going to based on honesty.'

Did he just look away momentarily? Is it guilt?

'What do you need to know sweetheart?'

'I need to know about the child you had with her. I fear Gabrielle will use the baby to come between us.'

Daemon was shocked. So his brother wasn't as innocent as he made out to be. A love-child! He certainly had not expected that?

'Sweetheart I told you everything about Gabrielle. There is nothing between us – it was a silly mistake made long before I met you. That child will never come between us, I promise you. Is that why you are so anxious?'

She had her answer – this was not Drew. She said it so softly he could barely hear her.

'There is no child. You're not Drew. Who are you?'

He kept his face as neutral as possible.

She had tricked him – how the hell had she worked out he wasn't Drew? What had he done to tip her off? He had been so careful.

'What do you mean darling? Of course I'm Drew. Who else would I be?'

Aislinn looked at her truth ring. It glowed sickly yellow confirming her worst fear.

'Who are you?' she screamed at him, 'and what have you done with Drew?'

'Calm down Aislinn, you're getting hysterical.' He grasped her shoulders in a vice-like grip.

'You're hurting me,' she whimpered in pain.

'You're just exhausted and overwhelmed Aislinn. It's been a big few days and I understand that you are afraid as it's your first time with a man, but you don't need to be afraid. I love you. Look at me, I am Drew Williams, the one and only,' he said as calmly as he could.

'You can try and convince me all you like,' she sobbed, 'but this ring does not lie,' she said pointing to her hand.

He knew there was nothing he could do to convince her otherwise.

Damn that ring! Damn Gabrielle, whoever she was!

'Let me go,' she said steely voiced.

'No I won't. I once told you that I would have you whenever and wherever I wanted you and that still stands. You are my wife and you will pleasure me as such.'

'That was you,' she cried remembering the incident in the tower room. She had been furious with Drew thinking he was acting very out of character. He was right – Falstaff had put an impersonation spell on this man, but who was he really? Why did he want to marry her? She had no answers and the possible scenarios frightened her. What scared her the most though was the thought that Drew could very well be dead.

'Please let me go or at least tell me who you really are and why Falstaff put an impersonation spell on you. He is behind this, isn't he?'

Daemon laughed, hollow and cruel that sent fear coursing through her veins.

'There's no spell Aislinn – this is me in the flesh and blood. I am Drew's long lost twin brother returning home to get my inheritance starting with you.'

She stared shocked at his revelation. Drew had not mentioned a twin. He could see the question in her eyes.

'No, my brother did not know about me, until the other day, that is.'

He still held her shoulders and she felt afraid. She could see the muscle in his jaw clenching.

'You're despicable. I won't be your conquest or the pawn in the war with your brother.'

He laughed again. 'You can protest all you like – you are attracted to me Aislinn. You've responded to my touch and kisses many times. I can make you happy if you let me. Believe it or not I do love you; that's why I married you, not because I am trying to punish my brother.'

'Get away from me. I only responded because I thought you were Drew. It's Drew I love, not you. You will never have my heart – if anything I hate you.'

'We'll see about that,' he growled in her ear spinning her around and pushing her hard up against the fireplace wall. The stone was cold and rough against her cheek and a sob caught in her throat. He lifted her skirts while pinning her to the wall and Aislinn knew instantly what his intentions were.

Help me Great One. Please don't let this happen to me.

Daemon fumbled with his trousers. It was difficult whilst keeping her pinned to the wall. Aislinn felt numb, as though her body had gone into hibernation and would not respond to fight him off, then she remembered the words that Ziah had spoken to her in Lionsgate.

You are the master of your own destiny.

She had always believed that and now this man was trying to take that from her – to override her free will and violate her against her wishes.

How dare he!

She felt fury rise up in her belly at what was about to happen, a rush of adrenaline that shook the shock from her and enabled her to fight.

He is not going to steal my destiny.

She stretched her arm out toward the fireplace and felt for the fire iron as he fumbled with her many-layered skirts. Her hand closed around the hard, cold metal and she pulled it toward herself.

Daemon had his pants down and she felt fear choke her. He pushed against her squirming body, cursing her for making it difficult. Aislinn gripped the fire iron tighter, the hard cold metal her only hope, and thrust it as hard as she could backward. She felt his body shudder; then heard him crash to the floor. She was too afraid to look. She turned slowly, pushing her skirts down trying to get her dignity back. He lay on the wooden floor, the metal iron protruding from his side, blood trickling from his mouth as he gasped for breath.

Aislinn dropped beside him, her nursing instincts kicking in. She was horrified at what she had done.

'Where's Drew?' she asked. 'He is the only person who can save you now. Tell me and I will get him to help you.'

Daemon coughed and then cried in pain.

'I'm sorry,' he said. 'I wanted you so much because whatever you may think Aislinn, I do love you.'

'Shh... it's all right. Where is Drew? He can help you.'

'He's at the old forge. Please forgive me.' He coughed again and bright red blood gurgled from his throat.

'Where is the forge?' Aislinn urged him.

The young man gurgled once more and then went limp, his eyes glazing over – the last light of life dwindling.

'Don't go,' Aislinn sobbed.

What was she to do now?

I have murdered a man and not just any man. I've murdered my husband's identical twin brother that no one knows about. No that's not right – I've murdered my husband who I thought was Drew but isn't. Oh lord even I can't get it straight in my head. No one will ever believe my story – it sounds so ridiculous. They will all believe that I was frigid when he made an advance and that I killed him for touching me. Worse, I'm still a virgin – my marriage has not been consummated. I even told Mama that just this morning I'll be thrown in prison for the rest of my life.

Wild thoughts ran through her head. What should she do with the body? She had to find Drew. He would know what to do. Aislinn closed Daemon's eyes – he seemed less scary that way- as though he were just asleep. She pulled up his trousers and buckled his belt. Then she gritted her teeth and pulled the fire iron from his body. It was too much. She ran to the door, flung it open and vomited all over the front step.

⌘

Another night in this godforsaken place.

Drew had not slept for days and his body ached from being unable to change position. He had tried calling for help to no avail. Wherever Daemon had hidden him was remote. He wished he had Aislinn's faith or her knowledge of how to talk to the Great One but as yet they had not had time for him to explore his beliefs. He still was trying to reconcile his scientific mind with the experience he had been through when they were almost burned at the stake. He could not deny that somehow a miracle had happened, but it was hard to throw logic out the window when you based your whole life on science and reasoning. He did not know how to live by faith.

He managed to drink a little from the dew that gathered each night on the creeper that invaded the old building and he ate a few blackberries growing on the bramble bush. He thought of Aislinn. She was the only thing keeping him sane and fighting. He had no idea how he would break this news to her. Would she even believe him? After all it was Daemon's word against his. They both looked alike – how would she tell them apart? What if she did not believe him?

Chapter 31

Lost and Found

"We lose ourselves in the things we love. We find ourselves there, too" –
Kristin Martz

AISLINN did not sleep a wink – it was hard with a dead body in her home. She covered the Drew lookalike with a thin cotton sheet. After she had cleaned herself up from the vomit and scrubbed her doorstep she scrubbed the fire iron and put it back where it belonged. Then she dragged his body over to the living area and behind the simple settee. She did not want to look at him till she decided what to do with him. She had to get rid of his body but where could she safely put it till she found Drew? She waited till daylight and then scribbled a note and placed it on her door before locking it securely. Then she saddled the horse and headed to Sherbrooke.

JUST MARRIED, direct all medical emergencies to Dr. Williams in Sherbrooke Village, the note read.

Hopefully that would buy her some time to figure this all out. Part of her wanted to run home to her parents and beg them to help her but another part didn't want them to know. They would be so disappointed in her – she had taken a man's life. She did not want to involve them in her sordid mess. Her only option was to find Drew quickly.

Please let him be alive!

She headed into the quiet village – most people were still sleeping which is what she was hoping for. She headed for the blacksmith. This was the only forge she knew of. He was up early building and stoking his fire ready for the day's work. He looked surprised to see a young woman so early in the day and especially one so beautiful travelling alone.

'Good morning Miss,' he said as she approached.

'Good morning,' Aislinn responded politely. She hoped he would not recognize her.

'You're up and about early. Is everything all right?'

'Yes all is fine, thank you. I have rather an unusual question for you. Is this the only forge in Sherbrooke?'

'That is an unusual question, but yes it is. Why do you ask?'

'I feel a little embarrassed telling you but I was recently wed and my new husband thought it would be fun to play a little romantic game.' She blushed at the lie but he smiled thinking she was coy.

'Anyway he left me a cryptic clue telling me to meet him at the forge as he has a surprise for me. He wouldn't be hiding in the back would he?'

'The blacksmith laughed. 'Well I think his plan went awry Miss, because there's no one here but me. He should have been a bit more specific. I wouldn't let you out of my sight if you were my new bride.'

'That is very kind. Where could he have meant if it were not here?'

'Well I don't know Miss. This is the only working forge in Sherbrooke.'

'You mean there are others that aren't working?'

'Only one that I know of but it has been closed down for over a hundred years. My great-grandfather used to work there before Sherbrooke established itself here.'

'Do you know where it is?'

'Certainly Miss, the village used to be about three miles down the road. The little white cottage with the honeysuckle was the old Inn. Of course there wasn't much to the village in those days – just the forge and the inn and that was pretty much it.'

Aislinn drew a deep breath. That was their home now. The forge was on their property. True she hadn't really explored the whole property yet due to the wedding preparations. It made perfect sense. The imposter would not keep Drew far from the home.

'Where is it in relation to the cottage?'

'Well let's see if I can remember. I'll do my best to explain it to you but I'm not sure I remember correctly. Nobody has been on that land for a while and there is a new family living there now I believe.'

Aislinn thanked the man for his help and he hoisted her back up onto her horse.

'I hope you find him and get your surprise,' he said as she turned to go. 'Oh and congratulations on your marriage.'

She smiled and waved as she left.

Aislinn urged the horse on faster and faster – this had to be the place. If it wasn't then she had no other clues and would not know where to go next. She rode past their cottage and followed the directions the man had given her. The grass became longer and the foliage denser as she made her way deeper into the property. Thorns scratched at her legs, hooking and tearing the fabric at the bottom of her dress. She did not care. She had to find this place. She stopped where she thought the forge should be – she saw nothing but thick bramble bushes.

⌘

Drew shook the chains again in frustration. When was Daemon going to take him from this place? He was hungry – blackberries were not very filling and he was afraid to eat too many. He missed the sunlight. This building was so engulfed in brambles that very little light came in through the broken stonework. Then Drew heard it. The soft noises a horse makes. Someone was here. Was it Daemon? Drew pulled himself up and tried to peer through the dense foliage. His face was scratched by a large thorn as he did so but he did not care. If Daemon was here to set his plan in motion he would not go easily or without a fight. He lifted the chains around his arms and tried to push the thorns open to see who was out there. He caught a glimpse and sucked in his breath seeing her sweet face, full of angst and frustration.

Aislinn's here.

Had Daemon brought her to taunt him? If he cried out he might put her life in danger and he vowed he would never do that. The bastard was clever. He knew that Drew would not resist if Aislinn's safety was at risk.

Drew kept quiet even though everything in him wanted to cry out.

'Drew,' Aislinn called, 'where are you?'

He waited breathing heavily.

'Drew,' she shouted louder. 'If you can hear me, call out please.'

He still did not know whether this was a trap.

'Drew, I love you. Please I need you – I've done a terrible thing,' she sobbed.

Her fear and brokenness surprised him. He could not help himself as he called out.

'I'm here,' he tried to shout but his words only stuck in his dry throat. He quickly drank a little water that had accumulated from the previous night's rain.

'Aislinn,' he shouted louder, 'I'm here.'

Aislinn froze. She thought she heard him calling.

'Where are you, I can't see you.'

'I'm in these brambles. There has to be a way in because Daemon came to see me.'

So that was his name. *Daemon.* She wished she had not found it out – now he wasn't just an evil man who impersonated Drew. Now he was a person with a real identity.

Aislinn jumped down from her horse and began to circle the bramble looking for a way in. It took her a while but eventually she found the entrance to the old derelict building. She pushed her way in getting scratched on her bare arms as she shielded her face. Then she saw him, tied up like a wild animal. She rushed over to him and flung her arms around his neck.

'You found me,' he said in wonder.

'Wait I need to see something first,' she said lifting his shirt. There on his left side just below his ribs was the birthmark as she remembered it.

'Darling have you missed me so much that you can't wait to get me naked,' he teased.

She burst into tears, deep sobs wracking her slender frame.

'It's going to be all right sweetheart, but we must get out of here before Daemon comes back.'

'He won't be coming back Drew. I've done a terrible thing.'

She told him what had happened through sobs as he held her. Now Drew understood why Aislinn had lifted his shirt. Of course his birthmark! That was the one thing his brother could not replicate. He thanked his lucky stars she had seen him with his shirt off or this whole scenario could have been different. He did not dwell on the fact that to make the connection she would have seen Daemon half naked. He did not want to think about her lost innocence. He loved her and they would find a way to move on.

They rode home and it felt good to be in his arms again. His body was bruised and aching but being free and together was all that mattered.

'What are we going to do with him Drew?'

'He told me of his plans to get rid of my body. I think we should just follow them and let it play out the way he planned.'

Drew filled her in on Daemon's plot, giving her details of his capture.

He looked down at his dead brother lying on their cottage floor. Aislinn had been so brave to stand up against him. She had not gone into too much detail other than to say that when she realized he wasn't Drew she fought him off when he became aggressive. He wrapped Daemon in a sheet and moved him to the little lean-to next to the cottage – he did not want Aislinn having to look at him any longer. He could see her guilt at what she had done – that and revulsion that she could take a human life.

'It's okay,' he said to her. 'It's not your fault – you did what was necessary to save us both.'

'I know that in my heart, but my head keeps accusing me and replaying the scenario over and over. What if I had just wounded him?'

'You would still be married to him then, Aislinn. Death is the only way you could have been free of him. Besides you didn't plan to kill him – just to stop him from hurting you. How would we have explained this to your family?'

'I don't know, shouldn't we just explain what happened?'

'No Aislinn – we have no evidence that you acted in self-defence or that you were even married to Daemon. They may think we plotted to kill him. We cannot take this to the lord of Sherbrooke. We will be separated and imprisoned. This is not going to ruin our lives. We will follow Daemon's plan. Leave the note on the door so that everyone thinks we are away. We will wait for nightfall to move his body. It is a way to Grimwood Forest but we must follow the plan as we can't have him associated with us. Drew hitched the little wooden wagon ready to leave when the sun set. They kept the shutters on the house closed and Drew bathed his aching muscles. Aislinn prepared him some of the food her mother had brought over. The irony hit her forcefully. This was food from their wedding and yet Drew had not even been at their wedding – he had not enjoyed the ceremony they had – heard the way she pledged to love him always. This was a mess, but at least she was free from being married to Daemon – that much was true. Still, she could not have her wedding over without having a lot of explaining to do. He had stolen that from her. She sat on the settee and closed her eyes for just a moment.

Drew watched her sleep. She looked exhausted and he guessed the physical and emotional toll of the last day had been immense. She was still beautiful even with all the worries of the world on her shoulders. He walked over and looked at the beautiful wedding gown she had worn. He took it from the hanger and placed it in a bag together with his clothes. Then he shook her gently startling her awake.

'It's time to go sweetheart.'

CHAPTER 32

THE COVER UP

"'We all make mistakes, have struggles, and even regret things in our past. But you are not your mistakes, you are not your struggles, and you are here now with the power to shape your day and your future"
–Steve Maraboli

THE LITTLE wooden wagon rolled down the road creaking and shuddering as it went over the bumps and through the rutted trail. Daemon's body was in the back covered with straw and bags of grain. Drew guided the horses along the track and Aislinn held his arm to keep her balance.

In a few hours they would reach Grimwood Forest. They had travelled all night and the journey had been difficult in the dark. They had no choice but to continue – it was imperative that they get rid of Daemon's body before daylight.

'Are we going to make it in time,' Aislinn asked anxiously.

'I hope so,' he answered urging the horses on faster.

The night sky began to lighten to a deep dark blue and the stars lost a little of their sparkle as the sun fought its way around the earth, waiting to peep out in orange and purple streaks.

'There it is,' he said pointing to the mass of forest that stretched ahead. We will have to go a little way in before we unload his body. The cart moved into the mossy forest deadening the sound of its wheels under the lush carpet of leaves.

'This will do nicely,' Drew said reigning the horses in.

He moved the grain and straw and pulled Daemon's body out with a thud.

He laid his brother out on the forest floor and then pulled the pockets of his britches out as though a thief had rifled through them looking for coin. He pulled off Daemon's boots and threw them in the wagon.

'What are you doing?' Aislinn whispered.

'No thief would leave a good pair of boots like these,' he said. 'We'll get rid of them on our way back. We will leave his horse and his empty money pouch with his initials on– that way they will know it is Daemon when they find him.'

Drew looked at his brother one last time.

'I'm sorry brother that you are not getting a proper burial but you put us in this predicament. When Gwen hears of this she'll see you are buried right. I'm sorry we could not have met under better circumstances. Rest in peace.'

Drew untied Daemon's horse that had been tethered to their cart, and gave it a smack on its rump scaring it off.

Aislinn felt sick. She had been doubly horrified by her actions when Drew had told her that Daemon was Gwen's brother. She had forgotten about Gwen and how this would affect her. She had just lost her father and now her brother was dead. She had done that to her. She also felt another measure of guilt. She had responded to Daemon's advances and kisses when she was in the castle at Griswold. She had taken picnics and rides with him and been none the wiser. She chided herself mentally and wondered how she did not know the difference. Surely she should have been able to tell it was not Drew.

After they left Daemon in the forest they made their way to Trenton.

'We need to be away from home a few days to prove that we had nothing to do with this,' Drew said.

Aislinn nodded numbly. It did not even bother her that they were not married and would be sharing a room. That was the least of their problems right now.

'Aislinn? Aislinn, are you listening to me?' he asked when she did not respond to him.

'Sorry Drew, what did you say?'

'I said I love you and that this is not going to ruin our lives together. We have overcome so many obstacles to get to this point. I don't want this to kill our love for one another.'

'Everything is possible for those who believe,' she said softly.

'What do you mean?'

'Regent taught me that. It means that I believe you love me and so it is possible that this is finally our time to be together as we have always dreamed.'

He was right – she could let this ruin their lives or they could thank the Great One that they still had each other. There was never going to be a good ending to this scenario. Someone was always going to die because Daemon had planned it that way. What happened did not make her a bad person. She was defending them as her father had tried defending their family years ago when Cillian attacked. They would not feel disappointed with her for fighting for love, fighting against evil. Why had she ever thought they would be disgusted by her actions? She tried to convince herself that it would be all right. She had to otherwise it would destroy them.

They rode in silence each with their own thoughts. Drew draped a protective arm around Aislinn and she leaned against him as the wagon rocked to and fro as it made its way toward Trenton. They felt relieved the task was complete. They were completely unaware of the pair of eyes that watched them as they tried to cover up the events of the previous day.

⌘

The Inn at Trenton was busy as always when they pulled up their wagon. It was midday and they were hungry and tired after travelling all night. Drew helped Aislinn down and then went in to get them a room. The innkeeper was delighted to see them again under better circumstances.

What brings you to Trenton? Not more illness I hope?'

'Nothing like that this time. We have just recently been married and thought we would come back to the place where it all began.'

The innkeeper was delighted to hear that romance had blossomed at her inn.

'Congratulations, please allow us to give you all your meals on the house while you are here as a thank you for all you did for the people of Trenton.'

'That is very kind thank you,' Drew replied. 'We will only be here for four days then we have to get back to our patients.'

They ate some lunch and then went up to their room to unpack.

'I hope you don't feel too uncomfortable sharing a room?' Drew said. 'I will sleep on the floor and you can have the bed.'

'Really Drew, that is not necessary. I think we have established that we love each other and I trust you more than anyone. You will sleep on the bed with me.'

They were too tired to argue. They climbed onto the bed and Drew wrapped his arms around Aislinn. Then they slept till it became late and the noise from the tavern wafted up to their room waking them.

'Are you awake,' she whispered.

'Mmm,' he replied planting a kiss on the nape of her neck.

'Good, let's go back to the pond Drew. I want to start over – to forget that any of this has happened. I want a new beginning.'

'Me too,' he said.

'

CHAPTER 33

RENEWAL

"And in great decay comes great renewal. Life finds a way out of the darkest spots"   - Tyler Knott Gregson

DREW had it all worked out. He could not sleep after their walk to the pond. This time he had not only told Aislinn he loved her but he had gotten down on one knee and asked her to marry him.

'Of course I want to marry you Drew, but technically we are already married in name. We could just go on from here but it wouldn't feel right to me knowing that the things I pledged were not to you and that you weren't even present at our wedding. How can we redo it without questions being asked?'

'Don't worry I will make a plan – just say yes Aislinn.'

'Yes, definitely yes,' she said kissing him.

When he had come to Trenton to help with the measles epidemic a few moons before, he had quarantined an old man who just happened to be the local priest of the village. Drew visited him regularly keeping the old man company through his infection as he had no family and they became firm friends.

You are just like a son to me,' he had said. 'If there is ever anything I can do for you in return for your kindness you have just to ask.'

Drew had not thought anymore of the priest's offer, now the time had come to take him up on it. There was something the old man could do for them.

Drew had left Aislinn at the Inn while he took care of their problem. He knocked on the door of the old church and the old man answered.

'Dr. Williams, how good it is to see you again. What brings you to Trenton?'

'Hello Father Norris. You are looking well. If you invite me in for a cup of tea I will tell you all about it.'

'Of course my boy – come on in.'

Drew smiled at being called a boy. He knew that he could not tell the priest what had happened and how his beloved had killed his brother. Instead he told him that he and Aislinn had been married only to discover that the priest who married them was not really a priest but an imposter looking to steal from the wedding guests. It was partly true – the imposter bit anyway – he just omitted to tell the old priest that the imposter was the groom.

'We cannot tell our families after all they went through to give us our dream wedding. Not only that but I want to protect Aislinn from shame. If anyone found out that we had been together in an intimate way without us really being married it would ruin our reputations in Sherbrooke. Our integrity in helping people is very important to us. We are devastated by what has occurred and want to make it right.'

'That is a terrible story,' the old priest said outraged. 'There seem to be more and more priest impersonations and it needs to be stopped. People pretending to be priests are robbing the poor claiming that the Great One will take their coin in exchange for saving their lives and protecting them from evil. It is a disgrace. I hope you have reported this in Sherbrooke.'

'I certainly have,' Drew said, 'however I doubt they will ever catch the rogue as the usual priest was away and he said he was the proxy priest. I guess we should have checked before we believed him.'

'Nonsense my boy! A man's word should be good enough. What is the world coming to? Bring your lady around for dinner later and we will perform the ceremony. Nobody needs to know what has happened to you both.'

'Thank you,' Drew said, shaking the old priest's hand vigorously, relieved that he had bought the story. Drew felt a prick of conscience at lying to the lovely old priest but he had to protect Aislinn at all costs.

⌘

Gwen felt concerned. Daemon was expected to return today and yet there was no sign of him. She felt alarmed and didn't know why. She had never worried about him being late before but somehow she felt something was not right.

'I am worried Legion. I don't know why.'

'I'm sure he's fine Gwen, and will arrive in the next couple of days. Daemon knows how to protect himself. He knows magic. Who could come up against that?'

'You're probably right,' she sighed.

Their conversation was interrupted by Holgrimm bringing word that Nuada had arrived at the castle.

'I will be downstairs shortly Holgrimm. Offer him some refreshment while he waits.'

Legion was nervous to face Nuada again. The last time he had seen him was when he was a young boy and he had fully intended for the young lad to be devoured by hungry animals in Grimwood Forest. He recalled the look of fear and horror on the boy's face when his parents had been killed. Granted he had not held the sword in his own hands, but he had given the order to kill his parents. He could not bring them back but he could try and make amends.

Nuada was not alone.

Of course he would not come here on his own.

Aedan was with him and both men looked suspicious and ready for any sign of treachery.

'Welcome,' Legion said. 'I suppose you are wondering why I have invited you here Nuada. Since my son's birth I have come to realize how short life is and what true value is. Previously I would have said power was the ultimate goal in life and you know I did anything I could to gain it – even at the expense of others.'

Nuada looked contemptuously at Legion.

'What do you want Legion? I have spent years fighting to let hatred go, to not allow your evil actions to rob me of my life and happiness. Bringing me here and dredging up the past is cruel.'

'I'm sorry Nuada, I did not mean to cause you any more pain than I have already. I want you to know that I am sorry for what I did to your parents and to you. I cannot take it back or make it right, but I want to make it up to you. I have some land that I would like to give to you to make amends. It is yours to do with as you will and it is choice farmland with river frontage. I would like to give something back to you. Please accept this as my way of asking your forgiveness.'

'I want nothing from you Legion. You are trying to buy yourself a clear conscience and I want no part of it.'

'Nuada,' Aedan interjected. 'Don't be so hasty. Perhaps it would be good for Legion to give for a change. You don't have to farm the land but it would be good to have some of the land your parents loved and gave their lives for.'

Nuada grunted. Part of him wanted nothing from Legion but Aedan was right – this land was meant to be his one day and Legion had usurped it.

'All right Legion, I accept,' Nuada said.

Legion smiled, relieved that he was willing to accept the offer.

'I will ensure the documents are drawn up and sent to you. In the meantime I will get one of my men to take you out to see the land if you wish.'

"We would like that thank you,' Aedan said. 'There is someone else who came with us and who would like to see you.'

Legion looked alarmed.

'Hello Legion, it's been a long time.'

Legion paled – he had not heard that voice in a very long time.

⌘

Aislinn had just finished bathing.

'Turn your back Drew, I am getting out,' she shouted from behind the privacy screen in their room.

'I'll leave you then,' he said. 'I have put the dress you are to wear on the bed. I'm taking you somewhere special tonight. I'll head down to the tavern and get us some cider while you dress.'

The tavern was beginning to fill up with the evening crowd. Drew asked for a cider and sat down in a corner away from the lively patronage. He did not notice her standing over him till it was too late.

'So we meet again,' she said sweetly bending over and kissing him squarely on the mouth.

"Gabrielle,' Drew spluttered pushing her away from him. 'What do you want? I thought I made it perfectly clear that we would never be together.'

'Well I think you were rather hasty in your decision Drew.'

'I don't have time for this. Aislinn is waiting for me upstairs.'

'I don't take defeat or rejection very well Drew. I have had a man watching your every move since you returned to Sherbrooke from the Dark Lord's castle. I would have turned up at your wedding and objected to your nuptials but that wasn't necessary since you never actually married Aislinn did you?'

Drew had a sinking feeling in his stomach.

'What do you want Gabrielle?'

"You of course, darling. If you don't leave Aislinn and come back to Arles with me I will be forced to tell the Dark Lord about how his brother-in-law died. So sad really how his own wife killed him. Sadder too that you helped her dump his body in Grimwood Forest.'

Drew was angry. They had been so careful not to be seen, but obviously not careful enough. He loathed this woman – she was selfish and manipulative.

'Do what you must Gabrielle. I would not return to Arles with you if you were the last woman on the planet. I doubt the Dark Lord would believe a woman who was scorned by an ex-lover,' he said sarcastically knowing they had never really been lovers.

Her face reddened and she spat the words at him. 'Suit yourself Drew; you've signed your own death warrant. I hope she is worth it.'

⌘

Aislinn dried herself off wondering what he had planned for the evening. She pulled on her undergarments and then stepped out from behind the screen. On the bed was her wedding dress. She ran her fingers over the beautiful silver embroidery remembering how beautiful she had felt in this gown.

Drew brought my gown. He must want to see me in this dress. He must have something special planned.

She stood looking at herself in the small mirror. She combed out her curls that were wilder than usual due to her steamy bath. Her blue eyes looked bluer than normal. She pulled back the front of her hair and wished she had something to wear in it. The door opened and Drew stood watching her. She was beautiful.

'Here, let me,' he said seeing her struggling to lace the back of her dress.

His fingers brushed her skin ever so gently as he tied the laces. She felt a shiver of excitement run up her spine. He could still make her weak with his touch.

'There,' he said admiring her in the dress. 'You look incredible. There is just one thing missing.'

He pulled out a beautiful pale pink rose that he had picked and tucked it into her hair.

'Now you look perfect.'

The sun had just set and the sky was awash with soft colour.

'Where are we going?' she asked as they wandered down the streets of Trenton. She felt self-conscious in her dress and felt the curious stares of people passing them on the street.

'We are having dinner with an old friend.'

'I didn't know you had friends here in Trenton.'

'Friends made during the measles epidemic. You'll like the old man. Don't worry; it will be a special evening you'll see.'

Dinner was delicious and they enjoyed the old priest's company. He obviously did not have visitors often as he was so animated and shared all his stories of weddings, funerals and some other strange things he had seen as a priest. Aislinn felt herself relax and found herself laughing again. It seemed an age since she laughed although that was not true – just a few days previously she had been deliriously happy on her wedding day. So much had happened in just a few short days.

'Drew talked so much about you when we were in Trenton with the outbreak. He would not let me visit anyone other than pregnant mothers to keep the contamination in check.'

'Well you would have cheered a sick old man up, but I can see why he kept you a secret,' he smiled winking at Aislinn.

Drew roared with laughter.

'Father Norris, you wily old man. You aren't supposed to be looking at pretty young girls.'

'Nonsense young man – I can appreciate the Great One's creation. I may be old but I'm not dead you know.'

They both laughed at the old man's wit.

'Now, let's get down to the issue at hand,' the old priest said after they had finished their meal. 'Drew has told me of your marriage plight and we need to make it right. I am appalled at how you have both been treated.'

Aislinn looked alarmed and glanced at Drew who warned her to say nothing just by his look.

'It is rather a vexing subject for Aislinn I'm afraid,' Drew interjected. 'She comes from a very reputable family who were spiritual leaders themselves so this has left her feeling distressed.'

What had Drew told the priest, surely not the truth?

She was pretty sure he would not be protecting her if he knew she were a murderer.

'I'm so sorry my dear for what you have been through. We will rectify it immediately and get you and your lovely doctor legally married.'

'You're willing to marry us?' she stammered.

'He didn't tell you?' Father Norris laughed.

'I thought I would surprise her. That is all right with you, isn't it?' Drew asked.

'I don't know what to say,' she laughed 'Thank you Drew, I can't thank you both enough,' she said hugging the old man.

'Well that has made it all worthwhile,' he chuckled.

Aislinn gazed up into Drew's eyes as he held her hands. They could have been then only two people in the world right then.

'Aislinn, my darling, I pledge to love you till the end of time, to protect you and share my every thought and dream with you, to be a husband and friend to you, the best father I can to our children. I promise to provide for you in good times and bad times. I love you and nothing past nor present, will ever change that. I give you this ring as a token of my love and commitment to you.'

He placed his mother's ring she had returned to him back on her finger.

'Drew, we have had so many adventures together the last few moons. Some have been good and some have threatened to tear us apart, but through it all you were there for me, protecting and loving me. You make me feel safe, you have shown me what real love looks and feels like and I would not want to be with anyone else. I love you and commit my life to you to be the wife and friend you deserve.'

'Aislinn and Drew, you have pledged your love for one another before me and the Great One who sees all. By the power vested in me I declare you to be man and wife.'

Father Norris blessed them and then said, 'Well what are you waiting for- you may kiss your bride Drew.'

⌘

'Great One, I must say I am surprised to see you,' Legion stammered, shock on his face.

'Don't be alarmed Legion. Is there somewhere we can talk alone?'

'Certainly, follow me,' Legion said escorting the Great One to his chambers.

'I wanted to congratulate you on the birth of your son. I see he has made quite an impact on your life.'

Legion smiled, 'yes he certainly has changed me, but surely he is not the reason you have ventured from Lionsgate to see me. Why have you really come? Did the Elders tell you of my refusal to pay for their sanctuary?'

The Great One laughed.

'Oh I wouldn't worry about that – in fact I think you were quite right to turn them down – those who seek me don't need a building to find me, they don't need rituals or rites to encounter me. I was very pleased with the way you handled them.'

'I don't understand then,' Legion looked confused.

'I think it is time you and I put the past behind us – that we bury the hatchet.'

'Why would you want to do that? I have done numerous evil deeds in the quest for power. I have hurt people for my own gain, even my own family at times and I have even killed your son to hurt you. Why would you want to reconcile with me? If anything, I deserve your fury and retribution.'

Remember when my horse ran you down? I could have left you then – most people would have seen a runaway boy, a wanderer and someone not worth wasting the time of day on. I saw something different then and I still do. I saw promise and potential. You have changed Legion – you are not the man you used to be and I am proud of you – I want to be a part of your life, your son's life. I am richer for knowing you. Yes, that may surprise you but when men do good, then the world becomes a better place.'

'I don't deserve this,' he choked back the emotion threatening to overwhelm him.

'That is the beauty of redemption and reconciliation – one doesn't have to do anything to deserve it. Will you accept my offer of friendship?'

'What if I disappoint you?'

'Why would you do that? You can only disappoint me if I have expectations. I can tell you now Legion I don't have any expectations on you or any other person in this world. My love is unconditional which means there are no conditions attached to my favour and love. The spiritual leaders would have everyone believing they have to lay down their lives to follow me, be obedient and pledge their loyalty to me to receive my grace – it is not true. If that were the case then my love could not be called unconditional. There is no man who cannot change – even the ones with the blackest hearts can change their way of thinking – I believe in you and I want to make this right.'

Legion wiped the tear from his cheek. He could not remember the last time he had cried. He went to the old man who held his arms open and hugged him, deep sobs erupting from the dormant volcano of emotions he had buried since his teenage years.

They were interrupted by an urgent knocking on the chamber doors.

'What is it?' Legion asked seeing Holgrimm with a castle guard.

He looked shocked to see his Master's red eyes but said nothing.

'Master, we are a little alarmed,' the guard said. 'A horse has arrived back at the castle and it looks like Daemon's horse, but there is no sign of him.'

'I want you to take some riders and go back toward Trenton to see if you can find him. If there is no sign of him on the road ask in Trenton where he may have gone. Someone must know something.'

Gwen appeared in the doorway, alarm on her face.

'I knew something was wrong,' she said quietly. 'I have a very bad feeling about this Legion.'

'Don't jump to conclusions my love. There may be a simple explanation. We will find him I promise. In the meantime there is someone I want you to meet,' he said indicating the Great One.

CHAPTER 34

INTIMACY AND ENMITY

"Radiate boundless love towards the entire world — above, below, and across — unhindered, without ill will, without enmity."
– The Buddha

THE MOMENT she had waited for so long had finally come. He was tender and loving as he unlaced her bodice. He kissed her neck and back with little kisses that teased and aroused her. When it was fully unlaced he turned her around to face him and pushed the sleeves off her shoulders, the weight of the fabric dropping the dress to the floor around her ankles in ivory waves. He lifted her off her feet removing her from the folds of fabric, her sheer undergarments not leaving much to his imagination. He could feel her warm body under the thin fabric and his hands wrapped around her curvaceous hips. His desire was not lost on Aislinn either.

She pulled at his shirt and lifted it over his head, enjoying the manly scent he emanated. She touched his chest wanting to remember every curve and muscle. She buried her head in his chest as she wrapped her arms around his hips. He felt her body shuddering before he heard the gentle sobs that came from her.

'Sweetheart, what's the matter?'

He saw her face and realized that she was remembering her time with Daemon just a couple of nights before. How stupid of me, he thought. Daemon must have hurt her after all.

She had been trying to be so brave but looking at him would dredge up all sorts of memories as they were so alike.

'It's all right Aislinn. We don't have to rush. I want you to feel safe with me darling, I am not him, I will never hurt you or force myself on you.'

He kissed her teary cheeks and her eyes.

Aislinn, smiled up at him through glistening lashes. He was right. They may look identical but their personalities were poles apart. He was not like his brother and she loved him even more for his sensitivity. She did want to be with him as a wife – to please him and show her love.

'I'm all right,' she said shakily. 'I want to be with you Drew. I guess I just needed to get my emotions out. I love you and I know you're nothing like him.'

Drew kissed her slowly and waited for her to make the first move. Aislinn lifted her undergarments over her head and dropped them to the floor. She stood before him, blushing and feeling self-conscious. Instinctively her hands moved to cover herself.

'Don't,' he whispered huskily. 'I want to look at you. You are so beautiful Aislinn. Don't be afraid,' he said gently. 'I will wait for you to be ready. You tell me when that is and I will be very slow and gentle.'

Drew did not want their union to remind her of Daemon's brutality or of the intimacy they shared. He wanted this to be her memory of what a marriage night should really be like between two people who loved one another.

'I love you,' he said.

'I love you too,' she said drawing him into her arms.

⌘

Gwen sobbed, her heart breaking as she looked at the broken and bloodied body of Daemon. Now they would clean him up and give him the burial he deserved on Skull Hill next to their father.

Whoever has done this will pay she vowed silently.

The guards had found him in Grimwood Forest and returned him home. They had found his saddle pouch attached to his horse and they handed it to Gwendolyn. She turned it over in her hands as though touching it would somehow keep him closer to her or bring him back.

'I want his killer found and brought to justice, Legion.'

'That will be difficult Gwen. No one in Trenton even saw Daemon so we have no idea who could have been tailing him.'

'Are you telling me that you are going to do nothing about this?' she challenged her husband.

'No, what I'm saying is that we will try and find out who did this but I can't promise you we will find the answer.'

'Well, I will never give up looking for the perpetrator. Sometimes I wish you would show a little bit of the backbone the Dark Lord had,' she said meanly.

Her words stung him but he did not let it show.

'Find who did this Legion,' she said. 'Money talks – it always does. Offer a reward for any information. In the meantime I will be moving back to my own chambers until you have found his killer,' she threatened as she stormed out of the room.

Legion let out a sigh. She was shutting him out – he could see how her pain made her withdraw and he feared for their future. Just when things had come right between them. He went back to his chambers to see if he could talk reason to her. She was nowhere to be found and her things had been moved. He felt sadness at what was lost.

'Master,' Holgrimm interrupted his thoughts. 'Someone is here to see you.'

'Can't it wait Holgrimm, or better yet get Drogus to deal with the issue.'

'She insists on seeing only you Master.'

'Very well,' he sighed, 'I will come down shortly. Have her wait in the parlour.'

Legion was surprised to see a beautiful young woman standing in his parlour. He had assumed it was a villager's wife needing assistance but this woman was clearly well to do and not from Griswold.

'Can I help you?' he asked.

'No, it is I who can help you,' she said smiling sweetly. "My name is Gabrielle and I have information regarding your brother-in-laws death.'

⌘

Aislinn bathed as Drew made up their bed. He pulled the sheet to straighten it and noticed the small blood stain. He paled. How was that possible? Aislinn had spent two nights with Daemon before she killed him. His brother had enjoyed taunting him with the details of their union.

'Sweetheart, there's something I need to ask you,' he said tentatively.

This could go horribly wrong leaving her angry with him but he had to know the truth.

'Yes,' she said as she poured water over her shoulders. The warm water felt good.

'You were with Daemon two nights after you wed. Did he hurt you in any way? He told me he was gentle with you. I couldn't bear the thought of him hurting you.'

Silence came from behind the screen as Aislinn processed just what he was asking. Drew cursed himself silently - he had offended her.

She stood up from the bath and covered herself with a wrap. The sheer cloth did not hide her wet body. She walked, dripping water over the wooden floor and stood looking into his worried violet eyes. She touched his cheek.

'Drew, what Daemon told you was not true. We never consummated our marriage as I was called out to birth a baby the night of our wedding. The next night I found out he was not you. You know the rest of the story. That was when I killed him. He was going to force himself on me and I couldn't bear the thought of him taking something that would be special to both of us. I couldn't let him do it. You were the first my love, and the only one for me.'

She had never seen him close to tears, but his eyes misted up as he pulled her in to himself.

'You beautiful, brave woman. I should know you better Aislinn Williams. You never cease to amaze me. Thank you Great One for making that baby come the night of the wedding,' he uttered looking up to the ceiling.

'All this time you thought I had given myself to another and yet you still wanted me?' she asked her voice muffled against his broad chest.

'I love you. Nothing can change that.'

'And I love you too,' she said dropping the cotton wrap to the floor, inviting him to explore her body all over again.

CHAPTER 35

ACCUSATIONS

"Don't make assumptions. Find the courage to ask questions and to express what you really want. Communicate with others as clearly as you can to avoid misunderstandings, sadness and drama. With just this one agreement, you can completely transform your life" - Don Miguel Ruiz

DREW held the letter in his hand, his face ashen. It was from Legion claiming that Gabrielle had told him the truth of the circumstances surrounding Daemon's death. Legion wanted to hear their side of the story. He and Aislinn had just returned from Trenton and were settling into married life. He had not believed Gabrielle would follow her threat through and yet feeling scorned, she had done just what she promised. She had been nothing but trouble in his life and he wished he had never met her. He could not tell Aislinn of this – she would suffocate under the guilt all over again if she knew that Legion knew the truth. Besides, he had once wanted her dead and he had vowed to protect her and keep her safe and now he would do just that. He would meet Legion and talk to him about what happened. He drafted a note and returned it to the pouch that was strapped to the Monwing's leg. These creatures still made him nervous. Thank the lord Aislinn was out birthing a baby. He watched the Monwing as it hopped a few steps and then took off into the sky to return to the castle.

That night as he picked at his dinner he thought about what he would tell Legion.

'Drew, are you even listening to me?' Aislinn asked.

'What, I'm sorry love what did you say?'

'I've told you twice already that our families are coming for dinner tomorrow.'

'I'm afraid we'll have to postpone sweetheart. I have received a call from the doctor in Trenton asking me to help him with new medical research he is working on. He wants my opinion before he proceeds with it. I said I would meet him tomorrow and discuss it with him. I'll only be gone a couple of days.'

'Really, could this not have waited a few weeks? - we've only just got back from our time away together and we've hardly settled in.'

'I know, but the world does not stop because we are in love and can't bear to be apart.'

She smiled. 'Well make sure you hurry back home to me.'

⌘

Drew rode into Trenton and headed toward the Inn. He felt bad about lying to Aislinn – he never wanted to keep secrets from her but he was left with little choice. He was still not sure what he would tell Legion. They had agreed to meet on neutral grounds in Trenton. He tethered his horse and asked the stable hand to water and feed the animal before heading into the Inn.

Legion had not yet arrived so Drew had some refreshment while waiting for him. It was not long before he appeared looking as though the world was on his shoulders. The two men shook hands and sat at a table.

'I'm sorry to drag you all the way here,' Legion said, 'but I had to hear the truth from you. Where is Aislinn?'

'Aislinn won't be joining us and I am sure you probably understand why. This is very awkward for her. I'm sorry that we have to discuss this – that my brother is dead.'

'Yes, I understand. This must be hard for you too. Sometimes I forget that Daemon was your twin. This Gabrielle woman, why does she hate you so much that she accused you and Aislinn of this deed?'

Drew quickly outlined his past with Gabrielle and how she had tried to convince him to leave Aislinn.

'I guess she just could not bear the thought of being rejected for another woman.'

Legion looked hard at Drew and could see his struggle.

'There's more to the story though isn't there? She didn't just concoct this story to hurt you. She has a witness Drew, someone who saw you and Aislinn leave Daemon's body in the forest.'

'Legion, I want you to know the truth but I also will protect my wife before anything – just as you would protect your family. There is more to this story, but if I share it with you I may place my family in danger and I cannot do that.'

'Drew, I owe you and Aislinn a debt of gratitude. Without you both, I would not have a family. I do not believe you or Aislinn would take a man's life unless there was a very good reason for it. You need to trust me. I know I have not really earned Aislinn's trust in the past but I am not that man anymore. Please tell me what really happened?'

Drew took a deep breath – should he trust Legion? He had heard horror stories about this man but the truth was he had never seen that side of him – he had only known Legion as he was now. His gut told him to trust the man.

He told Legion about Daemon's obsession with Aislinn which began when he was impersonating Drew during Gwen's confinement. He described how he had been abducted and how Daemon took his place at their wedding. He told of Aislinn's fear at discovering the truth and how she defended herself when he forced himself on her.'

'Aislinn never meant to kill him – she was only trying to protect herself Legion, but this scenario was never going to end well. If she had not realized who he was and defended herself, it would have been my body found in Grimwood Forest. He planned to kill me and leave me in the Forest so that Gwen would think it was him. He wanted my life. Nothing could have stopped Gwen feeling the grief she does – he planned it that way. We simply followed the plan he set in motion.'

Legion looked shocked. He understood how Daemon had fallen for Aislinn. He had once done exactly the same. Falstaff had forced them together in his game of deceit and this was the result. He was the culprit who should pay for this tragedy, but that would not happen as he was already dead. His interference and hunger for power had caused these tragic events. He could not tell Gwen. She would want Aislinn's head on a block and it would ruin her memory of her brother and her father. He did not want to start a war again with the Hamilton family or the Great One. He had promised he would never harm their family again and he meant to keep that promise. The Great One had reached out to him and given him a second chance – he had shown him that forgiveness for evil deeds was possible. Now he would have to forgive Aislinn and Drew for this mess that was forced on them by Falstaff's greed. No, he would have to lie to his wife and keep the truth from her – even if she never forgave him for not finding Daemon's killer. This was the punishment he deserved for all the evil he had done in the past. The circle was complete – there would be a reckoning for his past sins – not from the

Great One, but a reckoning of his own choosing – to protect others for a change. It was time he did the right thing.

'I understand Drew,' he said. 'I don't blame either of you for what happened, but Gwen must never know – she idolized her brother and I don't want his memory ruined. This must remain between us.'

Drew let out a sigh of relief. He knew it was a gamble.

'Thank you Legion, I wish it could have been different.'

The two men shook hands and Legion rose to leave.

'I must get back to Griswold Castle. Thank you for being honest with me. I hope you and Aislinn can pick up the pieces and get on with your lives. You both deserve that.'

CHAPTER 36

MISUNDERSTANDINGS

"The worst distance between two people is misunderstanding"
— Neetesh Dixit

SHERBROOKE - SUMMER 1627

'AISLINN,' Drew yelled at the front door of their cottage. 'Hurry up we have to go. This baby will wait for no one.'

She rushed around the living area trying to find her bag with all her equipment.

'Ready,' she said breathlessly running past him to her horse.

Each time she attended a birth now it was bittersweet. She and Drew had been married for three years and still she had not fallen pregnant. Initially she had just wanted the time with her new husband to get to know him. Then she began to worry silently that she could not give him a child. Every time she helped a new child into the world it was a mocking reminder that her body had let her down – that she could not experience what women took for granted. She tried not to let her worry show but every moon she would be disappointed yet again when her womanly cycle started.

They arrived at the homestead and could hear the woman screaming. Two children aged about ten and six sat outside with their hands over their ears trying to block out their mother's agony. Their fear was palpable.

'Why don't you take your little sister out to the meadow to play,' Drew said to the boy. He handed them each an apple.

'We'll call you when we've helped your Mother,' he said to the hesitant boy.

Poor kid, he wanted to be there for his mother but the look of relief on his face was obvious.

The boy nodded and took his sister by the hand as Drew followed Aislinn into the cottage.

⌘

'Papa, why does Mama not love me?' the three year old asked his father.

Legion's heart broke for the sweet child who looked up at him with serious eyes. What did one say when a child asked that question. He did not blame the boy for feeling rejected - he felt rejected too ever since Daemon had died. Gwen blamed him for never finding his killer and she had shut her heart away ever since that day. Now they were back to living as strangers in the castle. She had even turned her back on their son. He only had one present parent and Legion was determined that Phoenix would not feel unloved despite his mother's cold behaviour toward him.

'She does love you Phoenix – she just doesn't know how to show it because her heart is sore and broken.'

'Is it my fault Papa? Did I hurt her heart?'

'Never, my boy. It is no one's fault. Mama is just sad and hopefully one day she will get better. Until then we must just love her.'

The little boy nodded as though understanding far more than he should at three. Legion felt angry with Gwen. She knew what it was like growing up without a mother and how it had impacted her – now she was willfully doing the same to her own child. He wished he could shake some sense into her. There were times he was tempted to tell her the truth but he knew it would not take away her pain. She had chosen to wallow in it and the truth would just add to the pain she already clung to. In the old days he would even have found some poor sod who could have taken the fall just to appease his wife's disdain, but killing an innocent man for his own purpose was not something he did anymore. He did not want to become that man again – not even for his wife. He would not sell his soul again. She had to fight her own demons.

⌘

Aislinn sat opposite Rozanne and bared her heart.

'I don't know what to do Roz,' she said. 'You've been in this position before. How did you cope with being barren for so long? I have tried herbal remedies and other remedies but nothing seems to be working.'

'I know what you are going through Aislinn. It is the hardest place to be. Have you ever considered that it may be Drew that has the problem? Men don't like to admit they can't produce and so the burden falls on us to accept responsibility. The truth is that it takes both of you to make this child. You can't carry this burden alone. As long as you both love each other and share your feelings you will be all right. It took us many years to have Asher. It was only when we changed our lives and went to see the Great One that we were blessed with a child. As you know we have never had another. I think just letting go all our past hurts and drama helped us and of course being in Lionsgate made it possible. Perhaps you and Drew should make a trip to Lionsgate.'

Aislinn was not sure. To go to Lionsgate they would have to be honest about everything that transpired over the last few years. She was not sure she could look the Great One and Ziah in the eye and confess what she had done. How would he forgive her? She realized that her relationship with them had dwindled as a result of the events that had taken place. How had it happened? Regent still came by regularly to see how she was doing. He was a good friend but she could not even bring herself to tell him what had happened. Daemon's death was an ugly reminder that would not go away. Occasionally she still had nightmares of him forcing himself on her, of the sickening sound as the fire iron pierced his side, his dead, unseeing eyes looking at her, accusing. The irony was that she had defended herself yet she still felt guilty at times.

⌘

Regent was worried about Aislinn. Lately she was distant and something was weighing on her mind. He tried to get her to open up the last time he saw her, but she wouldn't.

'What's bothering you?' he had asked.

'Nothing Regent, I'm just a bit tired – work has been very busy lately.'

She may not have noticed the gleaming yellow stone in her ring but it wasn't lost on Regent. She was lying, but why? What could be so burdensome to her?

Now he stood outside her door and was determined that he would not let her brush him off.

'Regent,' she said surprised to see him. 'Come in.'

He hugged her and felt her wariness – not her usual exuberant self.

'What brings you here?'

'Well I could just lie to you and say I was in the area, but I love you too much to play games. What is going on Aislinn and don't say nothing? I know you better than that – something is weighing on you. I want to help.'

'Regent I love that you care about me so much but you can't fix this for me or protect me. I'm not that little girl anymore.'

'I'm not trying to fix you Aislinn. I don't think you're broken. I'm just trying to let you know that there are people who care for you and can share your burdens. Sometimes just letting your worries go will take a weight off your shoulders.'

She was silent.

'Let people in Aislinn. Let me in. What are you so afraid of?'

'I can't fall pregnant,' she blurted out. Regent looked surprised. It was not what he expected to hear.

'And this worries you?'

'Of course it does. We've been married three years and still there is no child. What if I can't give him a child? What if he leaves me?'

'So that's what's really worrying you. Drew loves you Aislinn – I've seen how he looks at you. He's not going to leave you. Have you shared your feelings with him?'

'No I can't. Please don't tell him I spoke to you Regent. As I said you can't fix this for me. Do you think the Great One could help me like he helped Rozanne?'

'I'm not sure Aislinn. I can't speak for the Great One.'

'Please Regent, I'll do anything. Let me come back to Lionsgate with you. You've always told me that anything is possible for those who believe. Well I've lost that belief and I need to get it back. Somewhere along the way I have lost myself – lost that unwavering faith I had. If I don't find it again having a child will never be possible for me.'

'All right Aislinn, but you need to let Drew know where you are going. I'm going to visit your parents. When I return be ready to leave.'

'Thank you Regent,' she smiled hopefully.

⌘

Regent was not the only person concerned about Aislinn. Imogene had been worried about her vivacious daughter's state of mind for a while now. Lately she seemed distant and worried all the time. The joyful enthusiasm that characterized her was lost or buried under a weight of some sort.

'Do you think we made a mistake?' Imogene asked Mac.

'About what sweetheart?'

'Well since we decided to create our own destiny and live our lives separate from the Elders and the clan, perhaps we have created confusion in our children. After all we gave all our time and energy to following the prophecies spoken over us and then things changed so suddenly and our beliefs were challenged and adjusted – maybe it was all too much for them.'

'That is ridiculous Imogene. Our children have seen the Great One face to face and experienced him. That is so much more valuable than following the Elders interpretation of who he is. Do you honestly believe we should have stayed under the Elders rule?'

'No, I know what we did was right. I wouldn't go back there for all the world but I don't want our children to suffer for our decision.'

'And they won't. We have never forced our opinions and beliefs on them and nor should we. They have to find their own way. I believe in our children Imogene – and the goodness of the Great One.'

'What about Drew though? Did we make a mistake letting Aislinn marry someone who did not believe in the Great One? Do you think that is why she seems unhappy?'

'I think you think too much,' he laughed. 'Aislinn is certainly not unhappy with Drew Imogene. Have you seen the way she looks at him?'

'Yes you're right, she does adore him, but something is bothering her.'

'She will tell us when she is ready Imogene. They are adults now and on their own journey. They have to work it out and seek truth for themselves. They have to have faith and believe for their own lives. That is part of the adventure of life. Give them time, they will work it out together, I am sure.'

'Ever the believer,' she smiled. That is what she loved so much about him. No matter what was happening he always believed that things would work out for the best. So far he had not proved her wrong.

⌘

Lionsgate was just as Aislinn remembered it – peaceful and vibrant at the same time. It was ageless this place. Regent ushered her in to the great hall where the Great One sat and ate with Ziah and Aedan on either side.

'Aislinn,' he boomed, his mouth full of food. 'So wonderful to see you. Come eat with us,' he beckoned her over to an empty chair beside Ziah.

Ziah hugged her as she sat next to him.

Thank you, it's good to be back,' she smiled. 'Mmm the food is just as I remember she said biting into a dish she could not identify –it just tasted good.

'Let's eat then while we catch up. I'm guessing you haven't come all this way to have supper with us, although we would have you anytime. Where is that dashing husband of yours?'

Aislinn smiled – he always knew what she was thinking and needed. She felt relieved to be here and about to share her deep, dark secret she had carried the last few years, but she also felt slightly afraid. What if he rejected her?

'Drew could not make it this time, but I promise I will bring him the next time I visit. He would love this place.'

'I'll hold you to that young lady – it's time I got to know the young man.'

They ate their fill and then strolled through the gardens of Lionsgate which instantly had a calming effect upon her. The beauty of their surroundings was undeniable, the sweet scent of the numerous flowers pervading their senses. Aislinn felt safe and her courage returned.

'Do you remember what Ziah told you when you were last here?' the Great One asked sensing her struggle to initiate the conversation.

'Yes,' she smiled recalling their last conversation. 'He said that I control my own destiny and that I must enjoy playing in the garden of life. He said no one man should ever have control over another.'

'So have you?' he asked.

'Have I what?'

'Have you enjoyed playing in the garden of life? Have you created your own destiny?'

'I want to but there are some things beyond my control.'

'Nothing is beyond your control Aislinn, unless you let it be.'

'Great One I can't have a child.' She blurted it out, all the pent up angst she had been feeling, fear and uncertainty in her trembling voice.

'I know.' He draped his arm across her shoulders, his gentle touch causing tears to flow down her face in rivulets. 'I've been watching you even though you have been keeping me at a distance. Why is that Aislinn?' he asked gently.

She dropped her head in shame. She couldn't bring herself to look at him. It was the truth – she had pushed him away because she still felt so guilty and ashamed.

'I know everything Aislinn. You forget that I see all that goes on. You have nothing to fear from me.'

'So you know then,' she said it so softly. 'Are you punishing me because of what I've done – because of what Drew and I did to Daemon?'

'Aislinn, is that what you believe? What happened to that young woman who was tied to a burning stake who believed beyond what was reasonable that we would save her – you even told Drew that we would come – you believed it then?'

'That was before I killed a man.'

'So you think that some things are unforgivable – that I would punish you for defending yourself. What would have happened if he had forced himself on you? Would that have been a better outcome?'

'No.'

'Did you intend to kill him?'

'No, I just wanted to get away, to stop him.'

'And you did, but not the way you intended. Aislinn I am not punishing you for killing Daemon – it was his own evil that caused that. What has been keeping you from having a child has not been me. The truth is that it is not me you fear but it is yourself you fear. Secrets have a way of imprisoning one – it is this secret you have been carrying that has held you back from conceiving. Deep in your heart you have not felt worthy to create a life when you took one. Your own thoughts have stopped you. Only you can change that. Ziah was right – you control your own destiny. If you continue to believe you do not deserve a child then you will never have one no matter how much you yearn for it.'

'I always thought I had forgiven myself for killing Daemon,' she said, 'but I don't feel any better – it haunts me.'

'Thinking you have forgiven yourself and actually doing it are two different things. As I said you can't forgive yourself when there are secrets. A secret will always remind you of something you are ashamed of – of something you want to keep hidden. When we hide things our subconscious makes us feel guilty. That is what has happened to you.'

I'm so ashamed- I never believed that I could be capable of killing a man and it's that thought that revolts me. I don't like who I have become.'

'That is not who you are Aislinn. One moment in our lives is not what defines us as people. You bring babies into the world; you help their mothers and families and heal the sick – that is who you are. You have a big heart but this one incident has clouded your vision.'

Aislinn looked at the beautiful old man standing before her. His kindness was too much. Tears flowed and sobs wracked her body as he enfolded her in his arms allowing all her pent up emotion to escape.

Crying was what she needed most.

'Thank you Great One,' she said as she wiped her red-rimmed eyes and he passed her a handkerchief. 'I'm sorry I kept you at a distance. I was so afraid you would not look at me the same way.'

He laughed, 'That does not make sense you know – you were worried I would treat you differently, reject you so to stop that happening you pushed me away first.'

Aislinn laughed with him seeing how ridiculous that was.

'Sometimes what you think you know gets in the way of the possible '

'What do you mean?' she asked.

'That when you believe something or think you know something, Aislinn, then you set yourself up to receive that very thing and that can sometimes get in the way of the possible. You thought that I would be disappointed and angry with you and that I would punish you. Since that was your belief and reality you made the possibility of conceiving a child impossible – your thoughts and feelings got in the way of the possible. Aislinn, I will never reject you or any person that comes to me. I am not like that. Even if you had killed Daemon intentionally, I would not turn away from you. People make mistakes – it is called life. You need to believe in yourself again as the beautiful, strong, kind-hearted person you are.'

'How come I always learn something new about myself when I am with you?' she smiled. 'You are right. I didn't realize it but I hated myself for what took place even though it wasn't my choosing. I am not going to do that anymore. I have too many people to help out there and if I am consumed by this then I will be of no help to anyone.'

'That's my girl. All I can say is that you are still going to help many children Aislinn – this incident is past and there is a glorious future ahead for you and Drew.'

She was glad she had come. Why had she waited so long? She would tell her parents what had happened. She prayed they would be as forgiving as the Great One. There was one other person she had to tell. No more secrets.

⌘

Gwen read the letter, her face deepening as she absorbed what was written in the document. She felt a mixture of emotions. Aislinn had saved her life when Phoenix was born – she had saved her child's life. She had always felt a debt of gratitude to the young woman. Now she had a letter from Aislinn outlining how her brother had died. She accused

Daemon of trying to rape her – of marrying her under false pretenses and of capturing Drew and plotting to kill him. That was very convenient since her brother could not defend himself. Well she would not let his name be tarnished by this woman. Legion was right about her all those years ago – she was a witch – she deserved to die. She was the one who captivated these men – first her husband and now her brother. She was the one who led them astray. Why should she absolve her conscience and move on with her life as though nothing had happened? Why should she be happy? She had ruined Gwen's family.

'It's not over Aislinn,' she whispered. 'I will destroy your family the way you have destroyed mine, if it's the last thing I do.'

EPILOGUE

SHE WAS not used to being on this side of the fence. One had to experience it to truly understand what it felt like. It was a pain that had purpose, a pain that brought joy even though it was unbearable at times. As another contraction ripped her body she moaned.

'You can do it,' he encouraged her. 'It's what we've been waiting for. Each one means our babe is closer to coming.'

'Are you repeating what I tell all my birthing ladies?' she laughed despite the excruciating pain. Now she understood when women said it felt like their insides were being ripped out.

'Well it's always worked for them, why not you?'

Aislinn looked up at the man she adored. He wiped her brow with a cloth and tucked a stray curl behind her ear.

'You can do this darling. I'm going to check now to see whether the babe's head is crowning. Don't push until I tell you to.'

'I can tell you it's a lot easier being that end,' she grunted, curbing the overwhelming urge to push.

'Ready?' he asked. 'On the next contraction, push as hard as you can.'

Aislinn felt the next wave of pain grow. She grunted and pushed as hard as she could, doing everything she usually instructed her birthing ladies to do.

She would be lying if she said she was not afraid of this moment even though she had attended many births. She had to consciously shut out Legion's words all those years ago that she and her baby would die in childbirth. The image he showed her of her future in the crystal was an image that would haunt her when she least expected it. It terrified her.

It's not the truth Aislinn – you know it isn't. You create your destiny; you know that, she mentally chided herself.

'I see baby's face Aislinn. You're doing so well. One more big push and our babe will be here.'

Drew's excited voice brought her back to the moment – everything would be fine and soon she would be holding her beautiful child. She tried to concentrate on the task at hand but it was difficult. She thought back to her time with the Great One. She was so grateful for his love and wisdom. She had returned and made right. She had heard nothing from Gwen – she did not know if Gwen even forgave her, but it had freed her from the awful secret she had. Hopefully it had given Gwen some closure too. The hardest part was telling old Dr. Williams what had happened. He took it the hardest of everyone and even blamed himself for putting them in such an awkward position and yet he was mourning a son he had never really known. It had taken time for Drew and his relationship to heal, but now they were determined to make it work – for him to be involved in their baby's life.

Her parents had been shocked to discover that Daemon had conned them all at the wedding. Imogene verified that Daemon existed and Aislinn had been shocked to find out that her mother had met him. The Great One was right. – keeping secrets always had a price attached. It had worked out well in the end – no one blamed her for protecting herself. She had come to accept that if she were in the same position she would have done exactly the same thing again. It brought her peace. With that peace, gratitude at what she had in her life was born. She had a wonderful man who loved her. That was all that mattered – the love she had of the people around her.

They had decided to make a fresh start when the secret was out, to renew their vows in front of their family and friends. Aislinn wanted her parents and siblings to witness her devotion to Drew. She wanted the special day that was robbed from her. On a beautiful summer day she and Drew stood hand in hand as her father remarried them – it felt as though the last cobweb of secrecy was blown away and a new beginning was unfolding for them both.

She remembered the day she realized her womanly cycle had not come. She had not been keeping track but she was certain it was later than normal. She dared not hope too soon. She said nothing to Drew. Then she felt her breasts grow tender and her disappointment set in, believing she was not pregnant. When she started throwing up her breakfast every morning she knew her body was changing and telling her something. That was when she told Drew she was expecting. He had been delighted swinging her around and then feeling her stomach and talking to the baby.

'Drew it is about the size of a grape,' she laughed.

'Doesn't matter,' he beamed 'It is our little grape.'

She was brought back to the moment as the next wave of pain came. This child was not a little grape anymore – it felt like she was birthing a pumpkin.

'Nearly there, Aislinn. Push,' Drew urged.

She gave it all, pushing as hard as she could, feeling the baby's shoulders slide free from their constraints, the gushing of fluid and then she heard her baby cry. It was the best sound she had ever heard.

⌘

Aislinn cradled the newborn in her arms.

'She looks just like you sweetheart,' Drew said looking at his tired but deliriously happy wife.

'No I can see you in her too. She's perfect Drew – a complete miracle.'

They gazed at their daughter, marveling at her tiny fingers and toes, a portrait of their love for one another displayed in human form.

'What are we going to call her? Have you decided yet?' he asked.

They had talked about names for months but not settled on anything yet.

'Yes, as soon as I saw her I knew what I wanted to name her,' Aislinn replied.

'Well don't keep me in suspense.'

'I want to call her Isabel. She is here because of the Great One's goodness to me. I won't make the mistake of shutting him out of my life again and I want her to know his goodness too.'

'That is beautiful – I love it,' he said.

'I also want her to be named Ailith, after your mother.'

'She would be honoured,' Drew said, his voice catching in his throat, emotion threatening to overwhelm him. 'Isabel Ailith Williams, welcome to our family – we are so delighted to have you with us.'

He kissed the child who had fallen asleep at Aislinn's breast. They were a perfect picture, mother and child.

⌘

The Great One looked in his Mirror of time. It was funny how people reacted to things in their lives - mostly they had to find some reason for the events they could not control or explain. It was human nature to blame someone or something else for the difficult things, the things they didn't like about themselves; the things they would not take responsibility for. It was always the darkness that made them do it, or even worse they believed it was he, the Great One, who was angry and was punishing them for their sins. What they did not understand was that it was neither. Darkness can only overtake people when they lose sight of who they really are – when they become blind to their own goodness and value. That had happened to Aislinn – she lost faith in herself and forgot how to believe in the impossible. Once that was lost she could not forgive herself. Still, she had found her way back again when she admitted she needed help and could not do it on her own.

He watched their family now and smiled. Aislinn held a special place in his heart and this baby would do some remarkable things in her time - he was sure of that. Aislinn and Drew were just starting their family and they would learn that the love of a parent for a child is all consuming and self-sacrificial.

He turned his attention to the Castle in Griswold and wished that Legion and Gwen could mend the cracks in their relationship, but she had chosen to follow the path of bitterness and hatred. He looked fondly at Legion – the prodigal son who realized it was better to be in a place of love than alone in the wilderness. Still, he held great hope for Gwen to find her way back from the darkness she was embracing.

Then there were the Elders of the clan. They each went about their rituals and daily tasks as though they had all the answers. He felt sad at how far removed they were from him. They believed that their service and rites connected them to him, but the truth was that all their striving did not equate to knowing him any better. He had seen how Elder Merek had manipulated Cillian to scare some of the villagers in Griswold by making them believe that the Dark Lord's refusal to build a sanctuary had caused hardship for them. Some had believed it but others had seen the change in Legion and had laughed it off. Cillian was a pawn and always would be as long as he allowed himself to be a victim. The Great One wished that he would start to live – that he would follow his heart and dreams instead of constantly seeking the approval of man.

Finally he looked at Eion and Rozanne. They had found the courage to live in freedom at last, to stand up to their fears and face them. Freedom demands courage – to step into the unknown and to take risks – they had done that and their lives had been transformed.

He loved them all deeply and he believed in them – each on their own unique journey of life. There would be some valleys and mountains yet to conquer – it was inevitable, but he knew they would be up for the task and he would be with them every step of the way, whether they knew it or not, loving them unconditionally all the way.

Life was an adventure and each of them would follow their hearts. Already they had written some of their stories in his golden book but this was only just the beginning – there was so much more to come and they had pages left to fill. He could not wait to read it.

⌘

ALSO BY CAROLINE HEMINGWAY

⌘

THE AWAKENING

BOOK 1 OF THE DESTINY CHRONICLES

One Family, One Tyrant, One Truth...

Mackenzie Hamilton and his wife Imogene always did what was expected of them. Leaving their homeland to fulfil the prophecies spoken over them by the Elders of the Clan, they journey to Griswold with their four children. There they encounter a power hungry tyrant who rules his people with fear and manipulation. When tragedy strikes and all is stripped away, tearing their family apart, they have to dig deep to find courage within to take back what is theirs and to discover who they really are. Will the mistakes of their past be their undoing or will their faith in the Great One be enough to conquer an evil that threatens to consume them?

A novel where tragedy confronts belief and victory depends upon it.

THE RISING

BOOK 3 OF THE DESTINY CHRONICLES

Aislinn and Drew Williams have devoted their lives to helping the community they live in. Their secure world is turned upside down when their eldest daughter Isabel dreams of becoming a warrior woman. This desire takes her to unknown territories where she faces challenges and hardships she never believed possible. Her belief system is rocked to the core when she comes face to face with a people she has been brought up to believe are evil and the enemy. Can their differences unite their tribes or will it drive a greater wedge between them?

About the Author

Caroline Hemingway lives in Melbourne Australia with her husband Hamilton and their four children. The Destiny Chronicles were birthed when she undertook putting pen to paper as a therapeutic exercise, discovering in the process a love of writing. This was followed by short stories and children's books she hopes yet to publish. She and her family are Foster Carers to children who are at risk in the community and she is passionate about human rights. She is also an enthusiastic blogger and loves all things creative.

THE RECKONING is Book 2 of the Destiny Chronicles. Other Titles in this series are THE AWAKENING Book 1 and the soon to be published third book THE RISING.

To follow Caroline's blog visit her website at http://carolinehemingway.wix.com/carolinehemingway